THE DEVIL'S LAIR

DE KYSA MAFIA
BOOK 2

PENNY DEE

The Devil's Lair

A De Kysa Mafia Romance
Book 2
Penny Dee

AUTHOR'S NOTE

Dear Reader,

Thank you for reading The Devil's Lair. It's a mafia romance so you can expect some darker themes throughout the story including murder. It also contains sexual acts and profanity. But the real focus of this sizzling, fish-out-of-water romance is how love conquers all. I hope you enjoy Bianca and Massimo's story as much as I enjoyed writing it.

Much love,

Penny x

1

BIANCA

Nine.

That's how many funerals I've attended in the last few weeks.

Nine men who died for the Bamcorda name. But none of them hit me as hard as this one.

I squeeze my eyes shut to keep my anger in check.

When I open them again, they focus on the man in the coffin in front of me.

Luca Bamcorda.

My father.

He lies stone-cold amongst a sea of white satin, his hands folded on his chest, his face pasty white. His thick hair is stiff with spray, and caked makeup barely conceals the bullet wound in his forehead.

A bullet courtesy of Don Nico De Kysa.

Hatred swirls in my blood and heats my veins when I think about the ruthless don.

His reign over this land has destroyed my family.

I glance over my shoulder at the poor showing of guests. When my father kidnapped Don De Kysa's wife, he did so without the permission of the families we were allied with, and when the De Kysa came looking for retribution afterward, our allies were quick to abandon us. They stepped back with their hands in the air and insisted they were never involved.

Now, they've disappeared into the shadows like the fair-weather assholes they are.

I turn away from the empty room to look at my father again. The mortician did his best to cover the bullet wound in his head, but no amount of makeup is going to hide the truth.

Not that anyone is here to goddamn see it.

Feeling a presence behind me, I turn around.

Tony Vinocelli, my father's consigliere, and his two sons, Giulio and Fausto, have entered the room.

Somewhere in the cold corner of my hardened heart, a small flame of hope and relief bursts to life. They care. Tears burn at the back of my eyes, because I didn't realize just how much I needed to know that today.

Tony takes my hands and gives me a respectful nod. "I'm sorry for your loss, Bianca."

"Thank you," I say, needing desperately to cry but holding back because a little voice inside me tells me to.

I want to ask him where he has been for the last week. Where were his sons? Where was anybody?

"There is much we need to talk about," I say to Tony.

I notice Giulio and Fausto give each other an awkward glance and feel a tightening in my gut.

"Forgive me, Bianca, but today is perhaps best left to mourn the dead," Tony says.

"Of course. Perhaps later we can discuss how to move forward," I reply.

"Move forward?"

"With a retaliation."

Again, Giulio and Fausto share a look.

Tony folds his hands in front of him. "There is no moving forward. No retaliation. It's over."

"Over? My father is dead—"

"And this is his farewell." Tony takes my hand again. "And our farewell to you."

A cold trickle makes its way down my spine.

They're not here to support me while I bury my father.

They're here to sever ties.

The realization is crushing.

But I don't react.

I won't give them the satisfaction.

He is just like the others.

Scurrying away like a frightened little mouse.

"Then you'd better go," I say sharply.

He can't get out of there fast enough, and with growing resentment, I watch the three of them walk away without so much as a glance back.

Rat bastards. They're fleeing the sinking ship along with everyone else.

When they disappear through the doors, I feel a wave of anger roll over me. Seeing the empty pews makes my heart hurt even more than it did before, and I look away; my father would be humiliated.

I lift my chin and reach for my papa's hands but recoil at the icy feel of his skin.

There is no coldness like the coldness of death—something I learned at an early age.

Ten years ago, I stood on this very spot and looked down at my mother's lifeless body, and when I touched her cold hand, I'd felt the icy pain of death slide through me.

Now it's cutting me to the bone once again.

Someone steps beside me. Harrison Tork, my father's accountant and trusted confidant. "It's time to go, Bianca. There is a car waiting."

No one else is here but the accountant.

He arranged all of this.

When everyone else fled, he hung around.

Which is to be expected.

Because when everything else is gone, money talks.

2

BIANCA

Three weeks later

"It sounds like you had a horrible time," Lilah says, taking a sip of chardonnay. "I'm sorry I couldn't be there, but Andrey was insistent we still took the trip to Europe."

"And you know I wanted to be there, but I just couldn't get away," my other friend Angelica says, also taking a sip from her wine glass.

Its lunchtime and we're dining at Sage Sprig, a restaurant on the waterfront.

"If I had been able to get off work I would've been there in a heartbeat," Jules, my other best friend, says. "But you know how demanding my job can be at times."

I look at my three best friends and try to force the fact

that none of them were there for me the day I buried my father out of my mind.

As well as the fact that I haven't seen any of them much in the last three weeks.

"I understand, life happens," I say, trying to ignore the knot in my chest. "I know you all have commitments."

I pick up my glass of wine and take a mouthful to wash down my lie.

The truth is, I don't understand. They are supposed to be my best friends but when my life collapsed around me, they were nowhere to be seen. Oh, their over-the-top floral arrangements came to the house, as well as the wine hampers and cards of condolences.

But a shoulder to cry on?

Not a single one.

I feel their guilty gazes on me, waiting for me to say something else, because heaven forbid they try and make this awkward lunch any easier on me. *My fair-weather friends.*

"You're here now, that's the important thing," I add with a forced smile. "I'm so pleased you invited me to lunch today. Perhaps we could make it a weekly thing again?"

I'm hurt by their lack of support but willing to put it behind me.

Because without my three girlfriends, who do I have?

Everyone scattered to the wind.

A look passes between Lilah and Angelica.

Okay, what was that?

Lilah plays with her diamond earring, a clear sign she's nervous.

"Is everything okay?" I ask, unease creeping into my gut.

Angelica glances at both Lilah and Jules before whatever

is on her mind gets the better of her, and she leans forward on her gold-bangled forearms and says, "Look, we've been talking and it's probably a good idea if we don't see each other for a while."

I stare at her as my world falls away beneath my feet.

"What do you mean?" I finally manage.

"It's not that we don't want to be your friend..." she says.

"But we have our own lives to consider," Jules adds.

Lilah gives me a pitiful look. "It's not our fault. Or yours for that matter. It's your father's fault. He created an impossible situation for all of us. Andrey says we need some distance. He has a business to consider and my friendship with you has already caused problems."

"And Edward says being an acquaintance of the Bamcorda is hurting his political ambitions," Angelica says, referring to her husband. "He's running for mayor and says we need to separate ourselves from what happened."

Edward didn't have a problem being tied to my family name when he was receiving big fat campaign checks from my father.

I huff out a breath as I look at my friends. "You guys are breaking off our friendship because of what my father did?"

"That sounds harsh," Lilah says, looking horrified.

"We're cooling our friendship, just for a while," Angelica assures me.

I turn to Jules.

My *very* best friend.

The one who enjoyed all the highs with me during the good times that included several overseas trips to exotic locations, frequent shopping excursions, and many, many meals at restaurants where the Bamcorda name got you a table no matter how short notice it was.

The one who spent so much time at my house she was basically family.

Please stand by me.

But she looks away.

"Jules?" I say her name with desperation. "Seriously?"

But she doesn't look at me.

And my heart breaks.

I have no one.

I remove the linen napkin from my lap and dump it onto my barely touched lunch in front of me.

"Well, I can see this lunch is over." I signal to the server for the bill. "Best I leave before I cause you ladies any further embarrassment."

"Please don't be like that," Lilah begs, as if I've just punched *her* straight in the heart.

Angelica straightens her back and doubles down. "It's not our fault, Bianca. Do you really think we want to do this? What your father did ruined everything for us too."

I glare at her. "How has anything been ruined for you? Have you lost the only parent you had left? Have you been made into a goddamn pariah in this town? Do people stare at you when you walk past like you have three fucking heads, only to turn their back on you?"

People from surrounding tables turn to look in our direction.

"Keep your voice down," Angelica hisses.

The server appears at the table with the bill, and I hand him my credit card.

"You don't need to pay for lunch," Lilah whispers.

"Bianca, that's unnecessary, we're happy to pay," Jules adds, finally looking in my direction.

"Consider it a final hurrah to our friendship," I say sharply.

"There is no need for dramatics," Angelica says.

"You're dumping me because of what my father did. I think the dramatics have already begun, don't you?" A pain hits me in the middle of my chest but I resist rubbing it. It's just my heart breaking. "I would never do this to any of you."

And I wouldn't.

When Lilah got busted for stealing ten thousand dollars' worth of clothes from an upscale boutique in Manhattan, and the media went crazy because she was married to a powerful businessman, I never left her side. I even got an assault charge when I shoved a paparazzi to the ground because he grabbed her on the boob to make her turn around so he could get a better picture of her tear-stained face. *Of course, he dropped it when he found out who my father was.*

When Angelica thought Edward was cheating on her, it was me who drove around the city with her, tailing his limousine when he was supposed to be busy working late. It was me who comforted her after we found him in the back of his limousine with two sex workers enjoying a delightful party for three. *Now there's something I can never unsee*. And it was me who held her hand when the story broke in the media and she was hounded by bloodthirsty paparazzi chasing all the juicy details. They called her *long suffering* and *clueless*, and it humiliated her as well as broke her heart, but I was right there, at her side, supporting her. Even when she took him back and told me he'd changed.

And Jules. The scholarship kid who became my bestie. Her family had no money but mine were loaded, so high school became so much more interesting and fun for her when we became BFFs. My money was her money. My trips to the French Riviera were her trips to the French Riviera. I shared everything with her. She got famous for being a New York *it girl* because of me, and she got to enjoy everything that came with it. And when she got herself twisted up in a scandalous love triangle with a very powerful and very married man, it was me who rode the terrifying roller coaster with her, ready at every turn to stand up for her. She's with a rich sugar daddy now, and even though he breaks her heart a lot, I'm always there for her when their relationship takes another dip, despite thinking she should kick his sorry ass to the curb.

But what's the point of reminding them of my loyalty?

If it doesn't matter now, then it never did.

I pick up my wine glass and drain it, fighting the tears stabbing at my eyes. *Because it will be a cold day in hell before I cry in front of these bitches.*

"Excuse me." The server appears beside me. "But the card was declined."

I look at him and frown. "What?"

"The card, it declined."

A sick feeling crawls into my chest. "Well, try it again. There is plenty of money on it."

My father left me forty-two million dollars in his will.

I might not have one goddamn person who cares about me, but I'm fucking rich.

The server looks uncomfortable. "I did, Miss Bamcorda. Three times in fact."

I don't have another credit card because Harrison says more than one card will get me into trouble, and because he takes care of my finances, I listen to him.

I glance at my friends. Lilah and Jules give one another an uncomfortable glance. While Angelica looks amused, clearly enjoying my humiliation. She's always been able to make me feel small, and she's loving seeing me hit rock bottom.

"There is obviously something wrong with your card machine," I say, feeling the flush of humiliation crawl up my neck.

"There is no problem with the machine, ma'am." The server looks even more uncomfortable. "Perhaps if we discuss this at the counter?"

"I agree. Let's do that." I stand, desperate for the floor to open up and swallow me.

Heat brushes my cheeks as I turn my back on my friends and follow the server through the crowded restaurant to a quieter area near the bar.

As he tries my card again, I nervously tap my manicured nail against the counter. My back tingles. I feel Lilah, Angelica, and Jules watching me from our table.

Don't cry. Don't give them the satisfaction.

I grab onto my anger to save me from my tears.

"This is ridiculous," I huff. "I can certainly pay for lunch."

The card machine beeps, declining my card again.

"That can't be," I gasp, digging into my bag for my phone. I bring up my accountant's number. But the call rings out. I try it a second time, but again, there is no answer.

An odd sensation churns in my stomach.

Fear.

I begin to panic.

What do I do in this situation?

I look at the server for help, but he's clearly pissed at my earlier reaction and isn't interested in showing me any empathy. Can't say I blame him. I can be a bitch when I'm cornered.

"I'm sorry," I say. "I'm not sure what to do."

Jules appears next to me. "Don't worry, I've got this." She hands the server her card which he swipes through the card machine, and within seconds, it beeps its approval.

I admit, there is a big part of me that wished it declined her card too. It would save me having to face the inevitable.

That something is wrong.

The server smiles smugly at me as he hands her the receipt.

"Well, I guess this is goodbye for now," Jules says, an awkward expression on her face. "I'll call you in a few weeks, or a couple of months, whenever this shitstorm has blown over." She pulls me in for a hug I don't want. "Take care."

She releases me and without another word, disappears out of the restaurant.

While I stand dazed and confused in the foyer, wondering what the fuck just happened.

"What do you mean it's all gone?" I ask, horrified.

I stare at the banking manager sitting behind the desk in front of me and feel the color drain from my face.

"Over the last couple of months, you've moved a lot of funds around."

My stomach knots. I haven't moved anything around. Harrison takes care of paying my bills. I simply use my credit card and it works.

"May I look at the statement?" I ask.

The banking manager, a woman in her forties with short blonde hair and gold earrings, slides the account statement across the desk so I can look at it.

My heart racing, I read each transaction. Five hundred and fifty dollars to the hair salon. Five thousand to Bentley's department store for the cute leather tote in the window that I fell for. Three thousand at Louboutin. Sixteen thousand at Prada. Twelve at Gucci. Twenty-three million transferred to an unfamiliar account last week. Another nineteen million moved into the same account yesterday.

Account balance: $1.75

A cold lump forms in my throat.

He stole it all.

"I didn't do this," I whisper. "I don't even know the account the money was moved into. It's not mine."

"Your accountant will know. Perhaps bring him down here and we can work it out together."

"That's the problem." I can't believe this is happening to me. "He seems to have disappeared."

3

BIANCA

Four weeks later

"FIVE HUNDRED DOLLARS."

I stare at Jonah, the woolly haired pawn broker who has been taking advantage of my predicament for weeks. He's a jerk. But now he's just upped his status from jerk to major asshole. Sitting between us on the glass counter is a six-thousand-dollar Gucci bag.

"You're missing a zero on that figure, Jonah. This bag is worth a lot more than five hundred and you know it."

"Maybe, but I don't see a lot of people lining up to buy designer bags from me."

I glance around the store. As far as pawn shops go, this one isn't too bad.

"I don't see the Fendi I brought you last week, or the

Birken and the Gucci I sold you the week before that, so don't tell me you haven't already off-loaded them to your black-market pals."

"You know, if you don't like my prices, you could always hold a yard sale," he says, knowing full well my ego wouldn't deal with the humiliation of peddling my designer accessories on the front lawn for all the neighbors to see.

"One thousand dollars," I say, barely getting the words out.

He peels off five one-hundred-dollar bills from a wad of cash he probably earned from selling my stuff to his shady friends for four times the amount he paid for them and drops them on the counter. "Five hundred. That's my final offer."

I think about the utility bills and the bright red OVERDUE stamp across the front.

I think about the IRS sweeping through my house three weeks ago and taking almost everything in it, after my sudden loss of millions caught their attention and somehow triggered an investigation that showed an outstanding debt my father never paid.

If I was broke before, I'm now almost destitute. I will have to sell the house soon.

"Fine, five hundred," I mumble.

He leans down. "You know, I wouldn't object to throwing in some extra cash for favors."

I cock an eyebrow at him. "What type of favors?"

His gaze drops to my lips. "The friendly kind."

Nausea bubbles up from my belly.

"You want me to give you a blowjob for cash?"

"I mean, if you're offering."

I grab him by the collar and yank him toward me. "I might need the money, but I'll never ever be desperate enough to bring my lips anywhere near your festering twig of a penis, so don't you ever insult me again with the suggestion, do you understand?"

He smirks and I let him go.

"There is a special place in hell for people like you," I say, snatching the money off the counter and walking toward the door.

"So I'll see you next week then?" he calls out.

I let the door close with a bang behind me.

Unfortunately, he will.

If I thought my day was going to get any better, then I was sorely mistaken.

When I arrive home, I find a man in a designer tracksuit waiting by the security gate.

I pull into the driveway. "Can I help you?"

"Are you the agent?" he asks impatiently.

He's young. All brains and no manners.

"Agent?"

He rolls his eyes. "Listen, I'm a busy man, and I don't have all day to wait around on the curb like a vagrant. Just give me the keys and let's get this done."

"What keys?"

"Keys to my house."

"This house?"

"Are you having a stroke? Yes, this house, 2300 Pilkington Lane."

"But this is *my* house."

He scoffs. "I don't think so."

I huff out a frustrated breath. A delusional dick in a designer tracksuit with a ridiculously large white zipper is the last thing I need right now.

"Listen, I don't know who you think you are—"

"Like I said, I'm the owner," he snaps.

Okay, enough. This guy has already wasted enough of my time. I grip the steering wheel. I need to get inside, sink into a warm bath, and drown my sorrows with some Ben & Jerry's.

"Get a life, loser." I hit the remote button sitting on my dash and the gates open.

I drive in, but before the gates close, he follows me in.

"Why have you got my gate remote?" he says, storming toward my car. "And I'll thank you very much to get off my driveway."

I climb out of my car and make a performance of pulling out my phone. "I'm calling the police."

"Go right ahead, it will save me the phone call. Do me a favor and tell them Brunette Barbie is trespassing on my property."

I don't make the phone call. Instead, I drop my phone back into my bag and pull out my gun. When I aim it at him, his bravado vaporizes in an instant and he throws his hands up. "Whoa."

"I said, get the hell off my property."

He grabs at the computer bag he has at his hip.

"I have p-proof the house is m-mine," he stammers, removing a folder from his computer bag. "The deed of sale."

Trembling, he thrusts the folder at me.

I don't take it from him. I just stare at him. Trying to figure out who the hell he is and what he's after. For a moment, I thought he was a reporter wanting to know more about my father and the shoot-out at the waterfront that claimed his life. A crime that two months later remains unsolved. *Because the De Kysa have one hell of a cleanup crew.*

But now I'm thinking he looks like one of those tech millionaire types. The ones who look like they live behind a computer, creating millions of dollars through code and innovation.

I put my gun back in my bag and cautiously take the folder from him.

Inside is a deed of sale and other contracts, and as I read them, my world falls out from under me.

Harrison, you house-stealing asshole.

It's funny what you think about when your life is crashing down around you.

Like right now, it's this asshole's zipper on his designer hoodie. It's thick, white, with big plastic teeth, and I have to resist the urge to reach over and pull on it just to watch those plastic teeth open and close, open and close... *and, my God I'm having a breakdown.*

"This can't be happening," I whisper.

But it's all there in black and white.

Harrison sold my house.

I know right now I'm supposed to face facts and deal with this like an adult.

But after the day I've had, I decide to go with denial instead.

I shove his documents back at him.

"Listen, Zippy, I'm sorry but you've been scammed. The person who sold you this house didn't own it. *I do.* So take it up with them." I start walking away but when he starts following me, I swing around. "Remember I have a gun in my bag. So I suggest you stop following me if you don't want me to shoot you."

Zippy steps back, suitably terrified, and I unlock my front door and slam it closed behind me.

4

BIANCA

Ten minutes later, my doorbell rings.

I consider not answering it and retreating into my bedroom to hide under my comforter until they go away. I know who it is. It's Zippy and his realtor coming to take my house away.

But I'm a Bamcorda, and we don't hide under comforters. We face our problems head-on. Or with a Beretta.

Either way, I know I have to answer the door and face what is on the other side of it.

Even if, deep down inside, all I want to do is sit on the floor and cry.

I suck in a deep breath and open the front door.

Zippy is there with his glamorous real estate agent who looks like she's been dipped in gold and sprayed with diamonds. A cool breeze blows in but her stiff blonde hair doesn't move.

She glares at me like I'm trespassing.

Or crazy.

"I've called the police," she says as a greeting. "You're trespassing on my client's property."

"And like I told Zippy, this is my house, and I didn't sell it."

She holds up a document. Again, the deed of sale.

"Wrong, you didn't own it. You gifted it to one Harrison Tork. He then sold it to my client."

"Listen, lady, I didn't gift my house to no one, so get your cheap manicured nails out of my face and off my property because…" I stop when I see the police roll into the driveway.

"Oh good, the cavalry has arrived. Now we might get to the bottom of this." The agent gives me a smug smile.

The two policemen walk up to where we are standing in the doorway. One is an older guy with gray hair, the other is much younger with large muscles and a serious face.

"So who's going to explain what is going on?" the older officer asks.

"I own this house and this lady is trespassing," Zippy says.

The frosty-faced realtor hands him some documents which he starts to flick through.

"No, I own it. From what I can tell, my accountant illegally sold it to him. But I am the rightful owner."

"The documents look legit," the older officer says.

"I don't care how legit they look. This isn't right." I glare at Zippy. "How did you even know this place was for sale?"

The realtor answers for him. "Mr. Tork sent me the listing photos. But I didn't need to advertise, this is a very sought-after area, especially this street. I had multiple offers within the day, all prepared to purchase the property sight unseen." She turns to the officers. "The gentleman selling it had all the relevant paperwork. If there is some kind of discrepancy, it is between this young lady and Mr. Tork. But it doesn't change the fact that my client is the rightful owner of this property."

"She's right," the younger officer says. "The law says this property no longer belongs to you."

I hear his words but my heart is too busy breaking for me to reply.

I feel gutted.

The world slows down.

I grip the doorframe to stop from collapsing in a heap because this is the final straw and I don't know what to do.

"I'll need time to move out," I whisper.

"We can grant you twenty-four hours," the older officer says. "If this gentleman agrees."

I look at Zippy.

Great, everything hinges on him.

I think about how I'd pointed a gun at him earlier.

Maybe I should've pulled the goddamn trigger.

He looks smug.

But my eyes can say a million things without me having to open my mouth. And right now, my eyes are reminding him I have a gun in my bag. They should probably be asking for forgiveness for pointing said gun at his face earlier, but I won't ever apologize for trying to protect what is mine.

He narrows his eyes. "Make it twenty-three and we've got a deal."

Twenty-three. The spiteful jerk.

When they all leave, and I'm finally alone to collect my

thoughts, I slide down the door and let my ass hit the cold marble floor.

I have twenty-three hours to get my things and leave. Not that I need it. After the IRS raids on the property and the fact that I've been pawning everything from Gucci to Birkin in the last three weeks just to pay the bills, I don't have a lot left to pack.

No money.

No house.

No things left to pawn.

I have to face facts.

I need help.

But who is left to help me?

Thanks to the De Kysas, I have no friends left.

Out of left field, Massimo De Kysa hits my thoughts like a cannonball.

Maybe he can help.

After all, we weren't always enemies.

5

BIANCA

Twelve months ago, way before all the shit went down

I DON'T KNOW why I do it.

One minute I'm in a club with Jules and Lilah—much to the torture of my long-suffering bodyguard, Vinnie, if his pained expression is anything to go by—and the next, I'm sneaking out the back entrance of the club and hailing a cab to take me to the Plaza on Fifth Ave.

There's no chance I'll get inside the hotel considering what is happening there tonight, but something in me just needs to see it for myself.

My father says it's a humiliation. An unforgivable disrespect. But the truth is, I don't feel the humiliation or the disrespect, and if it wasn't for his continual rant about it, I wouldn't even know how much Nico De Kysa has dishonored me.

But tonight, when I ran into my father on my way out to meet Jules and Lilah, and he saw the strapless, short blue dress I'd paired with my glittery Louboutins, let's just say my interest was piqued by his hurtful comments.

"Of course Nico would choose her over you. Look at what you are wearing. Bella Isle Ciccula has class and beauty and grace. And what do you have? A slutty blue dress that shows more skin than a whore."

Yeah, it stung. He'd been drinking, which is happening more and more since Nico De Kysa said he didn't want to marry me.

"Look at her and then look at you. What man is going to want a wife who looks like she gives it away to every Tom, Dick, and Harry?"

Fighting tears I would never let him see me cry, I fled the house, climbed into the SUV driven by my bodyguard, and raged a battle against the tornado of self-loathing and hurt whipping through me as we drove toward the city for another night at another nightclub.

Maybe my father had been right. Maybe I *should* have felt humiliated by Nico De Kysa instead of feeling that overwhelming relief.

Perhaps if I had, my father would have treated me more like a daughter and less like a prized auction piece.

When I got to the club, I tried to forget what he said. Tried to forget how crap he made me feel. Downed margaritas like water to help me forget.

But I couldn't get his voice out of my head, and his words

spun in my brain like a spinning top until I couldn't take it anymore.

Look at her and then look at you.

Spurred on by a need to see what was so spectacular about Bella Isle Ciccula—not to mention by the buckets of margaritas I'd downed since entering the club—the moment Vinnie was looking the other way, I disappeared out of the club and hailed a cab.

That's how I got to be here, sitting at the Pulitzer Fountain across the road from the Plaza, watching all the elegant guests arrive at the engagement gala for Nico and Bella in their fancy cars and designer clothes, while I drink cheap sparkling wine from the bottle I picked up from a convenience store on the way.

How did my life get to be so... *shitty*?

I'll tell you how.

I'm the daughter of a Mafia don who values power and status over family and love.

Oh, he knows I'm not a whore. He knows that, because he's protected my virginity like the freaking crown jewels since boys started to take notice of me. Because my Mafia princess virginity is prime real estate to my power-hungry father. Kept intact so he can broker the right deal with the right man.

Domenico De Kysa was supposed to be that man. Instead, he's marrying someone else—which is a relief, let me tell you, because now I've been given a small reprieve from having to give my body and life to a man I don't even know.

Not that I couldn't do with a bit of giving my body to someone. I mean, who is still a virgin at twenty-one?

father says. But he's right. I don't love Nico. Hell, I don't even know him.

"How old are you?" he asks.

"Twenty-two." I say the lie with confidence. But under Massimo's knowing gaze, I add, "In two months."

"You're young. Go and have fun. Kiss lots of boys. Kiss lots of girls, if that's your thing. Kiss both at the same time. Just don't sit here second-guessing yourself because the man you were supposed to marry has decided to marry the girl he has always loved his entire life."

"That's the thing, I want to do all of that but..."

I feel Massimo's curious gaze on me and my cheeks flame.

"But..?"

I huff out a breath.

"It's hard to do when your father sends you to boarding school and then has guards on you twenty-four seven so no one can even come close to kissing you. Let alone touching your precious Catholic-girl purity."

I don't know why I'm telling him all of this, but I can't seem to stop. It's like I could tell him anything.

He looks surprised. "You've never been kissed?"

"Not by a boy," I mumble.

"By a girl?" His eyes gleam, and mischief plays on his lips. "Do tell."

I can't help but laugh. Massimo is funny and charming, and it suddenly occurs to me that my nightmare evening is turning into something a lot more fun than my pity party for one.

"I mean, it wasn't a real kiss. She tried, and I got scared and turned away."

"You don't like girls?"

"I don't know what I like." I sigh. "I know it's pathetic. Twenty-one years old and never been kissed."

"It makes you unique. Not pathetic."

"What's wrong with me? Am I that hideous I can't get laid?" I say, slipping back into my self-pity. I hate it. But I can't help it. The wine has made me pitiful.

Massimo pulls a ghastly face. "Yeah, you're hideous. A real little monster. I can't stand looking at you."

"Oh, you're a funny man now," I say sternly, but I can't help but laugh. "Quit being so nice. At least if I was going to marry your brother, I would've been kissed tonight at our engagement party."

"I can see the whole no-kissing thing is a problem for you."

"Tonight it seems to be."

"I take it you're a virgin too."

I hide my horror behind sarcasm. "No please, don't hold back. Feel free to ask me anything."

He grins. "We're friends now."

"We are?"

"Yes, and friends share things. Friends also help friends out."

"What do you mean?"

"It means I'm going to kiss you now."

The way he looks at me sends a thrill down my spine. I lick my lips nervously and his gaze tracks the movement with keen interest.

Massimo De Kysa wants to kiss me and I want him to. I mean, I shouldn't, but right now I need to feel wanted.

"I-I—" Before I can get the words out, Massimo's lips are

on mine. Soft but confident and commanding lips. Lips that know what they're doing. I open my mouth and his tongue sweeps in and brushes against mine. My eyes close as I fall deeper into the kiss and my whimper falls between us.

A whimper that makes him groan, and the desperate sound sends fireworks through me.

My first kiss and it's making me see stars.

He slides his hand around my jaw, and the kiss deepens. The kiss I didn't know I was desperate to taste. The kiss spinning my world on its axis.

When he pulls away, I gaze up at him. Utterly kiss drunk.

"My first kiss," I whisper.

"Your first kiss," he repeats with a devastating smile.

Our eyes lock, and seconds later, his lips come back to mine. But this time there is something more urgent in them. Something unrestrained and needy. His hand cups my jaw again as his tongue drives hard into my mouth, and I melt into him, wanting more, *needing* more. Everything in me is on fire. My heart pounds. My clit aches and begs for more, more, more.

Unfortunately, he rips his mouth from mine.

"We definitely need to stop," he says, his voice ragged.

But I don't want to stop.

This time, I kiss him, and by the way he responds, he clearly doesn't mind. He takes my face in his hand and slides his tongue in my mouth and his groan is deep and rough.

But without warning, he rips his mouth away. "We can't do this."

"We can't?"

He tucks my hair behind my ear. "As much as I want to, I can't let this go too far."

"Why?"

"Because it would be taking advantage of you." He smiles and it's full of warmth. "And I might do a lot of questionable things but taking advantage of beautiful woman while they drown their sorrows beside the Pulitzer Fountain is not one of them."

He smiles and my stomach flips because Massimo De Kysa, the most handsome man in New York City, thinks I'm beautiful.

He helps me to my feet. "Come on, little monster, I'm taking you home."

"But your brother's engagement party—"

"It can wait. Come on."

He tries to lead me down the steps but I stop. Because I can see what Massimo is giving up because of me, and I don't want to ruin his night just because I can't get my shit together. "Please don't miss out on the celebration. I'm being a brat—"

"Yes you are. But I'm hardwired not to let a beautiful woman sit on the steps across the road from an engagement party of her *almost*-fiancé and drink alone."

He smiles and it's genuine, and something tells me I can trust this man.

Which is utterly ridiculous.

Yet, when he holds out his hand, I accept it and let him lead me across the road to his car.

We slide in the back and he gives his driver my address.

"You know where I live?"

He cocks a perfectly shaped eyebrow. "I know where your father lives and I know you live with him."

"Of course," I say softly.

When the limo starts to move, the privacy partition rises, leaving Massimo and I alone in the intimate space.

The numbness of the wine has gone, and I'm starting to feel foolish. Goose bumps pebble my skin and I hug my arms around my waist.

Massimo notices and removes his suit jacket.

"That's really not necessary," I say softly, the guilt setting in. He's missing the engagement party because of me.

"Are you going to fight me on everything? Kind of seems rude to me when I'm giving you a ride home." He winks, and I can't help but smile.

I accept his jacket and slide it over my shoulders. It's warm and soft and smells like him. Dark and manly and, oh my God, I just closed my eyes and inhaled the enticing scent like a weirdo.

"I'm sorry I dumped all of this on you," I say. "You must think I'm a real loser."

I look away, embarrassed. But he slides two fingers under my chin. "Look at me, little monster. I don't have a habit of hanging out with losers. So you must be wrong."

"You're just saying that to be nice."

Looking at him, he is fixated intently on me and it has me feeling anything but foolish. His look tells me he's not doing anything to be nice. He's doing it because he wants to.

We seem to be pulled together, like magnets, until he finally slams his mouth down on mine again.

We should probably stop this, I mean, there could be repercussions, but at this moment, I don't care. Instead, I slide onto his lap, my thighs either side of his hips, my panties pressing against the hard lump of his zipper.

I don't care if this is a stupid idea.

I want Massimo to take more than my first kiss. And going by the hardness pressing against my panties, he's more than interested.

I start to rock against the rigid outline and we both groan.

"This is a bad idea," he says between kisses, but unable to stop.

"The worst," I say, grateful that he doesn't.

The friction sends fireworks straight to my clit. I don't know how much longer I can hold back.

"I want you inside me," I pant, kissing him again, my pussy throbbing as I grind against him.

I reach for his zipper, but he stops me, pulling his mouth from mine. "That's a big step, little monster."

"I don't care." I turn his chin back to my kiss. "I want this."

And boy, do I.

Every cell in my body is screaming for it.

Only a zipper and a pair of panties separate me from what I am sure is a big cock. A big cock I want to smash my V-card to smithereens as I sink onto it.

Or maybe we could retire to his penthouse, and he could seduce me in his bed before he breaks me open.

I've imagined losing my virginity a lot of ways and with a lot of different people. But right now, those fantasies pale in comparison to the man beneath me.

His scent. His heat. The warmth of his skin and the magic of his kiss. I want to fuck Massimo De Kysa more than I want oxygen.

But he's cooled. His body language has changed. Although, it's obvious pulling away is hard for him.

He inhales roughly and slides his fingers through my hair. "You deserve better than this," he says, completely sober, his eyes searching mine. "And I'm not just talking about losing your virginity to a one-night stand in the back seat of this limousine. I mean you deserve better than all of this. The arranged marriage. Someone controlling what you choose to do with your body. Living by other people's expectations. No one can do you like you. Be who you want to be."

He's right.

But I keep my forehead pressed against his long enough to trap the heat between us. I tell myself any minute now I'm going to climb off. But our lips are so close and my body throbs and between my legs, he's hard. I shift against him and a new need blooms in both of us.

We both try to resist. We really do. But I linger there long enough for the need to become too much to ignore.

I start to move against him, only subtly at first, but he groans because I'm rocking against his erection and, dear God, I'm going to hell because this feels too good and I've gone past the point of no return. I start to rock harder and a desperate groan falls from his lips and it only pours gasoline over the raging fire inside me.

Massimo slides his hands behind my ass and begins to guide me over the hard ridge of his cock. Stars fly across my eyes. My panties dampen to a whole new level. I sink my teeth into my lip. He's going to make me come and I'm here for it.

I'm so fucking here for it.

He might not be taking my virginity but he's going to give me my first orgasm that I didn't give myself.

"Oh, my God," I moan. "I'm going to come."

He growls and I unravel on top of him. My head falls back and my throat arches. I cry out as the most heavenly sensation blooms through my body, the bliss spreading out through every nerve and fiber like warm water. I press my palm to Massimo's chest and can feel his racing heart beneath my fingers. His head falls back and his eyes lose focus as he comes beneath me.

Watching Massimo's face as he comes is like witnessing a work of art getting even more beautiful. It's raw and hot and spectacular, and knowing I'm the one who is putting that look on his face fills me with a confidence I've never felt before.

I press my forehead to his again and take in his scent as our bodies come down.

"Our secret," I whisper against his lips.

"Our secret," he replies.

I move off his lap and adjust my dress. My skin has cooled and I slide Massimo's jacket back over my shoulders.

He moves his hand along the seat to cover mine, and we ride the rest of the way to my home in a comfortable easiness. Which isn't surprising considering Massimo De Kysa is probably the nicest man in the world.

When we pull up to my house, he squeezes my hand.

I look at him and feel my heart flutter.

"Please don't tell Nico I was there tonight," I say softly.

His smile is beautiful. "Your secret is safe with me, little monster."

He kisses me and it's goodbye.

I don't watch him drive away. Instead, I slip inside the security gates and walk along the long driveway to the house and disappear inside.

For the tiniest moment, I let myself think about marrying Massimo. But like he said, he isn't the marrying kind.

Marriage is like setting fire to your life and a hoping it doesn't burn.

I'll probably never see him again but I kind of like that.

Tonight, he gave me my very own secret, one I can keep safe from all the prying eyes in my life, and one I can return to whenever I want to remember how it once felt to experience something real.

6

MASSIMO

The man tied to the chair is bloody and broken. He's also gagged but that isn't stopping him from trying to call me every damn name under the sun. Sweat beads on his brow, and blood and vomit and spit drip from his unshaven chin. He knows he fucked up. He knows he's going to die.

I stand in front of him. Far enough away that his blood and spit and desperation doesn't get anywhere near me or my suit. My arms are relaxed in front of me, a Beretta resting in my hands. "Are you ready to talk, Enzo, or am I going to have to beat some more manners into you?"

Enzo's hatred for me is rampant in his eyes. But he knows he's waging a losing battle. He nods, and I gesture to Matteo to remove the gag from his mouth. When he does, Enzo mutters *stronzo* under his breath, which earns him another strike to his jaw from Matteo. Enzo spits, and Matteo strikes him again.

"Enough," I warn them, my voice echoing through the underground garage.

Matteo steps away and straightens his cuffs. He removes a handkerchief from the breast pocket of his suit and wipes the blood and spit off his hands.

I don't move. I remain relaxed. My back straight. My shoulders square. My feet wide apart in a stance that says *I fucking dare you.*

"I'm going to ask you one last time, Enzo, who gave the go-ahead?"

"Fuck you," he says.

I point my gun at his forehead and take two powerful steps forward. "Say fuck you again and I plant a bullet in you."

"You're going to put a bullet in me regardless."

"Yes, I am. But you need to ask yourself if you want a quick death, or"—I aim the gun at his groin—"a slow and painful one."

He fights against his restraints to move his groin away from my gun.

"The choice is yours, Enzo. Now for the last fucking time, who ordered the ambush?"

A week ago, we were on our way to a meeting with the Draconi to discuss a territory truce. On the way, we were ambushed. We were in two cars. The front car took the brunt of the attack when a car smashed head-on into it. Two men climbed out and sprayed bullets like confetti. Three of my men died in the first car. By some miracle, I wasn't hit when they sent a wave of bullets into the second car. Matteo and I walked away unscathed. Unfortunately, Alex, who was with us, died from multiple gunshot wounds.

God works in strange ways.

I have no doubt I was the target.

It wasn't a message. It was an assassination attempt.

Somebody doesn't like me being the new don of the De Kysa.

It took three days to find out Enzo was one of the gunmen. Thanks to Damon, a tech wizard who is loyal to the De Kysa, we worked backward through CCTV footage to find the gunmen. By the time we found him, the second gunman was already dead. Turns out he pissed off the wrong guy during a poker game and was shot dead before I could get to him.

The Draconi said it wasn't them. The only reason I believe them is because it doesn't serve them to declare war like this.

Plus, my gut tells me there is a snake lurking out there waiting to strike, and they aren't Draconi.

No, that snake is a low-in-the-barrel scumbag called Marco V. He's a drug dealer who thinks he has some clout in this town but he doesn't. I have no doubt he thinks taking me out will give him some kind of street cred he couldn't earn any other way.

Thanks to Damon digging up more footage, I know Enzo has been hanging out with Marco V.

"You do this for that *stronzo* Marco V?"

His eyes flare.

Fucking bingo.

He doesn't need to say it.

"Fuck you, Don De Kysa, I'll see you in hell."

My bullet gives him a quick death. I'm in no mood to

play games. The quicker Enzo shifts off this mortal coil the better.

The same with Marco V. He will be fish food before the day is done.

Almost straight away, my phone vibrates in my suit pocket.

Its Dario. He's the manager of Lair, the club I own in the city.

"What?"

"Don De Kysa, you need to get down here."

"I'm busy. Whatever it is, you need to handle it. It's why I pay you."

"I appreciate that but, well, there's this woman here and she's pretty adamant she's not leaving until she speaks to you."

"Goddamn it, Dario, I said handle—"

"It's Bianca Bamcorda."

Well, that stops me.

Hearing her name flips my afternoon on its ass.

"Bianca is in the club?"

"Standing right in front of me," Dario says, unimpressed.

A flicker of a memory passes through me.

The lingering taste of a stolen kiss.

The lustful grind of her body against mine.

For a moment, sunshine breaks into the ever-present darkness in my head but disappears just as quickly as it appeared.

"What does she want?"

"She says she urgently needs to speak to you."

I haven't seen or spoken to Bianca since that night.

The timing of her sudden appearance makes me wonder if she knows something about the ambush.

Is she somehow connected with Marco V and the attempt on my life?

The De Kysa were her downfall. It wouldn't be a stretch to think she would align with a bottom feeder like Marco V to exact her revenge.

Again, the memory of her lips on mine hits me in the chest.

My sweet little monster, what are you up to?

"Fine. Tell her I'll be there in fifteen minutes. And, Dario, try not to upset her. Knowing Bianca, she might just shoot you."

I LEAVE Matteo to clean up the mess and head to Lair.

The exclusive club is in Manhattan. From the outside, it looks like your typical club offering cocktails and an ambient vibe. And for the most part, it is. There's a gleaming bar full of every bottle of alcohol you can think of. There are dancers in gold birdcages. There are comfortable lounges, tall tables and booths, and a dance floor. But for those looking for a little bit more spice and adventure, beyond the red-lit rooms of the club and accessed only by a long, dark corridor back-lit with pink neon light, is the Peep Arcade.

It's where guests pay to watch their fantasies play out before them. Where they can indulge their voyeuristic lusts in the privacy of a peep room. For the right price, the glass partition between the voyeur and the performer can disappear and their fantasies can come to life.

It's a business model that's served me well financially. But since my brother *died* and I became don, I've had to step away from it to focus on our other interests.

I park my Audi in the underground parking garage and take the private elevator up to the club.

Inside, I find Bianca sitting on a stool at the bar, her long legs crossed, her devil horns hidden beneath an abundance of dark hair. She swivels around when I walk in.

"Massimo De Kysa."

"Bianca Bamcorda."

We stare at each other. The last time I saw her, I kissed her, and then some.

I'd like to tell you I'd forgotten it. But I'd be lying.

That night, something unfurled inside of me. Something strange and new and intriguing.

I didn't act on it. And I never will.

But there was a moment between us that I can't forget, and right now, the memory of it has got a hold on me. Remembering the way her lips tasted, how soft and receiving they were. The way her desperate whimper hit me straight in the chest. The way I wanted more. The difficulty I had walking away.

After that, her father declared war between the De Kysa and the Bamcorda, and my brother killed him.

Now, we are the enemy.

And we've all been forced to do things we don't want to.

"I'm sorry about your brother," she finally says.

"Are you?"

My eyes narrow, and I do what I do whenever I face the enemy; I give her nothing but a stony-faced stare.

But she doesn't wither beneath it. "Yes, I am."

She sounds genuine. If I was the same man I was when I kissed her, I'd probably offer her a drink. But a lot has happened since then. A lot of water has gone under the bridge. A lot of blood too.

"You came here to talk, so talk."

We're not alone. Her gaze shifts to Dario lingering at one of the tables. He's checking something on his phone. Or pretending to. I don't doubt he's listening.

"Is there somewhere private we can talk?" she asks.

I lead her through the club to my office on the second floor. I take a seat behind my desk and gesture for her to sit.

"So what's this all about?" I ask.

"I need your help."

I'm silent as I wonder what could be so bad that Bianca Bamcorda crossed into enemy lines to ask for help.

"With what?" I ask, mentally noting everything about the beautiful woman sitting opposite me.

She's dressed up. But something isn't right. The Bianca I knew never left the house unless she was dripping in diamonds and gold, with a designer bag hanging over her wrist.

But this version is different. Her nails aren't done, her clothes are a little loose, and apart from a pair of diamond studs, she wears no other jewelry.

"My daddy died, his accountant took off with all my money, the IRS seized nearly all of our belongings, I've been evicted from my own home, all my friends have abandoned me, and I'm stone-cold broke. That about sums it up, I think."

Her words aren't flippant. They're cold and hard. She lifts

her chin. She might be scraping the bottom of the barrel coming here. But she still has her pride.

"And since your family are at the crux of this tornado of shit that has crashed into my life, I figure you owe me."

"Owe you?"

"Yeah, I don't have a daddy anymore. Your family did that."

I chuckle. I can't help it. This woman has a nerve.

But I kinda like it.

I narrow my eyes, observing her. "What do you want, Bianca?"

"What I want is my old life back. And because God hates me, you're the only one who can help me do that."

"What are you asking me to do?"

"I want you to find Harrison Tork and get me my money back." Her eyes blaze with dark emotion. "And then I'm going to shoot him in the face for what he did to me."

I'm not gonna lie, Bianca is a turn-on. Especially when that dark fire comes out of her.

"And exactly how do you plan to pay me for this?" I ask, a plan unfurling in my mind.

"Pay you?"

"You expect me to do this for free?"

"Your brother killed my daddy."

"And your daddy kidnapped my brother's wife."

"And it cost him everything. He made a mistake and he paid for it. Hell, I'm paying for it."

She lifts her chin defiantly but I see through her tough façade.

She's hurting. And damn, I feel that in my gut. Because I might not be the same man who stole her first kiss all those months ago but I'm not completely heartless. Bianca getting hurt is a tragedy of the war between our families.

And while I don't let her see it, I'm feeling Harrison's embezzlement tearing through my veins like poison.

"Finding someone who doesn't want to be found takes some resources," I say.

"Hence why I'm here. I don't have anyone left. No one wants to help. No one wants to be associated with me. But you're right, I will pay you. I will never be in debt to anyone, especially not a De Kysa."

"How do you plan to do that if you're broke like you say?"

"When you get my money back, I'll be rich again. I can pay you then."

"That's not how this works. I don't do pro bono. What if he doesn't have the assets anymore? What if they're buried so deep it takes time to get them back? I'll be out of pocket."

She looks around the room and I can almost see the cogs in her brain working.

Her big, beautiful eyes dart back to me. "I'll work for you."

My laugh is cold.

Bianca Bamcorda hasn't worked a day in her life.

Then I realize she's serious.

"Sorry, we recently filled the vacancy for spoilt Mafia brat."

I don't know why I say it. Perhaps it's because seeing Bianca reminds me of a happier time in my life that is unreachable to me now. A time when I didn't have the weight of the De Kysa syndicate resting on my shoulders. When my brother was the hard-knuckled don and I was the easy-going brother who could steal kisses from spoilt Mafia princesses.

When scumbags didn't ram you with their car and spray ninety rounds of bullets at you.

"Wow, you're mean," she says, and for a split second, she looks hurt and embarrassed and a broken sadness sweeps through her expression. But then it disappears quicker than a flash of light and she straightens her shoulders. "That wasn't necessary."

A foreign feeling tightens in my chest. *Remorse.*

"Forgive me, it's been a rough morning."

She doesn't know it yet, but after I deal with Marco V later today, Harrison Tork will move to the top of my shitlist and I'm going to get her money back.

She lifts her chin. "I may not know a lot about a lot, but you shouldn't underestimate me, Massimo De Kysa."

"Is that what I'm doing?"

She swallows but doesn't say anything. Actually, that's not true. Her silence is very telling. She's not leaving here until we formulate some kind of deal.

"Fine, you start behind the bar tomorrow night. Do you know how to fix a drink?"

She scoffs. "I might be a spoilt brat, Massimo. But I'm not useless."

7

BIANCA

Except, apparently when it comes to pouring drinks, I am as useless as a glass hammer. I don't know my simple syrup from my liqueurs and I can't keep up.

Who knew taking a drinks order could turn into a dumpster fire of epic proportions?

It's a busy night and the bar is three people deep and I'm flailing like a fish out of water.

I can remember the orders. That's the easy part. It's working out what alcohol goes where and in what glass, while the customers wait with increasing impatience, that proves to be difficult.

This isn't a dive bar. It's not just beer, wine, and basic spirits. It's all about bottles of expensive champagne that cost more than the average rent, and fancy cocktails in even fancier crystalware.

A man in a suit leans against the bar. "Four shots of Clase Azul Ultra."

"Of what?"

"Clase Azul. But make sure it's Ultra not Reposado."

"Yeah, but what is Clase—what did you call it?"

"Clase Azul Ultra."

Yep, still no clue. "And that would be a..?"

I can see his mental eye roll.

"It's a very expensive tequila," he says impatiently.

He's already had to wait fifteen minutes as I labored through the last four orders and his patience has hit its quota.

"Coming right up," I say with a confidence I absolutely don't possess.

Why can't these people drink something I know?

"Do you have any idea what you are doing?" snaps Natalie, the other server, when I bump into her as I look for the bottle of *very expensive tequila*. She grabs it off the shelf, slams four shot glasses onto the bar and fills them before I can blink an eye.

Although, I can hardly blame her for being pissed at me. When I showed up for my shift, the very unimpressed club manager, Dario, kind of dumped me on her and the other server, Elsa.

"This is the new girl. Make sure she doesn't fuck up too bad."

There was no time to train me. Clearly I was going to have to learn by diving into the deep end, and here we are. In mixology hell.

My customer hands Natalie his credit card, and she slaps it into my palm. "Do you think you can handle taking payment, or do I need to do that for you too?"

I shoot laser beams at her from my eyes before running his card.

If there's one thing I know, it's how a credit card machine works.

The next customer wants a Tom Collins. Which as luck would have it, I know how to make, thanks to my uncle Deno who used to drink them like water whenever he would visit from Boston. When I was a kid, I'd make them for him, and he'd shove a dollar bill in my palm every time I brought one to him. He said working for money gave a man a good sense of purpose, and I should learn it young. He died when I was fourteen in a car bomb meant for my father, and I haven't earned a single dollar bill since then.

The next four orders are for champagne. Something else I have a lot of experience with. Thankfully, it gets me away from the bar when I have to take the ice bucket and glasses to their tables. Which also gets me away from Natalie and her hateful energy.

I get that she's pissed because I'm more of a hindrance than a help. But it's more than that. She decided the moment she met me that I was the enemy. Which is fine by me. I'm not here to make friends.

I'm doing what I need to do to survive.

When it's time for my break, I head outside to the alleyway for some fresh air.

Except I'm not alone.

A girl in a glittering bikini and fishnet stockings leans against the brick wall, enjoying a cigarette. I recognize her. She dances in one of the giant gilded cages.

"Rough night?" she asks.

"I'm hoping this is rock bottom and the only way is up," I joke.

She offers me a cigarette, but I shake my head.

"Is this your first job tending a bar?" she asks.

"Is it that obvious?"

"As obvious as a bomb."

"And as destructive, it would seem."

She shrugs. "You'll get the hang of it."

"I don't know, your faith may be misplaced."

"I'm Lavender, by the way," she says.

"Bianca."

She drags on her cigarette. "So what leads someone who has no experience pouring drinks to look for a job in a bar?"

"Desperation."

"I can respect that."

I exhale roughly. "Natalie doesn't like me."

She smiles. "I wouldn't worry about that. She doesn't like anyone. Well, not until she gets to know them."

"I'm not sure she's interested in getting to know me."

"She's wary of new people, is all."

I don't care if she's wary of me or not. She pushes me too far, and I don't care how much I need this job, I'll push back.

A set of headlights cut into the darkness.

"Shit." Lavender drops her cigarette and crushes it into the concrete with her boot. "We gotta get back inside."

The way she hustles me toward the door takes me by surprise. "Why, what's wrong?"

"That's Dario, and if he sees us out here, he'll get mad." With a worried look on her face, she glances down the alleyway.

I'm learning a lot of things tonight.

One, I suck at tending a bar.

Two, I'm not sure I'll ever get better at it.

And three, Dario scares Lavender, and going by the look on her face, he scares her a lot.

8

MASSIMO

"This is a bad idea, Mas."

My stepsister sits behind her desk and eyes me suspiciously as I stand at the observation window overlooking the club. I turn away from her to watch Bianca serving drinks at the bar.

I lift a glass of scotch to my lips. "It will work out."

As I say it, Bianca fumbles as she pours tequila into a row of shot glasses and knocks two of them over.

"How can you be so sure?" Eve asks. "For all intents and purposes, she's the enemy, and you just let her in behind enemy lines."

"You know the old saying, keep your friends close and your enemies closer."

"Thanks, Don Corleone. But this isn't *The Godfather*. This is real life, and you're walking a dangerous line."

"I always walk a dangerous line," I say dismissively, my

gaze fixed firmly on Bianca. Christ, she just knocked over a tumbler of expensive scotch, splashing it across the front of the customer's shirt.

"I'm serious, Mas. This could go south real quick. How do you know she's not up to something? She's a Bamcorda."

"And they're demolished. Scattered to the wind. Every alliance was broken the moment Luca Bamcorda went against the De Kysa. She's got nothing left."

"Don't underestimate her, Massimo. I have a feeling Bianca has a giant pair of lady balls on her. She's got nothing to lose."

I turn back to my view of Bianca. "I have eyes and ears on her. I know what she is doing every second, every minute, every day. If this is a play, I'll find out what game she is playing and beat her at it."

"Fine, but don't say I didn't warn you."

Eve is the only person I will allow to question me. In the years since our parents met and married, we've become close. For some reason, we just click, and she's become one of my closest confidantes. Which came as a surprise to both of us considering how resistant she was initially when her mother came home from a cruise suddenly engaged to the old don of the De Kysa family.

A precocious nineteen year old, she had a lot to say when they got married.

Now, she's as much a De Kysa as I am.

She leaves her chair and joins me at the observation window to watch Bianca. "Oh God, it's like watching a newborn foal trying to walk for the first time."

"It's her first night."

"Yeah, but she isn't a natural."

She's right. Bianca isn't a natural. But that smile, fuck, no wonder the customer laughs it off. Somehow it manages to be bright and beautiful but awkward and apologetic at the same time.

I feel Eve's questioning look searing the side of my face.

"What," I ask, knowing she's got a lot more to say about the matter.

"Why are you really doing this?" She tilts her head. "Does this girl mean something to you?"

Her question triggers the memory. And for the first time since Bianca walked into my club, I let myself recall the last time I saw her.

Never in a million years would I have imagined kissing Bianca Bamcorda in the back of a car while driving through Manhattan.

But here we are.

Kissing like hungry teenagers. A needy groan falls between us, and I realize it's coming from me. She whimpers in response, and I know I'm beyond stopping now.

She begins to rock against me, and fuck, I want this.

I know this is all kinds of wrong.

But the way she kisses, goddamn, she tastes like sweet wine and berries all wrapped in a gentle softness that's driving me crazy.

I'm so fucking hard it hurts. And if she keeps rubbing her sweet body against mine like this, then I'm going burst.

"This is a bad idea," I force out between kisses.

"The worst," she agrees.

Yet I can't stop kissing her.

She begins to rock harder. I know what she's doing. She wants to take her satisfaction from me, and hell, I'm down with it.

I grab her ass and pull her back and forth over my cock.

"Oh, my God," she moans. "I'm going to come."

She grinds harder, her panties pushing up and down my hard cock, and dear God, I just want to unzip my pants, push those panties aside, and sink my cock deep into her wet pussy.

Her thighs grip me tighter.

"Massimo..." she whimpers.

Our eyes meet. She sinks her teeth into her lips, and behind my zipper, my cock explodes with my orgasm.

My fingers press into her hips, controlling the rock of her body against me as both our orgasms roll out of us.

She softens on top of me and presses her forehead to mine.

I'm not sure what I've just done. Probably broken some cardinal rule in Luca Bamcorda's mind. But it was just a taste, and damn if I don't want more.

"MASSIMO?" Eve brings me back to the present.

I turn to face my stepsister.

"No," I say, pushing away the memory and the emotion it stirs in my chest. "She doesn't mean anything to me."

Eve keeps her gaze on me, scrutinizing my face, obviously wondering if I'm telling the truth or keeping something from her. But I have the best poker face in the world, and no one will ever know what happened between Bianca and I that night.

Our secret. My little monster and me.

"Well, don't say I didn't warn you when this blows up in your face, or worse..."

I turn away from the window to look at her. "Worse?"

"You fall in love with her."

I start laughing. But it's humorless. "You know that falling in love and all that comes with that plague isn't on my radar. Never has been and never will be, sister dearest."

"Sure. Keep telling yourself that. But not even the great Don Massimo De Kysa is immune to cupid's arrow."

"You read too many romance books."

She folds her arms and lets out an amused chuckle.

"What?" I ask.

"I just realized something," she says. "Nico is going to lose his mind when he finds out you hired a Bamcorda to work for you."

9

BIANCA

The bar is busy again, and the next couple of hours go by real quick.

Later, during a lull, I decide to try and make peace with Natalie. I'm determined to make this work and having Natalie in my corner would help.

She's wiping down the bar when I approach her.

"I think we got off on the wrong foot," I say, giving her my most beguiling smile. "I'm sorry if I did something to offend you."

Natalie stops what she's doing and looks at me. "So you're apologizing to me, but you don't know what you're apologizing for?"

Okay, this is going to be a little harder than I anticipated.

"I guess so."

She raises an eyebrow. "So you're not really sorry, you're just telling me what you think I want to hear."

I have to fight the urge to grit my teeth and ball my hands into fists, and instead, plaster another charming smile on my face. "For the sake of peace."

She thinks for a moment and then smiles. "Sure. Why not."

I'm surprised. "So we're good?"

She shrugs. "If that's what you want to call it. Yeah, we're good."

I relax a little. Although, an awkward silence falls between us.

"It's gone quiet," I say, looking around the bar.

"Because a lot of people have either already been in through the Peep Arcade or have just gone in."

"Peep Arcade?"

She narrows her eyes. "You know what this club is all about, right?"

The way she's looking at me makes me feel like an idiot.

"Yeah, of course."

After leaving Massimo's office yesterday, I googled the club. One of the articles called it *an innovative club concept with a hot and spicy twist.* I figured the hot and spicy twist was the girls in the cages.

A small smile twitches on Natalie's lips. "You know what, I've got this. Why don't you go and explore the club. Check out the Peep Arcade." She gestures to the far wall of the club where there is a closed door. If I focus hard enough, I can see the faint glow of pink light peeking out from under it. "Your access card gives you entry to any part of the club. Go check it out."

"Are you sure?" I look around for Elsa. "What if it gets busy again?"

"Elsa will be back in a minute. Go before I change my mind."

I hesitate. Why is she being so nice to me when two minutes ago she wouldn't have poured water over me if I was on fire?

"Oh my God, stop being such a princess and go," she snaps.

Not one to look a gift horse in the mouth, I do as she says and disappear into the crowd.

I slip past the two gilded cages where dancers weave and twist their bodies to the music and make my way toward the door at the far end of the club. Above it is a sign, *Welcome to the Peep Arcade*. A strange shiver rolls through me and I hesitate. I look over my shoulder and see Natalie watching me.

This is probably some kind of trap. But fuck her. I rip open the door and am immediately drenched in pink neon light sending my senses into overdrive.

The sound of the club disappears as the door closes behind me and I follow the long corridor deeper into the Peep Arcade.

Eventually the corridor breaks off into a larger room where there are twelve doors.

I try the first door but it's locked. That's when I notice the sign above the door. *Peep Show in Session*.

I know I shouldn't. But my curiosity gets the better of me, and I use my employee card to swipe open the lock and slip inside.

Immediately I'm absorbed by the darkness and the soft scent of something sweet. Jasmine maybe? Or rose? It's so subtle I can barely make it out.

There's a dark curtain separating the entrance from the room behind and as I slowly part the silk to peer inside, my heart begins to hammer in my chest.

It takes a moment for my eyes to adjust and for my brain to make sense of what I am seeing.

The area is dark, but the room on the other side of the giant glass partition is brightly lit.

Music throbs in a slow, seductive beat through the surrounding speakers.

On the other side of the glass, a man in bondage gear is jerking off toward the audience, his big hands running over a heavily pierced cock.

While on this side of the glass, a man has a woman pushed over a table and is fucking her, his hips thrusting in time with Bondage Man's stroking hand.

What kind of club is this?

Shocked and not knowing what to do, I slip out unnoticed back into the glowing pink light as my mind scrambles to figure out what I just saw and why my body feels so suddenly awake.

The heavily pierced cock. The thrusting hips. The seductive pulse throbbing between my thighs.

Go back to the bar, my inner voice warns. But before I can stop myself, I slip into another room.

I don't know why.

To try and understand where I work, maybe?

To make sense of what is going on here?

Because some perverse part of me liked the thrill of standing in the darkness and watching?

In this room, there is a man and a woman sitting at the

table. Her hand pumps his cock as they both stare at the action on the other side of the glass. They're watching two men fuck against the glass.

I shouldn't be here.

But I can't move away.

The woman senses my presence and looks over. I freeze, certain they're going to lose their shit at me. But she smiles and signals to me to join them. "Don't be shy... come join us."

The man looks over. He's handsome. Tall. Dark. Scruffy jaw. A ginormous cock jutting out from his suit pants.

I lick my lips.

The woman's hand continues to glide over it.

I want to know what that feels like.

The thought hits me from out of nowhere, and a thrill zaps through me and lands right between my thighs.

"Wanna come play, baby girl?" the man asks. Pleasure shimmers on his face and he sinks his teeth into his lower lip. He lets out a moan as the woman palms the head of his cock. "But make it quick because I'm gonna come soon, baby..."

I realize I want to see that.

I want to watch him lose control.

I want to see him come and hear how that sounds.

What the hell?

"I'm sorry," I choke out.

I turn away and flee the room.

I run along the glowing pink corridor and out to the main club where Natalie is behind the bar, smirking.

Be calm.

She only did this to shock you.

And possibly to get you fired.

I know girls like Natalie.

Because I used to be one.

Before I can reach her, Dario steps in front of me.

"Why are you coming out of the Peep Arcade?"

Lust and shock and excitement still fog my brain. I shake my head, "I... I was..."

"The Peep Arcade is for patrons of the peep rooms. Only certain staff provide service to those areas. Why were you in there?"

"I didn't know." I frown. "I'm sorry."

"Did you go into any of the rooms?"

I pause for long enough that he puts two and two together.

"For fuck's sake. Guests pay for privacy. You don't enter a room without invitation, got it?"

Wanna come play, baby girl.

A new wave of heat spreads through me.

"I knew you would be trouble," he mutters.

"I didn't know about the peep rooms."

"Everyone in this city knows about the peep rooms." He frowns. "Get back to work, and don't let me catch you this side of the club again."

With flushed cheeks, I walk away and head back to the bar where it's growing busy again.

Was I so busy fucking up my new job I didn't pick up on what kind of club this was?

While I pour a whiskey and soda for a customer, I side-eye Natalie.

"Happy?"

She smiles smugly. "Very."

I turn away to serve another customer.

She'll keep.

10

BIANCA

It's two a.m. by the time I leave the club and head home.

Home is a fleabag motel just out of the city. A single-level dump with rooms by the hour and an interior décor that dates back to the seventies.

I don't even bother with the light. Even with the lights out, the room glows with unnatural red light from the neon vacancy sign.

Feeling deflated, I sit on the edge of the bed and let my shoulders sag with fatigue and the overwhelming reality that is my shitty life.

I lie back and shove a pillow over my face.

Harrison fucking Tork is going to pay for this.

A sudden noise from next door tells me Rosa, my sex-worker neighbor, has a client with her, and by the rapid banging of the headboard against our communal wall, he's going hard at it. "Call me daddy," I hear him pant. "Call me daddy, little girl."

I pull the pillow tight around my ears and wonder how the fuck life has come to this.

My other neighbor is an old rocker who used to be a roadie for some major band in the nineties. I don't see or hear much of him because he likes to keep to himself, but he seems nice enough. By now, he'll have cooked his heroin and gone on the nod.

I jump when the banging headboard turns into a rapid pounding against the thin walls.

"That's right, you bad girl, take daddy's big dick."

If I weren't so tired, I'd cry. Surely this is the lowest of the lowest point in my life.

A knock at my door makes it through the layers of pillow around my ears, as does Rosa's client, who isn't quiet as he comes.

"Ahhhhhhm take my load, you bad girl, take daddy's load."

Nausea rises in my gut when I look through the peep-hole and see who is on the other side of my door.

Snake. The manager.

I huff out a rough breath and try to summon the strength to deal with him as I open the door.

"Snake," I say with a fake smile. "It's late."

"I was up watching my shows. Saw you pull in."

Snake is the reason I check for hidden cameras in my room, especially in the bathroom. Although, I'm probably giving him too much credit. He's not what I'd call motivated. Certainly not in self-care anyway, if his stained singlet and yellow teeth are anything to go by.

"What do you want?"

"Just to see how you're settling in. I do that for my long-term guests." His eyes roll up and down my body, and I swear they leave a trail of slime in their wake. "Thought I'd check up on you, make sure you is okay. This side of town can be hard on a sweet girl like you. Lots of shady people doing lots of shady things."

Despite the nauseating scent wafting off his unwashed body, I plaster a smile on my face. "Thank you for your concern. But I know how to take care of myself."

His eyes flare, and I can only surmise he's misinterpreted what *taking care of myself* actually means. He licks his lips and gives my body another lewd sweep, and I know he's picturing me *taking care of myself*. "Is that so?"

He adjusts the front of his filthy jeans and I want to puke.

"Well, it wouldn't be the first time I've had to use my Beretta. In fact, I'm pretty handy with it. Better still, I'm not afraid to use it."

Snake gets the warning. But I think it excites him.

"You is a feisty one," he says with a lewd chuckle.

"You know what else I am, Snake? I'm a good shot. You might want to remember that the next time you knock on my door in the middle of the night."

He straightens and holds up his hands. "Whoa, lady. I was just being friendly is all. No need for you to get the wrong idea. I only wanted to let you know I'm just over there if you need anything."

Sure.

"And I only want to let you know that I won't ever need anything. So no more midnight knocks at my door, got it?"

Before he can utter another word, I close the door, pull the safety chain across, and double-check the lock.

I exhale roughly as I lean against the door and watch Snake slither back to his office through the window. He stops to pick up a half-smoked cigarette butt from the gutter and dusts it off before shoving it into the back pocket of his jeans.

Full of fatigue and nausea, I fall onto my bed and fight the tears pricking the back of my eyes. I squeeze them shut, will them to stay closed, and pray I don't get murdered in my sleep.

11

MASSIMO

The next day, I make good on my vow to make Marco V fish food.

Despite being surrounded by hired guns when we arrive at his apartment, they are no match for me and my men.

After taking out his frail security, I find the lowlife drug dealer in his bedroom, his pants around his ankles, about to climb on top of an unconscious girl on his bed.

"Hi, Marco, remember me?" I say, my weapon drawn and pointed at his head. He lunges for his gun on the bedside table but I shoot off a couple of his fingers before he can reach it.

He falls onto the bed, grabbing his hand in pain, his small dick turning flaccid between his legs.

The girl on the bed groans but still doesn't come around.

Jesus, she looks young.

"Not a very friendly welcome," I say, strolling over to him. "Anyone would think we weren't friends."

"You shot me," he yells, clutching his hand as he rolls around on the bed. "You motherfucking shot me."

I aim for one of his knees and pull the trigger. "Oops, I did it again."

He cries out in agony.

I don't usually get my hands this dirty. But this one is personal. In the ambush, I lost Alex, a loyal *capo*. I also lost three other men who were loyal to the De Kysa. Marco needs to pay for it. It's how I do business. You take out one of my men and the entire De Kysa clan will come crashing down on you, led by me in the flesh, coming to burn your kingdom down.

"What are you doing?" he yells.

"I know it was you who ordered the ambush. So this is my retort."

Another shot. Another knee.

"You fucker." He moans like a wounded beast, angry and in pain. "I'll kill you. I'll motherfucking kill you."

"You tried, remember? Ninety rounds and not one of them hit me. So far I'm three for three. Want to make four for four?"

"Fuck you, Massimo. Your days are numbered."

"Maybe. I'll let fate decide. Until then..." I point my gun at his forehead. "This is from Alex." And I pull the trigger.

Blood spatters across the bed, but still, the girl doesn't wake up.

On the way out of the room, I tell one of my men, "Get her to a safe place. Then call an ambulance."

My cleanup crew will dispose of Marco and his men in

the Atlantic. It will take some time, but no one will know we were even here.

It's why I pay my men the big bucks.

And why the De Kysa rule the city.

A FEW HOURS LATER, I'm at one of the De Kysa warehouses, checking a cargo of bootleg moonshine ready for shipment when Matteo walks in.

"Did you get the new campaign of surveillance in place?" I ask him.

"Yes, there are eyes and ears on her at all times. More than last time. She does anything, and we'll know about it."

This isn't our first campaign of surveillance on Bianca. The truth is, we've had eyes and ears on her since her father died. We wanted to know who she was aligned with and what she was planning.

When Nico died, and I became don, I increased the surveillance on Bianca because all reconnaissance showed there was nothing brewing. No planned retaliation for Don Bamcorda's death, and it didn't feel right.

It felt like we were missing something. So I probed deeper into her life. Paid people stupid amounts of money for information. Put more eyes on her. Now, those eyes have increased even more.

"Anything to report?" I ask him.

"She's not much of a bartender. According to Dario, she spills drinks on customers. Fucks up orders. The customers seem to like her, though, from what I've seen. But who wouldn't. With a juicy ass like that."

"Your hands go anywhere near that ass and it'll be the last thing you touch. She's off-limits. Got it?"

He lifts his brow, amused. But has the sense not to say anything.

"What else have you got on her? She look legit?"

"She doesn't make any calls either, landline or cell."

"Public phone box?"

"No, nothing. This girl has no one. No family. No friends. No allies."

Damn, why does that twist in my chest?

Matteo continues, "She's definitely all work and no play. She's either at work or at home."

My phone rings before I can ask where home is. The name Crazy Joe lights up the screen.

Crazy Joe is an undercover agent who infiltrated The Long Road Diablos, a notorious motorcycle gang the Feds were after. One day while I was visiting the clubhouse to supervise a deal between us and the MC, I recognized him.

I could've blown his cover and he'd be dead. But I knew I'd be sitting on a pot of gold with Crazy Joe in my pocket if I didn't blow his cover. And I was right. Crazy Joe has given us vital information when needed, and its impact has been significant.

But just because I didn't blow his cover or the operation, doesn't mean Crazy Joe is happy about it. He shows his appreciation by giving me the information I need, but the fucker resents the hell out of me for forcing his hand.

"What the fuck do you want this time?" he barks into the phone.

"You didn't answer when I rang. Remember our deal? When I ring, you fucking answer."

"I was sitting in a room with ten other Feds, and you want me to take a phone call from the don of one of the biggest crime syndicates in the country? I don't think either of us want the lid blown off our secret. But the next five minutes are all yours. What do you want?"

"I want you to find out everything about Harrison Tork. He was an accountant in New York City. I want to know everything there is to know. His address, his family, his everything. Hell, I want to know where he eats his goddamn breakfast each morning."

"You got any other information on this accountant?"

"He stole forty-two million dollars from an associate of mine. He managed her accounts following her father's death and then he vanished. I want him found."

"I've got a contact in white collar crime. They do this shit in their sleep. Leave it with me." He pauses. "Tell me, will the information I give you lead to his demise?"

"Do you really want to know the answer?"

"No, I'm a federal agent, you probably shouldn't answer that. I'll get back to you when I have what you need."

He clicks off the phone call.

I ring Dante, my driver. "Meet me out the front."

"Okay, I'll be there in five."

He's there in three.

"Where to, boss?"

"Lair."

THE CLUB IS THRUMMING with energy when I arrive. I move through the crowd, catching Bianca's eye as I pass by the bar.

Our gaze lingers, and I feel that all-too-familiar kick in my chest before she looks away to focus on her customer. Tonight, she looks stunning in a halter-neck top that shows off her tanned shoulders and pushes her impressive cleavage together. Her hair is piled on top of her head, and she wears a thick black choker around her slender neck.

She's beautiful.

Two women come up to me and immediately drape themselves around my shoulders, one whispering a blatant invitation in my ear, while the other runs her hands up my chest. But I don't stop to talk to them; I just grin at them and keep walking so their arms fall away.

When I'm a few steps further into the crowd, an older woman wearing nothing but a glittering see-through sheath winks at me as I walk past and mouths, "Call me." Her name is Sheri. Somewhere in her late forties, she likes to fuck hard, and her appetite is insatiable. I don't usually go for seconds, but Sheri is an exception. She isn't needy, she doesn't expect more, and best of all, her feelings don't get hurt if I don't call.

But it's been a while. Weeks. Months, maybe.

I glance over my shoulder to see she's giving me a tantalizing grin, inviting me to follow. But I give her a wink and keep walking in the other direction.

When I reach my office, I take a seat behind my desk and close my eyes, letting the dull thud of the club's music lull me into a quiet moment.

But it doesn't last.

Dario steps inside my office, and the hair on the nape of my neck prickles with annoyance.

"Got a minute, boss?"

There's something slimy about him.

"What do you want, Dario?"

He slides into the chair across from me. "I want a word about the new girl."

"What about her?"

"She's a pain in my ass, Massimo."

Dario doesn't realize it yet, but he is walking on thin ice.

I tilt my head. "Is that so?"

"Who is she?" he demands, forgetting his place. "She's not a fucking bartender, that's for fucking real."

I glare at him. "You might want to remember who you're talking to," I say in a low, dangerous tone.

Realizing his mistake, Dario pales. "Of course, I'm sorry. I meant no disrespect."

"And yet, here we are."

He thinks for a moment, his shifty eyes darting about as he tries to get on my good side. "I'm sorry, Massimo."

"What has she done that's got you so worked up about her?" I ask, not interested in his apologies.

"She can't pour a drink. She spills shit on customers. And on her first night, I caught her coming out of an occupied peep show looking all hot and bothered. If there's one thing we shouldn't tolerate, it's staff getting off for free."

My interest in this conversation has suddenly piqued.

So my little monster likes to watch.

My cock is showing some interest too.

Bianca looking hot and bothered as she flees a peep show is something I wouldn't mind seeing.

"Did you discuss this with Bianca?" I ask.

"I told her she isn't to visit the arcade."

"And has she been into the arcade since you told her not to?"

"No."

"Then where is the problem?"

He frowns. "I don't like her. She's up to something. Something just doesn't feel right. You need to fire her ass."

Sometimes Dario doesn't know when to shut the fuck up.

I suddenly wonder if he's hit on her and she's turned him down.

No, he wouldn't go there with her because he knows she'd probably knee him in the balls for trying.

I cock an eyebrow at him. "You're telling me how to run my business now?"

Again, Dario's eyes widen with fear. "I'm sorry, Don Massimo. I mean no disrespect."

"So you keep saying. How about we clear this matter up right now so you can fuck off and leave me to continue with more important matters. Bianca is here until I say she isn't, got it? Just like you are—which is looking like it might not be very long if you keep coming to me with this shit. Have I made myself clear?"

Dario pales. "Yes, Don Massimo."

"Good, now get the fuck out of my sight and go do your fucking job."

He retreats out of my office and I lean back in my chair.

Bianca might still be the enemy but I'll be fucked if I let some squirrely piece of shit talk smack about her.

12

BIANCA

It's another busy night, and again, I struggle to keep up. As usual, I fuck up one order after another, and even manage to tip a dirty martini down the shirt of an actor whose face is familiar but whose name escapes me. He laughs it off, but it just adds to the big pile of stupid I already feel. I have to face it, I suck at this job. But I'm not going to let it beat me.

If I want to eat, I have no choice.

I feel him the moment he walks in. But I suspect everyone does. He's like an approaching storm, dark and ominous and thrumming with insurmountable power.

Massimo's wearing black pants and a black button-up shirt with the sleeves pushed up, revealing two forearms covered in tattoos. When he walks, it's with the confidence of a man who knows he is king.

Women and men alike turn to watch him as he walks deeper into the club and takes a seat in one of the booths.

Natalie collides with my shoulder as she reaches for the ice scoop. "Less perving and more serving."

Whatever.

I turn to my next customer who orders two glasses of a ridiculously expensive whiskey for himself and the cheapest bottle of sparkling wine for his date. He's all expensive suits and heavy cologne, while she's as pretty and sweet as they come.

"It's supposed to be date night," she says, looking crestfallen. "Surely we can indulge a little. I've never had real champagne before. Perhaps I can tonight?"

"Darling, when you bring home the bacon, you can have anything you like from the top shelf," he says in a voice dripping with condescending bullshit. "Until then, you get what I give you."

He's a jerk.

And going by her dejected expression, this isn't the first time.

I slide his two glasses of Macallan across the bar and turn to retrieve her champagne. Except I don't get the cheaper sparkling. I grab her a bottle of the expensive stuff. Real champagne that makes you hear angels sing with every mouthful.

"That's not what I ordered," the jerk growls.

"No, but like your very lovely date said, it's date night. And around here, that means something, so it's on the house." I give her a wink and she smiles brightly.

But the jerk balks at the offer and decides to be a dick and look the gift horse in the mouth. "That's ridiculous. What moronic business gives away a free bottle of expensive champagne? It's easily a hundred-dollar bottle."

I nod toward the two glasses sitting on the bar between us. "It's the same price as those two whiskeys."

He doesn't appreciate the innuendo. "Does your boss know you give away hundred-dollar bottles?"

"Of course not. If my boss knew what was happening, he'd throw you out for being a dick. He treats the ladies how they're meant to be treated; it's why all the ladies love him. Me, I'm half your size, so throwing you out seems like a lot of effort. Besides, your date looks like she could do with a fun night out, so I'm going with the free-bottle option instead. But those whiskeys, they're not free, mister, so that'll be a hundred dollars please. Cash or card?"

He stares at me like I just slapped him with the bottle. His jaw tightens, and if he grits his teeth any harder, they'll shatter.

He glares so intently at me it's like he's trying to will my head to spontaneously combust.

Finally, he bares his teeth and says, "Card."

He holds up his platinum card which I take from him gleefully and run through the card machine.

When I hand it back to him, he leans on the bar and tilts his head toward me so no one else can hear. "If I were you, I'd keep your opinions to yourself."

It's a threat.

And I don't do very well with those.

I lean closer to him. "If I were you, I'd enjoy her company while you can. Because let's face it, buddy, you're punching above your weight. I know it. You know it. And by what I've seen tonight, she'll know it sooner than you can say, '*I need to be schooled in how to treat women.*'"

Again, the jerk lets his blazing glare speak for him.

It's like a face-off between Titans. I won't look away until my last breath. And he knows if he looks away that I've won.

It takes Massimo interrupting us to bring it to an end.

"Is there a problem here?"

The jerk keeps looking at me, and I keep looking at him. *Tell him, I fucking dare you.*

"Are you the boss?" he asks Massimo without removing his glare from me.

Massimo leans against the bar, his interest piqued. "I own the establishment. Can I help you?"

Finally, the jerk looks away. The standoff is over.

"Thanks for the free bottle of champagne," he says to Massimo before ushering his date toward a booth at the back of the club.

Massimo turns to me. "We're giving away free champagne now?"

"This club is about good experiences, right? Well, I figured she needed one. He's a condescending jerk, Massimo. And I know I shouldn't get involved, blah blah blah, but come on..."

I expect him to be annoyed. Instead, he fights the smile tugging at his lips. "So the little monster has a heart."

"Yes, a very, very black one, but a heart, nonetheless. What can I get you?"

"A Macallan. And bring it to my booth."

"Are you going to fire me?"

"If I wanted to fire you, I'd do it right here. I don't need to sit you down to do it." He gestures to the cheap jerk sitting at one of the tables toward the dance floor. "You were right when you said I'd throw him out for being a dick."

"You heard that?"

"I hear everything," he says.

And I don't doubt him.

"One Macallan coming up."

He walks away and it takes a lot to rip my gaze from him. The way his body moves when he walks is like crack to my swoony black heart.

I turn away and pour his whiskey. I'm under no illusion that entertaining thoughts about Massimo and what he might look like under his clothes is doing me any favors.

When I take his drink to his booth, he's tapping a message on his phone and looks up. "Take a seat."

I slide into the booth, observing him across the gleaming table.

He's changed a lot since our night together. There is something harder about him. Colder.

He smiles, and it takes me back to the first time I felt those lips on mine. Their taste. Their warmth. The way they took command. And I remember so clearly how he made me feel like no other human being had ever made me feel. *Wanted.*

But that man is gone, and our encounter is nothing but a memory tucked away in a locked box somewhere in my heart because I have to remain focused on getting my money back.

"Dario tells me he caught you sneaking out of the Peep Arcade."

My eyes dart to his. *Dario, the little rat.*

"To be fair, I didn't know what the arcade was," I say.

"You were surprised."

Is an understatement.

"Yes."

"A pleasant surprise, I hope," he says, taking a sip of his drink.

"I wasn't expecting to see what I saw." Massimo's gaze warms my skin. "I didn't realize this was a club for voyeurs."

"And now that you do?"

I like it.

"I want to know more."

His eyes flare but his expression doesn't change. He's composed. His strong jaw set. His body relaxed.

"It interests you?" He asks.

"I think so."

I hate that my voice sounds feeble. But what's a girl to do when the most handsome man in the world is sitting opposite you, looking all gorgeous and kissable, and you know how he tastes and feels beneath you when you come on his lap.

Oh Jesus. Focus.

"Lair offers a lot of different fantasies, Bianca. What is your pleasure?"

He doesn't shift his intense gaze from me.

My cheeks grow hot.

What is my pleasure?

I sink my teeth into my lips.

"I don't know," I whisper.

"Then maybe you'll find it here." The seductive rumble in his voice hits me right between my thighs.

My eyes dart to his.

"I'm not going to have sex with you," I say, clearly

suffering from a fatal disconnect between my mouth and brain.

He cocks an eyebrow. "I didn't realize I was offering."

Heat dusts my cheeks again. *Of course he wasn't.*

Embarrassment sets my tongue racing. "One minute you're telling me about fantasies, and the next you say you're going to take me to a peep room to watch one..."

"As one of the employees of this club, you should know what the peeps are all about. Of course, if it's not your thing, that's your prerogative. No one is expected to do anything they don't want to. Eve looks after the performers and the running of the Peep Arcade. You won't be expected to be involved. But if you're curious—"

"I am," I blurt out.

I don't want to be the naïve prude anymore. My virginity and lack of experience are like weights around my neck. I want to change and become someone new if this is my life now.

I want to experience it all.

Starting with a peep show.

"I want to watch a show," I say eagerly.

Too eagerly.

And Massimo notices.

"I want to understand what this place is about," I say.

He takes another sip of his Macallan. "Tell me, what do you think it is our clients want?"

"To watch people have sex?"

He shakes his head. "No."

"No?"

"What they want is prolonged arousal." His voice is smooth and hot, and my gaze drops to his beautiful lips as he talks. "Because it's the key to a mind-blowing experience. When they watch their fantasies play out on the other side of the glass their brains become flooded with the neuro-transmitter norepinephrine and their bodies get antsy. The tension builds. Their physical need grows. Their entire being lights up with hormonal chemistry. Then the dopamine kicks in and everything gets just a little bit harder and a little bit hotter. That's what they're paying for. That build up. That conjuring. Because the higher the mountain, the bigger the fall. And when they finally come and the sero-tonin and the oxytocin surge through their grey matter, it will literally blow their minds."

I lick my lips. "So you're selling them better orgasms?"

A seductive smile tugs at his lips. "Yes."

His dark orbs study my face, and I buckle under the weight of them.

Suddenly I'm back on the steps of the fountain across the road from the Plaza with his lips taking ownership of mine and my body exploding with a thousand little fires beneath his touch.

I drop my gaze, afraid he'll see right into my skull with those knowing eyes of his and read my mind.

But it's too late. The energy between us shifts. I can hear it in his silence. He's thinking about that night too.

"We haven't talked about the night out the front of the Plaza…" he says.

Bingo.

"It won't be a problem," I say quickly.

"I didn't say it would be."

"Lots of people work with people they've made out

with," I say with crushing stupidity. Why does this man reduce me to an overtalking weirdo under his searing gaze?

"Is that what we did? Make out?"

"Okay so *make out* was a bad choice of words."

How about, *the night I begged you to take my virginity?*

Inwardly I cringe. But I won't let it get the better of me. "We kissed, and I wanted you to take my virginity."

"Yes, so I recall."

"But you didn't. So really that night wasn't a big deal and it shouldn't be weird between us."

"If I remember correctly, we did a little more than kiss."

The image of him pulling me back and forward over his erection until we both come sends an arrow of heat right into my core.

I shift uncomfortably in my seat. "Yes," I whisper.

"Even if we had gone there, it wouldn't be weird. We're different people now, Bianca." He toys with his glass but his eyes never leave mine. "I'm sure you've since found a more suitable person."

I look away, afraid of what I'll reveal to him if I keep looking at him. "Well, I've been busy."

I clear my throat, embarrassed. I don't know why I told him that, but he's always been able to open me like a book, and clearly, nothing has changed.

He lifts his whiskey to his lips. "I see."

Embarrassed, I stand up. "Well, if that is all?"

"Be here tomorrow at five p.m."

"For what?"

"A peep show."

I swallow thickly. "You want me to watch one with you?"

"No, tomorrow I am vetting a new dancer. It will be a good opportunity for you to see the process."

"But—"

The air feels tight. And those dark eyes, oh my God, they burn with unfathomable darkness.

"I'm not asking, Bianca. You want to see one, then be here tomorrow at five."

13

BIANCA

My encounter with Massimo doesn't leave me all night.

The look on his face. The tone in his voice. The way he slow blinks while throwing me a heated look. It's all on repeat in my head.

Which does nothing good for my focus. I fumble and mess up orders more than I ever have.

God, my body aches to be touched.

By him, that little voice whispers. *It aches to be touched by him.*

By closing time, I'm exhausted, and I'm wound so tight with sexual tension it's no wonder I snap when Natalie decides to give me attitude about how much I suck at this job. It's like a match striking the side of a matchbox.

"What is your problem with me?" I demand.

And it's the opportunity she's been waiting for.

"I'm tired of spoilt little rich bitches like you thinking you should get everything so easily," she bites.

"You know what, I've had enough. You have something you want to say to me, go for it. Get it off your chest."

Natalie rolls her eyes. "Would it even make a difference?"

"Yeah, it would. So how about you drop the tough bitch act and give me a chance?"

"How about you go back to your penthouse in Manhattan and make a TikTok or something."

"Ugh, you're so original." My words drip with sarcasm.

"Thank you." She flashes me a fake smile. "I wish I could say the same thing about you. Poor little princess who can't pour a drink to save herself, but give her an iPhone and her daddy's money, and she's somehow better than everyone down here in the trenches actually working for a living."

"You're a real bitch, you know that?"

"And you're a joke."

I snap.

I can't help it.

Maybe because her words grate against my vulnerable side and sting me.

But one minute the glass of red wine is in my hand.

The next it's empty and the wine is dripping off Natalie's face.

Her eyes widen as she gasps in disbelief. "You entitled fucking loser."

She grabs the soda hose and sends an arc of water at me, hitting me in the face.

So I throw the closest thing I can get my hands on, a punnet of glazed cherries sitting next to the limes. I grab a handful and throw them at her.

She drops the water hose and shoves me.

I shove her back.

She slaps me.

I slap her harder.

She grabs my hair and we both fall to the floor, grunting as we wrestle, pull hair, and roll around in water and red wine like two teenage girls in a cat fight. It's not my first. I went to a boarding school full of rich, bitchy brats all vying for the crown of queen bee. I'm kind of ashamed to admit it now, but I was the biggest brat of all, and that crown was mine.

And look where it got you.

Finally, after much yanking and grappling, I'm able to straddle her and push her arms down at the side, pinning her to the floor.

"Alright, you win," she pants.

I'm out of breath too and realize this is the most exercise I've had in months.

I pin her wrists tighter. "I'm sorry, I can't hear you. What did you say?"

She rolls her eyes. "I said, you win."

I lift a brow at her. "That's what I thought."

I release her arms and rise to my feet. But the moment I step over her, I slip on the wet floor and end up on my ass.

Natalie starts to laugh, and I can't help it, I start laughing too. And then we're both laughing so hard neither of us can get up off the floor.

Eventually, Natalie crawls to the other side of the bar and sits with her back to the wall. I drag myself through the water and alcohol to sit next to her. We're both soaking wet.

Clothes clinging to us. Hair drenched. Both breathless from laughter.

She wipes her lip, and blood smears across the back of her hand. "You've got a mean right hook, princess."

"Good to see I actually got something right tonight." I lean my head against the wall.

We're both silent for a moment, trying to catch our breath.

"You're not as bad as you think," she finally says.

"No, I'm worse."

She laughs. "No, *I* was worse."

"You?"

"My first night of serving in a bar, I set someone alight."

"What—how?"

"They wanted flaming sambuca shots. When I set them alight, I somehow knocked one over the guy buying them, and whoosh, he lost his eyebrows."

"Nooooooooo, what did he do?"

"He asked me out on a date. I felt bad, so I agreed."

"And..?"

"And then I married him." She holds up her hand and wiggles her finger. The big diamond ring glints in the dull light. "It takes a while, but you'll get used to it."

"I'll take that as a compliment."

She turns her face to me. "Truce?"

Her eyes roam my face, scrutinizing. A small smile tugs at her lips.

She gives me her hand and I shake it. "Truce."

From the other side of the bar, a head appears. It's a woman with a blonde pixie cut and dimples.

"Hi, I'm Eve, Massimo's evil stepsister. You must be

Bianca, the enemy. Nice to meet you. Now do you mind telling me what the hell you're doing on the floor?"

ONCE WE'RE DRIED OFF, Natalie and I join Eve at one of the booths. The club is completely empty now. All the other staff except us have gone home for the night.

A glass of neat scotch sits in front of each of us.

"So you're Massimo's stepsister?" I ask.

"Guilty," Eve says, lighting a cigarette and draping her arm across the back of the leather booth. "My mom came home from a cruise engaged to their father, and I gained two brothers overnight. It's been life-changing to say the least."

If there's one thing I know about, it's overnight life-changing events.

"I was resistant at first. I knew the De Kysa name, I mean, who doesn't, right? But I was scared for my mom. I mean, Gio De Kysa had a reputation, you know. Old school Italian Mafia. Connected. Ruthless. There were some rumors about him killing his first wife. Well, according to Google. But it turned out he really is just a big softie. He treats my mom like a queen, and she laps it up." She grins. "Once I started to come around to my mom marrying the old don, I realized I'd gained two brothers. Granted, they weren't exactly the brothers I'd dreamed about growing up as an only child, but we quickly became close."

"You were close to Nico?"

Her gaze drops to the scotch in front of her. "We were getting there."

"I'm sorry he died," I say.

She lifts her gaze and regards me with a curious look. "Even after the loss of your father?"

"Even after the loss of my father," I say.

I feel Natalie's eyes on me. "That's cool, princess. Forgiveness is a big thing."

I glance at her and she gives me a wink. Which is in stark contrast to the daggers she usually sends my way.

"I adore Nico," Eve says, then quickly adds, "I mean, I *adored* him. But Massimo and I were always closest. I guess because Nico died before I had a chance to get really close to him. But Massimo, he and I just clicked right away. He's changed a lot since Nico's death, but I still see the old Massimo every now and again. Especially since your arrival."

"Really, how?"

"Well, he visits the club more since you started."

"Yeah, probably to make sure I'm not going to accidentally burn it down."

Natalie laughs. "Well... I mean, there have been a few close calls."

"Says the girl who set fire to her future husband."

She grins as she raises her scotch to her lips. "And I'd do it all over again."

"It took a lot of guts coming here to ask Massimo for a job, given your history. You've got some lady balls on you, and I like that." Eve clinks her glass against mine.

I take a sip of my scotch. I've never tried it before. I'm a champagne kind of girl who enjoys cocktails with her girlfriends on the weekends. But this is something completely new, like liquid fire that burns a volcanic path of heat through my chest. I start to cough.

I push it away but Eve pushes it back. "Keep going, it gets better."

I lift my scotch in a toast. "Well, cheers to us getting through a night without killing each other."

"Barely," Natalie says, clinking her glass to mine.

I'm under no illusion that we're friends. But it's nice to have some girl talk again.

14

BIANCA

The next day, I arrive at the Peep Arcade early before Massimo shows up so Eve can explain the process of the peep shows and what they offer to the clients.

"It's an exclusive club. Clients pay a yearly membership to participate in the peep arcade."

"So anyone can join?"

"If they have the hundred k for the membership fee."

"A hundred thousand dollars!" My eyes almost pop out of my head. "What do they get for that amount of money?"

"Exclusivity. People with money like to be a part of something elite and limited. They also get treated very well. We cater to their every whim. From their favorite alcohol and food to very enjoyable membership evenings that are invitation only. They alone are a major attraction. There is a lot of money in this city, and a lot of people want to spend it on their pleasure."

I had no idea anything like this existed. Now I'm intrigued.

Eve continues. "All our clients receive a digital portfolio of all the performers available. Options range from burlesque dancers to multi-partner sex. The client can select what they want to see the performers do. From dancing and simulated masturbation to full sex, bondage, MF, MM, MFM, MMF… you name it, we cater for it. All for an exorbitant price, of course. But our clients are rich, some of them filthy rich, and they like to pay to watch their fantasies play out in front of them under the cloak of anonymity."

"The performers can't see them?"

"The glass screen separating the performers from the patrons has two options: transparent or dark mode. When the patron selects the transparent mode, the performer can see them. When it's in dark mode, they cannot."

"And the performers and patrons are always separated?"

"Some performers like audience interaction, but not all of them. The clients have to let us know prior to the booking if they want to participate because certain things need to be arranged."

"Like what?"

"Health checks, for one. And security checks. This club is a safe place for everyone. If someone wants to bang a performer, we need to make sure our performers are safe."

"Gotcha."

"But most people just like to watch while getting a hand job off their other half."

Wanna come play, little girl.

The memory flashes briefly in my mind. The stroke of a woman's hand up and down a giant cock. The drawl of pleasure in his groans. Even now, it still sends a spike of pleasure between my legs.

"Right, got it." I smile and try to ignore the pulse in my clit.

Eve smiles. "Do you have any questions?"

"Yes, slightly off topic. But how old are you?"

"Twenty-one."

"Wow, I didn't pick that."

"How old did you think I was?"

"Mid to late twenties. You have the confidence of someone who has been doing this a while."

"That's because I used to work here during college breaks. A few months ago, I decided it was way more fun working here than going to college, so Massimo put me on as executive assistant to the old manager. The manager had a heart attack a couple of months back, and since then, I've been overseeing all of it. Believe me, no one is more surprised than me that I am actually really good at this. I never thought I'd be scheduling dildo sex sessions for rich men in suits who like to watch while dancing their hand in their pants. But hey, when it's your calling, it's your calling, right?"

I don't just like Eve, I think I actually love her.

"That's the thing about Massimo. He knew I could do this. Even when I didn't, and he gave me the opportunity to prove to myself that I could. He's like that." I'm only vaguely aware of someone entering the arcade. "Speak of the devil."

I turn around to see Massimo behind me, and my stomach tightens. He looks insanely hot in his fitted midnight-blue shirt, black vest, and black pants.

"Ladies," he says with that smoky drawl that only ramps up the throbbing need between my legs.

His gaze lingers on me, and mine on his, and something tight and delicious pulls between us.

"Well, I'll let you kids catch up." Eve puts a warm hand on my arm. "Enjoy your first peep show."

She walks away, and suddenly I feel nervous.

Massimo offers me his arm. "Ready?"

I take his arm. "No, but when has that ever stopped me?"

STEPPING INTO THE PEEP ROOM, we're immediately cloaked in darkness. Massimo guides me to the table and chairs in the middle of the room, and we take a seat.

It's cooler in here, and because it's so dark, all my other senses have kicked into gear. It smells clean with a subtle hint of sandalwood mingled with whatever sorcery Massimo is wearing.

Honestly, a man shouldn't smell as good as he does. It makes me want to press my face to his skin and drown in his scent.

Massimo pours us a glass of champagne from a waiting bottle.

"I shouldn't, I've got to work my shift after this," I whisper.

"One glass to ease your nerves." He hands it to me.

"Thank you," I whisper again.

"Why are you whispering? We're the only ones in here and we're not doing anything wrong."

He's right. But sitting here in the dark with all my senses

on hyperalert, it feels so... *wicked*. My nerves tingle all the way through me, right down to my toes.

But it's also a little intimidating.

I have so little experience with this stuff it makes me anxious.

Yet, I feel safe with Massimo, like nothing bad can touch me when I'm with him.

I've been surrounded by Mafia bad boys my whole life. Ruthless killers. Psychopathic soldiers. Brutal hitmen. But no one has ever made me feel as protected as he does. Because I know if it came down to it, Massimo wouldn't let anything happen to me.

And I don't know how to feel about that.

We're meant to be rivals, but somehow we're not.

Not when you strip away all the family rivalry, and all the bloodshed and egos that led to stupid decisions and unforgivable acts. We're just two people whose lives were tainted by the actions of others, sitting in the dark about to watch a near-naked woman dance for us while sexy music fills the room.

Oh God.

I take a desperate gulp of champagne, and whoa, it's heavenly.

On the other side of the glass, a light goes on, and seductive music slides through my body.

A girl appears, and she's dressed in a lingerie set that looks expensive. And sexy. *So sexy*.

She starts to dance, and she's mesmerizing. Long legs. Beautiful blonde hair. A body I could only dream about. And you can see she's enjoying what she does as she gets lost in the music, moving her body.

I turn to watch Massimo, but he's making notes on his phone, occasionally lifting his eyes to watch the dancer. It suddenly occurs to me that this isn't sexual for him. Oh, I'm sure he appreciates it. Who wouldn't appreciate a beautiful woman dancing to a sexy song in front of them? But she doesn't interest him, other than she wants to work for him.

I relax, no longer feeling as if I'm out of my depth.

This is a job interview.

I sit back in my seat and sip my champagne.

When it's over, and the girl disappears, I turn to Massimo. "She was really good."

"She was."

"Did she get the job?"

"She did."

I drain my glass, and like a gentleman, he refills it with more Cristal.

He puts down his phone and gives me his full attention. "So what do you think of the peep room?"

I look around the dimly lit room. It's comfortable. Well appointed. Lux but comfortable. Immaculately clean.

After all, people indulge in their wildest fantasies in this room.

"I like it. I can see why *The City* magazine calls it 'exquisite and delectable' and *The Online Chaser* describes it as 'the club to blow your senses, no pun intended'."

He laughs, and I really like the sound of it. "You googled Lair?"

"I wanted to know what I was getting myself into today."

His smile slowly fades. "I hope it didn't disappoint."

"Not at all."

The temperature in the room has increased. Or perhaps

it's the champagne. Or maybe it's the way Massimo is looking at me. Those dark eyes, as black as midnight. It feels like they have their own source of molten heat as they fix on me.

The air seems to spark. Goosebumps pebble my skin. All because of the way he's looking at me.

I have to clear my throat.

"Do you come to a show regularly?" I ask.

"I used to indulge. But that has changed since Nico passed away and I gained new responsibilities."

His face shows no emotion when he mentions his brother.

"Currently, I only vet the performers, but eventually, I will give that responsibility to Eve as I'm pulled further away from the club."

"I'm sorry about Nico," I say. "When I heard the news I thought about you."

The words are out before I can stop them.

I put down my glass. I think the champagne has gone to my head.

His eyes dart to mine. "You did?"

"Of course. He was your brother, and you were close. It hurt to know you'd be hurting."

Something flickers in Massimo's eyes. Surprise. Maybe gratitude. I don't know, because he doesn't say anything.

"For a while, I thought he faked his own death," I say, unable to stop myself, because yep, the champagne has gone to my head and invaded my vocal cords. "I mean, it seemed so unreal that he survived all those years as a don, only to get shot by an ex-lover. But then I remembered the world we live in and how predictably unpredictable it is."

I play with the stem of my champagne glass, remembering the day I learned he'd died. My friends had just dumped me and I hadn't left my bed for days. The news came on the TV, and I sat up so quickly my bowl of popcorn tipped over and scattered across the bed. Don Nico De Kysa had been shot dead by an ex-lover.

"I would've thought you felt his death was some kind of retribution," Massimo says, his voice sharp but not cold.

"Me too," I say honestly. Because this champagne is an apparent truth serum. "Truth be told, I kind of wished he did fake it."

Massimo turns fully toward me. "Why would you wish that after he killed your father? I thought you would blame him for everything that followed your father's death."

"No, I blame the fallout on the people who did those shitty things to me. Tony and his sons. Harrison. My supposed friends. They didn't do that because my father was dead. They did those things because they're assholes." My throat is dry, so I take another sip of champagne, which, given my loose tongue, is probably a bad idea. "My father was a bad man, Massimo. I learned a lot of things about him in the weeks following his death. But he was my father, and I loved him, and in his own way he loved me too. But he woke the devil when he kidnapped Bella De Kysa, and I know if someone kidnapped the person I loved, it would awaken the devil in me too."

"You sound empathetic."

"For once in my life, I am. Because there is a lot of time for self-reflection when you're lingering at the bottom of the barrel. It's also a giant reality check when you wake up broke and friendless and actually have to fend for yourself. You start to see things in a different light. I thought Nico had faked his death because there was a part of me that wanted him to still be alive."

"Why?"

"Because too many people die in our world for too many stupid, unnecessary reasons. If my father had just gotten over Nico marrying Bella instead of me, life would be completely different." I toy with my glass. "The night on the steps of the fountain..."

"The night you ravaged me in the back seat of my car?"

"The night you stole my first kiss." Amusement tugs at my lips but it fades. "You told me he was in love with Bella, always had been and always would be. It made me grateful he had picked her. Because I realized I wanted to be loved like that. Someone to love me so big that nothing else could get in the way." I push my champagne away, knowing I've said too much. "And then for him to die... it seemed so unfair."

"Life is unfair, Bianca. That's why you have to fight for what you want."

I lift my gaze to his. "And what do you want?"

"If I knew that, I could start searching for it."

"Come on, that sounds rehearsed. What do you truly want, Massimo?"

"I want to find the sonofabitch who has your money and help you shoot him in the face."

15

MASSIMO

I wasn't lying when I told Bianca what I wanted.

Finding Harrison has become my number one priority.

It's time to fix some wrongs, because if there's one thing I can't stand, it's a double-crossing asshole.

If a man doesn't have his word, then he doesn't have anything, my father used to say.

The De Kysa network of people is globally vast. We have alliances with people in almost every country. From North and South America, to across Europe and Asia. Hell, we have friends tucked away in the smallest towns in the smallest countries. Because our word means something. We are loyal but deadly if crossed.

Meaning, there is no place Harrison can hide now that he's pissed off the devil.

After the peep show audition, I retreat to my office,

trying to drown out Bianca's words and the memories of that night on the steps and all that happened afterward.

Sometimes, I'm just so bone-tired I want to sleep for a million years.

But not alone.

Because I'm starting to realize things are changing in me.

I've spent years fucking myself into a mindless oblivion where coming was the only goal, and emotions did not exist. Another face, another body, no commitment, no feelings. *No big deal.*

But it's getting old.

And I'm not too much in denial to not recognize that feeling this way coincides with the arrival of Bianca in my life.

But I'm a realist and know it's pointless entertaining any thoughts about it. Because we would never stand a chance. Love doesn't thrive in our world. It dies in a hail of bullets and blood and bad deeds. Only a lucky few get out alive. Like Nico and Bella.

My phone rings. It's Crazy Joe.

"The name Dario Rancini mean anything to you?"

"Why?"

"If you're involved with him, you will want to uninvolve yourself."

Darkness slides through me. "Tell me what you know and don't leave a goddamn thing out."

16

BIANCA

It's a quiet night at Lair. Which is a godsend, since I'm preoccupied after spending time in the peep room with Massimo. But I've only managed to spill a drink on one customer tonight, so I'm taking that as a win.

Later in the evening, a group of suits saunter in and immediately take ownership of the corner booth. Four of them, all looking as important and entitled as the next. They order a bottle of champagne and vodka cocktails.

I take the tray of drinks over to the suits in the corner of the room.

"Good evening, gentlemen," I say, placing the champagne in the center of the table

One of them whistles. "Now that's some gorgeous real estate I'd like to explore."

He sweeps a gaze up and down my body.

"Real estate I could spend a lot of time enjoying," his friend with the red hair adds with a crude lick of his lips.

I let their disrespectful comments slide because I know how to pick my battles. I need this job, and schooling these leering pricks is going to take more time than I'm willing to spend with them.

"Are you on the menu?" The first guy asks.

I cock an eyebrow at him. "Do you see me on the menu?"

"No, but I'm hoping." He grabs my wrist.

"You keep grabbing at me, and you'll be hoping for a new set of balls."

"Don't be like that, baby, I'm just being friendly."

I look at his fingers gripped around my wrist. "And I'm warning you, get your goddamn hand off me."

He throws his hands up in surrender. "Okay, okay, no need to be a bitch about it."

I ignore him and finish placing the drinks on the table.

Next thing I know, Mr. Grabby slaps my ass and grabs a handful of cheek.

"Juicy," he laughs, squeezing it tight.

Oh hell no.

I swing around and throw a vodka and soda at his face.

"What the fuck?" He shakes off the liquid. "You fucking cunt, this is an Armani suit."

"And this *real estate* is a no trespassing zone, asshole."

He raises his hand to slap me, but I slap him first, right in the nuts, and he bends over with a wince.

"No means no, asshole."

His friends start laughing at him. Which only infuriates him further.

"Fucking slut..."

Dario appears out of nowhere. "Is there a problem here?"

He glares at me before turning his attention back to Mr. Grabby.

"Yes, your waitress is a cunt. I want her fired."

"My apologies, Mr. Donnington. I'll send a new server over right away, and I'll make sure they bring you a complimentary bottle of champagne."

Mr. Grabby glares at me. "Yes, do that. And make sure she is more professional than this slut."

That's twice he's called me a slut.

A third, and I'm going to go to my locker, pull out my last remaining Gucci handbag, remove my gun, and bring it back here so I can shoot him in the face.

Not really, but fantasizing about it sure as shit beats standing here listening to his name calling.

Dario yanks me by the arm and drags me all the way into his office.

"Do you have any idea who the fuck that was?" he fumes.

"Yeah, an entitled prick who thought he could put his hands on me without my permission."

Dario actually rolls his eyes. Which infuriates me.

He really has no care for any of his staff.

"That was Alastair Donnington. Tech magnate. Worth a billion fucking dollars."

"And I'm Bianca, a broke waitress who doesn't have two pennies to rub together. What's your point?" I put my hands on my hips. "Or are you saying because the asshole has money, it allows him to do what he likes to me?"

I'm furious.

How many other girls here have endured this bullshit?

He scoffs. "That's rich coming from you."

"Excuse me?"

"Talking about entitled pricks, exactly how much of daddy's money did you spend before Domenico De Kysa put a bullet in his fucking brain?"

My fingers curl into a ball.

I'm two seconds away from punching this loser in the nose when Massimo says his name sharply. "Dario."

We both swing around to find him standing in the doorway.

"Don Massimo," Dario says, his tough-guy demeanor suddenly vaporizing like smoke in the presence of his boss. Immediately, I realize he is afraid of him. And I kind of don't blame him. Standing in the doorway in a suit that fits perfectly over his muscular frame, Massimo cuts a powerful figure. A man you don't want to fuck with.

A strange delight flutters in my belly, and I'm suddenly wondering what he looks like under that custom-made suit.

All hard lines and slabs of muscle, I'm sure.

"To what do we owe the pleasure?" Dario asks nervously.

"This is my club."

"Of course, it's just we don't usually see you here on the weekends, especially not on a Sunday night."

Massimo ignores him. "What's happening here?"

"I'm sorry you had to witness this. But Bianca has just insulted an important guest."

"Is that so?" Massimo slides his dark eyes from Dario to me. "Exactly how did she do that?"

"Threw a drink at him and then..."

Massimo's gaze lingers on me. "And then?"

"She hit him in the groin."

Massimo doesn't remove his eyes from me. "Is that so?"

Oh crap, he's going to fire me.

But even with that in mind, I lift my chin defiantly. "Yes, I did those things."

I can almost feel Dario's glee at my admission. He wants Massimo to set me alight just so he can watch me burn, and it's got him excited.

"She's trouble, Don Mas—"

"Leave us," Massimo interrupts.

"But—"

Massimo finally rips his gaze from me and gives Dario a dangerous look. "I said get the fuck out."

Dario pales beneath his vicious glare and obeys. "Of course, I'll be out in the club should you need me."

He practically bows at his boss before retreating out of the room, leaving Massimo and I alone.

"So you threw a drink and punched one of my guests in the cock?"

The way he says cock hits me right between my thighs.

"Yes."

"Why?"

Again, I raise my chin. "I'm not desperate enough to put up with someone putting their hands on me without permission."

"And I am not the kind of man who would expect that of you."

"I warned him. He didn't listen."

"So you resorted to violence."

"Sometimes in those circumstances, that's all you've got left."

"I understand."

"You're not angry?"

He lifts an eyebrow. "I rarely issue warnings and usually go straight to the violence, so no, I'm not angry."

I relax a little and fold my arms to show him just how relaxed and unfazed I am. "Good."

"Good?"

"I was hoping you hadn't drunk from the same cup of assholery like your manager has and expect your staff to put up with that kind of behavior in your club."

"I expect my staff to be treated with respect."

"Have you told Dario that? Because I'm pretty sure he isn't on board with that particular philosophy."

"What would you suggest I do then?"

"You're asking me for advice?"

"No. I'm simply curious as to what you would do."

"Is shooting him in the dick an option?"

Amusement tugs at his lips. "Let's pretend this is your club. What would you do?"

"I would kick his ass to the curb and find a new manager. Someone who knows how to treat their staff with respect and actually care about them."

"Done. Do you want the job?"

"Excuse me?"

There is no way he just offered me the position.

"Dario was correct in saying I don't visit here on a Sunday night. But tonight, I'm here for a very specific reason. He's been stealing from me, and by the end of the night, he will know with great clarity what happens to people who steal from me."

A thrill zips up my spine.

He's going to kill him.

"Why are you telling me this?"

"Because by the end of the night, I'm going to be short a club manager, and I want you to replace him."

Two things are vying for my attention in my head right this minute.

One, the fact that he's going to make Dario pay for his crimes, which let's face it, isn't going to bode very well for Dario.

And two, he's giving me a promotion.

A promotion because I suck so bad at mixing drinks?

"Why me?"

"Because you demand respect and give it in return. You're personable, and according to Eve, the staff all love you... even Natalie, which is a feat in itself."

"She was a tough nut to crack, I'll give her that."

"I trust my instinct, and my instinct is telling me you'd do the job right."

"But I've never done anything like this before."

"So you'll learn. Besides, Eve oversees everything, so look at it more like an executive assistant role to her." He folds his arms and regards me with those impenetrable eyes. "Or are you trying to talk me out of it because you're afraid?"

"I'm not afraid."

Am I?

Is that what the knot in my chest is all about?

I'm afraid of letting him down?

Massimo.

A De Kysa.

The De Kysa.

Oh hell no.

"I'm a Bamcorda," I blurt out, reminding myself of why I

will never be afraid of a De Kysa or anything to do with them.

"We all have our faults," Massimo says with a wicked smile touching his lips.

A *sexy* wicked smile that sends another tingle through my body.

"You seriously want me to be involved in running the club?"

"Looks that way."

"I'm the daughter of your rival. I was lucky you even let me in the door, and now you're giving me more access to your world."

"Not my *world*, my *club*." He pushes off the desk to stand in front of me. He towers over me, all broad shoulders and power. "You know this place is very separate from the family business. You won't be privy to anything I don't want you to be."

Standing this close, I can see the lighter flecks in his deep obsidian eyes and every long, dark lash that surrounds them.

And Jesus, what cologne is he wearing?

It's like a spell being cast, one that makes you so high you don't care what happens to you.

"So what do you say, little monster, do you dare?"

Massimo holds out his hand.

I reach for it and shake. "Dare accepted." I can't help but smile.

It never fails to surprise me how quickly life can turn on a dime.

Sometimes it's a bad twist of fate.

But sometimes it's good.

17

MASSIMO

I put a bullet through Dario's skull within an hour of my meeting with Bianca.

He knelt before me, apologizing for stealing from me and begging for his life.

I could've forgiven him for his theft. Taken a few fingers and let the asshole live out his years with only a pair of thumbs.

I could've made it quick, too.

But I did none of the above. Instead, I drew it out. Toyed with him. Like a cat toys with a mouse before he rips it apart and devours it.

Why? Because Dario was doing more than just stealing. He was involved in trafficking. And trafficking is one thing the De Kysa don't tolerate.

To add insult to injury, he was also meeting with those

involved with it in my goddamn club. Making phone calls on my goddamn phone. Bringing filth into my goddamn space.

His offences were numerous.

The reasons to kill him abundant.

First, I'm a De Kysa, so the Feds have got eyes and ears all over me, just waiting for me to fuck up somehow so they can take me down, and Dario was laying out the red carpet for them. If they caught even a whiff of me being tied to something like that, then I'd be sitting in a six-by-four cell by sundown.

Secondly, the moment you think trafficking is an acceptable career choice, you and me are going to have a problem. I trade in fantasies and corporate warfare, I even do a little killing, but I don't fucking traffic people.

Thirdly, I'm not blind. The girls hate him. And it's my experience that there is never smoke without fire.

And lastly, he kicked a stray cat on our way out to the alleyway, and goddamn it, that shit is just vile. Hurting animals is a sign of weakness, and I don't surround myself with weak people. And I certainly don't have them running my club.

So I made him beg. Gave him a glimmer of hope. Made him think perhaps he could talk his way out of the giant pile of shit he'd landed himself in.

Then I took all the fingers on his right hand.

Then all the fingers on his left.

Because trafficking sickens me to my gut and I wanted him to feel the pain.

And then I shot him dead.

~

Back in the club, I open a new bottle of Macallan in my office. I don't like killing people, regardless how much of an asshole they are, but it's an unpleasant necessity in my position. The moment you show weakness is the moment you lose the fight. And in my world, that means you die.

When I check my phone, there is a message from Crazy Joe.

"Harrison Tork is still off radar. But we were able to access his financial records. He transferred money out of an offshore account to another one only a day ago. But this is the strange thing. That account was closed, and the money sent somewhere else. We're trying to find the new location of the money, but there are a lot of firewalls in place. If I were a betting man, I'd say your boy has been double-crossed."

I sit back in my chair.

So the double-crosser has been double-crossed.

I met Harrison a couple of times when the De Kysa were still involved with the Bamcorda, and I occasionally visited the Bamcorda compound.

One thing about Harrison, he might be clever with numbers, but he's no intellectual con man. I know for a fact he wasn't the only one involved with stealing Bianca's money. He pushed the buttons, but someone else was behind it.

Apparently, a new someone else is now in control.

Meaning, finding Bianca's money just got a lot harder.

18

BIANCA

To celebrate my promotion, I visit my very own heaven on Earth.

Bentley's on Fifth.

It's one of the most luxurious department stores on Fifth Avenue, where the air is thick with opulence and designer labels are in abundance, and it is even scented with their own signature fragrance that smells like luxury.

As soon as I step inside the palatial store, my spirits lift.

I stop to inhale a deep, appreciative breath, and straight away, my dopamine levels shoot up. I might be broke now, but this is my happy place and these are my people.

I move from designer to designer, taking it all in.

The smell.

The lights.

The glittering display cabinets.

The dazzling array of designer labels.

It's like coming home.

If I didn't think it'd get me kicked out, I'd get down on my knees and press my cheek to the cool marble floors and thank it for welcoming me home.

I can't take the grin off my face as I absorb the haute couture heaven surrounding me. I used to lose hours in here. Not to mention, drop a sizable amount of money that would make anyone weep. Which, in hindsight, feels kind of ridiculous now that I actually have to work for my money.

But still, this place makes my heart sing.

I pick up a ridiculously expensive scarf and slide it through my fingers, relishing the softness and the delicate way it falls. It feels like pure luxury and elegance. Like it's been woven from angel wings and dyed with rare hues found along the river Nile.

I smell it, and it even smells ridiculously luxurious.

"Oh my God, that looks divine on you. It'd be a crime if you don't buy it."

I recognize the voice before I even turn around.

Lilah.

But she's not talking to me. She's talking to Jules, who is trying on a stunning cocktail dress that probably costs more than what I'd make at Lair in a year. They're across the aisle from me, standing in front of a mirrored wall where Jules turns and twirls in the stunning silk dress.

I quickly duck behind a display gondola to watch my ex-best friends.

I'd like to say they looked like they were suffering greatly without me. But going by their laughter and the fun they're having, it's more like they're thriving without me. They look good too. Lilah is as well put together as always in a Lacroix pantsuit, and Jules has finally gotten the bangs I've been telling her to get forever. She must be finally spending some of her sugar daddy's cash on a new wardrobe too, because she looks fabulous.

Stealthily, I move toward them, ducking from rack to rack so they don't see me, and hide behind a display of evening gowns to watch them. They look like best friends, and my gut twists, and my heart aches with longing.

Jules and I used to come here all the time. We'd shop until our feet hurt and then indulge in the cute baby cakes and glasses of Verve Clicquot at the store's a la carte café while pretending we weren't rubbing our feet under the table because walking for hours in four-inch heels is hard work and hurts.

Jules decides to buy the dress, and I watch her and Lilah talk and laugh as the sales assistant rings it up for her.

Go over there, the little voice whispers.

But the truth is, I feel too hurt and broken by how they treated me, and if I'm really honest, I feel embarrassed. I look down at my jeans and t-shirt and think about the crappy motel I now call home, and the car that is on blocks because someone stole my wheels while I was sleeping.

"It's perfect for the Balboa Charity Ball next Friday," Lilah says to Jules.

I gasp. The Balboa Charity Ball is like the Oscars for the who's who of New York society. I used to get an invitation every year because my daddy used to send them a hefty donation in my name. The event is lavish and ostentatious, and over the top. *And in what fucked-up universe am I not invited and my two fair-weather friends are?*

"Angelica will love it too," Lilah adds.

Correction. My *three* fair-weather friends. Ugh, this sucks.

With a heavy heart, I watch my ex-best friends walk away, their arms laden with bags of shopping after what looks like a big shopping day. Bentley's. Saks. Bergdorf. Tiffany's. They've done the rounds.

It's not until they disappear onto the street that I let out a rough breath.

It hurts.

It hurts real bad.

But I try not to let it affect me. After all, I'm in Bentley's, my favorite place on Earth. So I try to put on a happy face and focus on some retail therapy—without actually participating in the retail bit.

I've never window-shopped in my life, and it's hard not to buy anything, especially the elegant dress on display in front of me. It's a Bianchon gown made from the softest red silk which feels heavenly against my skin. It's been months since I've felt anything this magical. I sigh as I press the silk to my cheek because it feels so soft and rich, but I'm quickly brought out of my daydream by a sharp clearing of the throat.

"Can I help you?" a pinched-face assistant asks.

It's then I realize I'm caressing the silk like it's a boyfriend.

I drop it. "I'm sorry, I'm just looking."

"Then you should probably look with your eyes and not your hands."

The sales assistant must be new because I don't recognize her.

Her gaze sweeps over me and her expression sours.

Somewhere in her twenties like me, I feel her judgement like it's a bucket of cold water splashing all over me.

I bite my tongue and move away from the dress to look at a selection of shoes created by a designer known for their elegant stilettos.

Unfortunately, the assistant follows me, bringing her cloud of judgment with her. It's then I realize she probably thinks I'm going to steal something.

"Can I help you with anything in particular?" she asks.

"Nope, I'm just looking. I come here a lot."

"Hmmmmm," she says dismissively. "But not lately."

Again, she does another judgmental sweep of her cold blue eyes up and down my body.

"Well, now I'm back." I pick up a pair of four-inch heels and study the immaculate stitching and craftmanship.

She folds her arms and narrows her eyes at me, and I'm kind of taken aback. Usually it takes people a while to take a dislike to me. But she decided the moment she saw me that I was not her kind of person.

She folds her arms. "I think you'd better leave."

"Excuse me?"

"I don't think we have anything here that's suitable for you."

"Oh, you don't?" I put down the shoes and take a step toward her, meeting her cold gaze with my own blazing one. I lower my voice so she knows I mean business. "See that surprises me considering I've been shopping here since my mama brought me to Bentley's in my Versace stroller and Baby Dior romper. And since then I've dropped the most astronomical amounts of money here, the kinds of numbers that would make your eyes water and your jaw drop." I lean closer. "Amounts that would remind you of the difference between someone with money and someone who serves people with money. Now how about you leave me the fuck alone and—"

Not the least bit impressed by my monologue, she walks to the nearest counter and picks up a phone. "I need security down here in section five."

I glare at her. "Are you kidding me?"

She gives me a cold look. "I can assure you that I don't kid."

"Fine." I hold up my hands in surrender. "I'll leave."

"Not before you show me your bag."

"What the fuck?"

"No need to get aggressive."

"Aggressive..?" I look at her name badge. "Anastacia, if I were to get aggressive, you'd know about it."

"If you don't show me your bag—"

"Why are you asking to see inside my bag? I haven't done anything wrong."

"Because I have reason to believe you might have taken something that doesn't belong to you."

I put my hands on my hips. "And what reason is that?"

She gives me another one of those judgmental sweeps up and down my body.

I cock an eyebrow at her. "Well?"

She looks at me as if I am the bane of her existence. "I must insist you open your bag and allow me to see the contents inside."

"And I must insist you go to hell."

Things kind of go downhill from there.

I make it to the front door, but the moment I take a step

outside of the building, the security officer arrives, and I get hauled away to the security office beneath the building.

Remember the scarf I was falling for when I spied Lilah and Jules?

Yeah, in my sudden preoccupation with seeing my best friends go on about their best lives without me, I accidentally put it in my bag.

"I swear to God, I have never stolen anything in my life," I plead to the security officer when he calls the police. "It was a simple mistake. I saw my friends, well, my ex-friends, so I quickly hid behind a display of evening gowns so they wouldn't see me, and somehow I must've put the scarf in my bag without thinking. I'm not a thief. Really, I'm not. I used to shop here all the time."

But the security officer isn't having any of it.

When the police arrive, they drag me away like some criminal in handcuffs, and I am charged with shoplifting.

19

BIANCA

Just when I think things couldn't get any worse, the situation takes a dive for the bottom of the barrel.

"So this is what you do in your spare time."

I look up when I hear the familiar voice.

Massimo.

He's standing in the doorway looking stupid sexy in a black button-up shirt and black pants. His sleeves are pushed up his forearms, showing off his tattoos.

I straighten in my chair and the handcuffs around my wrists jangle. "What are you doing here?"

"I heard a rumor that New York's finest had a scarf-stealing thief down at the station. Thought I'd come check it out for myself."

I roll my eyes. "Who told you?"

"I have eyes and ears all over this town."

"Are you having me followed?"

Of course he is.

Not that he'd ever admit it.

"So why are you here? Come to gloat about seeing me in cuffs?"

"I know there's a witty comment to be made about cuffs here, but I'm short on time." He looks at the officer sitting at the desk writing something up. "Is she free to leave?"

"As a bird," the officer says with relief. "But I warn you, it's at your peril."

Okay, let's back it up a bit.

So after I realized no amount of tears or pleading was going to get me off this stupid shoplifting charge, I might've become a little sassy. And by sassy, I mean really mouthy. But that's only because I am having the mother of bad days.

But I wasn't rude to the officer. I find that so distasteful when someone is only trying to do their job without judgement and then someone comes along and screams at them.

But I *was* emotional. In fact, I'd probably even go as far to say I was exhaustingly emotional. The poor officer wasn't expecting me to unload my life's problems on him, but once I started, wild horses weren't going to stop that shit from pouring out of me.

He gives Massimo a tired look and says, "Go with God, my friend."

Much to Massimo's amusement.

On the way out, Massimo pays my fine. When I protest, he says, "Just add it to the debt you already owe me."

And, of course, I have to agree or end up spending a night in jail for the great scarf-stealing crime that didn't actually happen.

His sexy black car is parked in a *No Parking* zone, and we slide in.

"Where to?" Massimo asks me.

I think of the motel I'm staying at, and it's the last place I want him to take me.

So I lie and give him the address of an apartment complex in Midtown where an old friend of mine from my party days used to live. I know the building code, so at least I'll be able to get into the lobby and fool Massimo into thinking I live there.

"You didn't have to come down to the station," I say.

"And what would you have done about the fine?" he asks.

"I would've done my time in jail like a pro."

Which is a lie. Chances are, I would've cried like a baby. Since I've been doing that a lot today.

Massimo chuckles, and I decide I like the way it sounds. In fact, today he seems a lot more relaxed than I've seen him in a while.

I look around the interior and wonder if it is the same car we kissed in on the night of Nico and Bella's engagement party. It looks the same. Feels the same. I look over my shoulder to the back seat. Same buttery leather. Same gleaming chrome.

"You looking for something? Or just reminiscing?" he says with an evil twinkle in his eye.

"I'm working out my various escape routes."

He grins and starts the engine. "Don't bother, I've got the child lock on."

I roll my eyes.

"Want to tell me what happened at Bentley's?" he asks as he merges into traffic.

"No," I say, a little more petulantly than I meant to because I'm embarrassed. And if I'm honest, I'm still a little hurt by how my friends could move on so easily and be so wonderfully happy without me. "I mean, it's not fair, you know. One minute I have this great life with these great friends, and the next, I'm hiding from them behind this gorgeous, *and I mean gorgeous*, red silk Bianchon gown while they shop gleefully for the biggest event on the social calendar that guess what, I am no longer invited to."

My emotions get the better of me, and I charge forward into my second meltdown of the day. Because life sucks big dog balls, and I don't have the energy to stop it.

"And then some pinched-nose sales assistant gets all crotchety because I'm caressing this Bianchon gown like a lover, but it has this to-die-for red silk that's as soft as a baby's breath, and I haven't felt anything as sweet and pure on my body in what feels like forever, and I couldn't stop wishing I could just know what it feels like to wear. And I know there is so much worse going on in the world. But that was my world, and I don't even know who I am outside of it. And that sales assistant hated me, Massimo, I could tell, from the moment she saw me she hated me, because I'm poor and friendless, and I fondle dresses I can't afford."

I let out a pathetic sob.

"Wow," Massimo says. "No wonder you stole the scarf."

I swing my tear-stained face to him and promptly start to cry in earnest.

"Oh sweet Jesus," he whispers.

But he takes pity on me. "Your friends sound like bitches."

Which cheers me up immensely.

"Want me to have them killed?" he asks.

"Thank you." I sniff back tears and smile. "That's so kind of you to offer. But I have better plans for them."

"That sounds like revenge talking. Now I'm intrigued. What's your evil plan, little monster?"

"I'm going to get my life back, Massimo. I'm going to land on my feet, and I won't stop until I'm done."

His amusement fades because he knows my determination is nothing to joke about. He knows Harrison is going to pay for what he did to me.

We're both quiet for a moment—him because he's concentrating on the traffic, and me because I'm thinking about all the things I'm going to do once I get my money back. First stop will be Bentley's for that red dress. Second stop will be to show up at the Balboa Ball looking so fabulous my ex-friends will see just how magnificent and wonderful I am without them.

Even if it's a lie right now. At least I'm breathing and relatively healthy. With a roof over my head and a job.

And not in prison.

I sneak a look at Massimo. It's stupid to admit, but watching him drive is a turn-on. Hell, who am I kidding. Anything this guy does at this point is a turn-on.

But I'm not going to let him distract me from my goals.

Find Harrison.

Shoot him in the face.

Buy dress.

Make ex-friends green with envy.

They might seem frivolous to some, childish even, but at the moment, they're all I've got.

I steal another glance at Massimo. His profile is perfect.

Thick hair. Smooth forehead. Beautiful eyes. A nose people pay good money for, but one he was born with. The kind of cheekbones you only see on runway models. Full lips that know how to make a girl come in the back seat of your car as you pull her back and forward over your erection.

The memory roars out of the dark depths of my brain and spreads heat all over my body.

I remember that night as if it was yesterday.

The way his lips tasted. The way his fingers dug into my ass as he made us both come.

It's because I'm in the same car, I tell myself. *Same leather. Same scent invading my senses.*

I push my thighs together. I really need to get laid.

He pulls the car up to the curb, and for a moment, I forget this is the fake address I gave him.

"Why are we stopping here?" I ask.

"Because you live here."

Realizing my mistake, I try to cover it up but only make the situation worse. "Yeah... of course... I was lost in thought..."

"About?"

You and how you made me come in the back seat of this car.

"Stuff." Is my great response.

I'm flustered because I suck at lying, and now I can't get my seat belt to unlock.

I jab at the buckle, but I'm suddenly all fingers.

Massimo leans over to help, and I'm suddenly engulfed in his heat and that addictive scent that is pure him. He unlocks the buckle with ease, chuckling as he does so.

I barely get the words out. "Thank you."

"I can't sit by and watch a damsel in distress, even if seeing you tied up is kind of hot."

"What do you mean?" I whisper, slightly inebriated on his scent.

He leans closer so his lips brush my ear. "It means I would very much like to see you in cuffs again."

Bells and whistles ignite inside me, and that achy need that's taken up residence between my thighs since he arrived at the police station skyrockets to a relentless throb, forcing me to squeeze my thighs together.

He settles back in his seat as if he didn't just set my body on fire. "I'll see you tomorrow." He gives me a devastating grin. "Just try not to get arrested between now and then."

20

BIANCA

The next day, I start my new job with Eve. Essentially, I'm her PA, helping her with the day-to-day running of the club, like reviewing rosters, chasing up various supply orders, and making sure all the administration tasks get checked off.

Eve runs a well-oiled ship. She can be flippant and breezy, but when it comes to business, she is as professional and diligent as they come.

She also seems relieved that I'm here to help. Dario didn't appear to do a lot more than walk around the bar looking moody.

At the end of each day, we confirm the roster to make sure everything is in place for the night's performances.

"What is this number in the last column?" I ask.

"That's how much the performers get paid."

My mouth drops open. Some of the numbers are astronomical.

"John and Jared are getting paid twenty-five hundred dollars for a thirty minute performance?" I want to know who John and Jared are and what the hell they do for thirty minutes that earns them twelve hundred and fifty dollars apiece.

"John and Jared cater to our clients who like to watch two men together," Eve explains.

"You mean they—"

"Have sex, yes. But there are blow jobs and other things besides the actual penetration. It depends what the client requests."

I look at the other names on the list.

"Judge Julie? What does she do for forty-five minutes to earn nine hundred dollars?"

"She wears a judge's gown over a PVC bikini and spanks a submissive. She also allows suggestions from the clients. She's very popular. I think she's on twice tonight."

Indeed she is. She'll be taking home eighteen hundred dollars for ninety minutes' worth of spanking.

"Jerome Big Dick Collins for four hundred dollars?" I can't help but laugh at his name.

"Don't laugh, his name is an understatement. He's one of our sex butlers, and he has a twelve-inch cock."

There's a lot to unpack in that sentence.

"A sex butler?"

"Yes, he'll serve drinks naked. He's very popular for obvious reasons."

"Twelve inches' worth of reasons. Wow. I've never seen one that big."

Who am I kidding?

I haven't seen one at all.

Unless it's been on Netflix.

"How is any of this legal?"

Eve laughs. "Legalities don't matter to the De Kysa. I mean, Massimo abides by the law where necessary. But in other areas, it really comes down to who you know and how much you're willing to pay them off."

Which is typical. My father had lots of people paid off.

"People really pay this amount of money to watch these people perform?"

"Our clients pay for the complete experience in pleasure and fantasy. The performers, the butlers, the food, and drink. It's one big package customized to their desires. Then we pay the performers their cut."

"How long do the peep shows last?"

"Usually a client will book the room for two hours and schedule several different performances. So someone who likes to watch dancers may book ten dances for the two hours. Some clients mix it up and have a dancer perform, then bring in new performers for a sex show."

"What's the longest anyone has booked the room?"

"I won't name names, but there was a rock star and his wife, and they spent about five hours in there. Watched four sex shows and three dances. Spent a fortune on champagne as well."

And I had no idea any of this even existed.

I look back at the roster.

"Candy Cane. What does she do for three hundred?"

"Candy Cane is one of our private dancers. She'll dance for clients. Usually half an hour."

"Just dance?" I ask.

"Yes, just dance."

Three hundred dollars.

I stare at the figure on the paper as an idea begins to unfurl in my head.

Eve notices. "What does that look on your face mean?" When I give her a toothy grin, it clicks, and she starts to shake her head. "Oh no, you're not thinking what I think you're thinking?"

"If you're thinking I'm going to become a performer, then yes, you are thinking what I am thinking."

She groans. "No, that is a very bad idea."

"Why? It's good money. And I am the very definition of someone needing good money."

"Because Massimo won't like it. You're friends. He doesn't let friends perform."

"Why not?"

"Because he likes to keep his private life separate from his professional life."

"Then we don't tell him."

She laughs as if it's a ridiculous notion—which it probably is. "You'll never get away with it. He vets every new performer."

"So, I'll wear a wig and a mask for that performance. He'll never know."

"You know he's a Mafia don, right? He's alive because he can see through all the masks and metaphorical wigs of those who try to fool him." She shakes her head. "This is a bad idea."

"Sometimes bad ideas pave the way for those in debt, Eve."

"Can you even dance?"

I'm mock offended. "My mom enrolled me in dance the

moment I could walk."

Dancing is probably the only thing I'm good at.

She looks pained as she asks, "Is there anything I can say to talk you out of it?"

"No, because I have three hundred very good reasons why this bad idea is a very good thing."

TWO DAYS LATER, I'm wearing a long red wig and a masquerade mask while getting dressed behind a privacy screen in one of the club's dressing rooms.

Eve chews her fingernail. "Remember, he wears a gun. If he finds out it's you, he'll probably shoot you first and me second."

"You worry too much. He's not going to know it's me," I say, securing a gun garter around my thigh.

I step out from behind the privacy screen, and Eve's eyes light up.

"Oh my God, you look hot."

I'm wearing an ankle-length lace robe over a red bikini set, and black thigh-high boots. The robe buttons from the belly button up, leaving the rest open, so when I walk, the slinky lace swirls apart to reveal my legs and bikini bottoms. I look like a sexy, gunslinging vamp who's just stepped out of the Wild West.

"What song are you performing to?" Eve asks.

"'I See Red' by Everybody Loves an Outlaw."

"Oooh, yeah, it's a fitting song."

It's a powerful revenge song, and it's kind of my anthem now.

For the past two nights, I've been practicing my routine in my motel room, and I'm pretty sure Rosa has fucked a few clients to it, while the roadie on the other side of me probably wished it wasn't playing on loop while I practiced my moves in front of the chipped mirror on the wall.

"I'm still not convinced this is going to work," Eve reminds me for the millionth time.

"Ye of little faith. I only have to conceal my identity for three minutes and thirty-eight seconds. It'll be a piece of cake." I click my fingers as if it will be the easiest thing in the world to pull off. "Besides, the lighting I've chosen is low, so it will make it harder to see my face."

Yesterday, I met with Stu, the lighting tech, and deliberately selected a dim, shadowy setting for the audition.

I'm serious about making this work. Three hundred dollars a pop will help me out of the hole Harrison dropped me in.

And truth be told, dancing in front of Massimo and knowing I could get caught kind of excites me.

21

MASSIMO

I arrive at Lair just after three. It's two hours before opening, and the club is empty, except for Natalie and the new bar girl Eve hired to replace Bianca. They're behind the bar getting everything ready for the night.

When I walk through, Natalie gives me a nod, while the new girl's face lights up, and her eager eyes track me all the way through the club.

"Oh God, he's even sexier in real life," she says to Natalie as I pass them.

"Eyes in front, perv, the boss is off-limits," growls Natalie.

Which kind of makes me smile because if Natalie is one thing, it's consistent.

Leaving the main club through the rear door, I enter the pink-lit corridor leading to the arcade where Eve is waiting for me.

"So who am I here to see?" I ask her.

She checks her notes on her iPad. "A solo performer. Miss Hellfire. She's a dancer."

"Does she perform any sexual acts?"

"No."

"Interested in performing with anyone else?"

"No, strictly solo. She's looking for two nights a week."

"Anything else I should know?"

"She's new. I don't think she has much experience with this kind of thing."

Eve looks uncertain. She chews her thumbnail—a nervous trait.

"Something wrong?"

"No," she says a little too quickly. "It's just, well, it might be a waste of your time. She's very inexperienced."

I can already see her in my head. Young and inexperienced and lured to dance at Lair by the obscene amount of money we pay our performers.

But if anyone has the balls to get behind the glass and interview for the job, then they're worth seeing.

"You must've noticed some potential in her for her to get this far along in the process."

"Yeah," Eve says unconvincingly.

I lift a brow at her. "What's going on, evil stepsister?"

"Nothing. Enjoy the show." She shoves the iPad at me and practically runs out of the arcade.

Inside the peep room, I settle in the seat and scroll through the information on the iPad. Apparently, Miss Hellfire is a twenty-something redhead from Idaho who likes walking around her house naked and lives to dance.

The lights come on behind the glass, and Miss Hellfire

appears like a blast of sensual energy as "I See Red" bursts from the speakers.

And fuck me.

Miss Hellfire is stunning.

Legs for miles in thigh-high boots, which just happen to be my one and only weakness. Lashings of red hair tumbling down to her tiny waist. Big eyes behind a masquerade mask.

And then I see her lips.

Those luscious red lips.

Luscious red lips I am well acquainted with.

Because of the mask, it's hard to see her face, but she could wear a thousand different masks and I'd always know it was her.

Bianca.

My body reacts almost immediately. It's like every cell explodes with arousal.

I pour a scotch and take a big mouthful.

I may not know a lot about a lot, but you shouldn't underestimate me, Massimo De Kysa.

Behind the screen, Miss Hellfire dips and parts her firm thighs, revealing a captivating view of her bikini-clad pussy, and my cock thickens in appreciation.

I should put an end to this. But hell, I can't tear my eyes off her, let alone stop her. The way her body moves. The tantalizing way her hips sway in time to the music. The way her body looks in the red bikini she's wearing. My breathing quickens, my pulse races. I haven't felt this level of excitement in months.

I drain my drink and quickly pour another. But there is no chance I'm getting whiskey dick. I'm hard as fuck.

She stands and turns her back to me, and after undoing

the buttons of her robe, it slips to the floor, revealing the juiciest, luscious ass I've ever seen.

Round.

Perky.

Fucking perfect.

I have to undo the top button of my shirt and sit back in the chair.

My cock aches behind my zipper.

I can't rip my eyes from the glass—from Miss Hellfire's mesmerizing dance in black lace and a tiny red bikini.

Images of tearing it from her body and sinking into her sweet, wet pussy send a wave of heat through me.

My palms sweat, dying to hit the button on the table beside me that requests the glass petition be removed.

But I won't.

Not ever.

Instead, I sit frozen to the chair with my pulse racing and quickening breath.

She drops to her haunches and parts her knees, and I see another flash of the red bikini. *Fuck.* What I would give for a taste of what is behind that tiny strip of red fabric.

I grip the glass of scotch in my hand so tight my fingers ache.

I want her. I want her so bad it hurts.

Too bad I won't ever be able to touch.

Because I've done bad things.

Things she can never know.

~

After the lights go down and Bianca disappears from the peep room, I remain seated. Every nerve and fiber in my body hums with need and a restless urge I know I can't satisfy.

My little monster has moves.

She would be a draw card, for sure. A popular addition to the Peep Arcade lineup.

Yet, the thought of sharing her with others sends a hot rush of possessiveness through me.

I leave the peep room to find Eve in her office. She looks up from her desk.

"You seriously think I wouldn't know?" I say.

She swallows. "What?"

"Miss Hellfire is Bianca."

She huffs out a breath. "For the record, I told her it was a bad idea. But Bianca insisted she wanted to try it, and who am I to deny her the opportunity?"

"She's not going on the roster."

"She wasn't any good?"

On the contrary, she was very good.

I look away, and my shrewd stepsister picks up on it. "She was good wasn't she? Why don't you want her performing... oh my God, Massimo, don't tell me you're developing feelings for—"

"Don't insult me by finishing that sentence," I growl. *A little too quickly.*

Eve leans back in her chair and eyes me for a moment before adding, "You need to let her have this, Massimo."

"Why?"

"Because I like her. And I think she needs this."

"She's paying off her debt to me by working for you."

"It goes deeper than the money. I think it feels good for her to shed her skin and be someone else while she's in that room. She's been through a lot because of who she is. Let her be someone else for a while."

What Bianca doesn't know is that I will not be taking any payment for finding Harrison. But I don't tell her because I know she needs to feel like she is in control. And when you're paying, you're in control.

"Fine, but you don't book her for anyone but me."

"You're denying her the chance to earn more money."

"Only. Me."

"But—"

"Twice a week. Two songs. Five hundred dollars."

Eve's mouth drops open; she's speechless. Which is saying something.

I walk out of the room before she can come up with something to say.

I'm walking a thin line.

But if I can't have Bianca in reality, at least twice a week, I can have her in my fantasies.

22

BIANCA

Ecstatic and buzzing after my audition, I catch up with Eve in her office.

"Oh my God, that was just as amazing as I thought it would be," I say, my enthusiasm bubbling out of me as I lean against her desk.

But Eve looks uncomfortable.

"What?" I ask.

"I was hoping you'd decided your first dance would be your last, you know, get it out of your system and move on."

"Not a chance. It felt incredible dropping my inhibitions and being someone other than poor little broke Bianca for the duration of the song." I sit down opposite her. "What did Massimo say? Did he like it? Am I going on the roster?"

She doesn't look me in the eye, but she nods. "Yes, you're on the roster."

"Yes!" I'm so excited I jump up. Finally, something I am good at. "When do I start?"

"Our IT girl is updating our website and client list as we speak."

"So I might get a client soon?"

"Yes."

"And Massimo didn't realize it was me?"

Again, she doesn't meet my eye. She focuses on whatever is in front of her on the computer screen. It's then I realize she's preoccupied because I probably interrupted her doing something.

"Sorry to burst in here like that; it's just that it was a real rush auditioning for something I really enjoyed. And now that Massimo has approved Miss Hellfire to perform... I don't know, it just feels good to know I'm helping dig myself out of this hole I'm in."

Eve looks up and smiles, and it's genuine and warm. "That's great, Bianca. You deserve to feel happy about this." She thinks for a moment and then adds, "In fact, we have a client requesting someone just like you. I'll send them your file and see if they're interested in booking you."

"Really?"

"He's a good payer too."

It's hard to contain my excitement, and I leave Lair on cloud nine.

It looks like things are starting to look up for me.

Even the grime and seediness of the Last Stop Motel can't dampen the buzz I feel after dancing my first peep show. But the real buzz was knowing Massimo was watching me. I try not to overthink it, but who am I kidding, I'm going to overthink this because it is what I do. I got off on Massimo watching me, and it's probably because I'm either falling for my boss slash enemy slash kiss thief, or I'm crazy. Or both. *Probably both.* But I also feel grateful knowing I am one step closer to paying Massimo what I owe him for finding Harrison.

When I let myself in to my room, I feel the prickly unease settle over me, but I force it to the back of my mind. I do my usual search for cameras, now a habit because I don't trust Snake, and thankfully, I still don't find any. Except, while I'm searching, it suddenly occurs to me that it's not just cameras I should be looking for, and that Snake might not be the only person who might put video and audio surveillance on me.

My father used to have an associate called Lawrence who used to plant bugs in homes or vehicles when my father asked him to. I met him once, and he showed me what they looked like. Said if ever I came across one, I should either get rid of it or use it to my advantage and feed whoever had put me under surveillance a lot of false information.

George, my father's head of security, also gave me the speech about bugs and RG transmitters, and at the time, I thought it was all a bit over the top, and I didn't pay a lot of attention because I wanted to go shopping with Jules.

The sudden recollection has me running to the landline in the room and, what do you know, there it is, stuck to the back of the console, almost too small to see. A tiny black bug transmitting all of my words back to whoever is listening.

Not that it will be netting them any information. I literally don't talk to anyone when I close the door behind me.

Yeah, that's right, whoever is listening, I really am a lonely loser who has no friends.

A further search nets me two more bugs. One plugged into the wall socket beneath the desk in the corner, and another one in the bathroom hidden beneath the vanity.

Massimo.

The invasion to my privacy ignites my temper like a match to gasoline.

"Asshole!" I yell into the listening devices. "Asshole. Asshole. Asshole."

I'd like to say I storm back to Lair like a bat out of hell to confront Massimo, but that's impossible to do when your car is still on blocks because someone stole your tires in the middle of the night so you have to take a cab through busy New York traffic.

It takes me thirty minutes to get there, but my temper is still boiling by the time I reach Lair.

Clearly, Massimo was expecting me because he's sitting behind his desk with that amused grin on those stupidly kissable lips and is completely relaxed as I spin into the room like an EF5 tornado and throw the surveillance devices onto his desk in front of him.

"This is a complete breach of my privacy," I yell at him.

"And?"

"*And* how dare you!"

He rises from behind his desk, and it's like watching the devil rise up from hell—all dark energy and villainous intent but sexy and delicious and very, very enticing. Every female instinct in me wakes up, despite knowing it would be very bad for me let him get too close.

"How many times do I have to tell you. I have no alliances left. No bad intentions. When are you going to trust me?"

He takes a step toward me, and the pounding in my heart skyrockets to new levels.

"You of all people should know how betrayal works. You very rarely see it coming if you're too busy looking the other way. The only way to protect yourself is knowing what your enemy is up to when he thinks you don't know."

"I'm not the enemy!" I cry. "I'm the girl in the blue dress whose first kiss you stole."

The words rush out in a surge of emotion and I immediately regret them.

Much to Massimo's amusement.

His lips twist, and one perfectly shaped eyebrow lifts. "Stole? If memory serves, you didn't complain."

"Because my mouth was full of tongue."

His black-as-black eyes burn as he steps even closer.

"Do you really think I'd let you into my club without knowing what you are doing when you're not here?"

The way he's looking at me, it's like fire and ice. Fire because standing this close to him is like being absorbed into a wildfire of physical attraction and lust, and ice because all the confidence I found in my anger has been suddenly doused with icy water as he moves even closer to me.

"Perhaps I should kiss you again, see if it helps your memory."

I gasp. "You wouldn't dare."

He steps even closer. But I don't move because I'm being dragged into his orbit.

A wicked look moves over his handsome features. "You should know by now, little monster, you should never dare me to do anything because I might just do it."

23

MASSIMO

Christ, I'm in hell. I'm still hard from watching her dance, and now she's yelling at me, her eyes wild, the gloss on her lips gleaming every time she opens her mouth to call me a name. Fuck, I should be putting a stop to it because all I want to do is bend her over my desk and fuck this need for her out of my body.

I stalk toward her, and her wild eyes widen. She takes a step back until the back of her thighs hit the edge of my desk.

"You need to remember who you're talking to," I growl.

My phone rings.

Thank fuck for small mercies.

It's Matteo.

"What?" I snap into the phone.

"We've found an address for Harrison Tork."

"Where is it?"

"In the city."

Now that's a surprise. Either he's visiting, or he never left.

Which tells me something doesn't add up.

A criminal accountant who steals a fortune from his unsuspecting victim doesn't hang around if he has any brains.

Especially when his victim has ties to various criminal elements.

He should be living it up in a tropical island somewhere, completely off radar.

"Can you confirm a sighting?" I ask.

"No. But we're here, out the front of his brownstone. You want us to check it out further?"

"No, send me the address. I'll leave now. And, Matteo, nobody does a thing until I get there."

I hang up. I'm still hard as fuck, but this can't wait.

Which is going to give me a painful set of blue balls.

"What's wrong?" Bianca asks.

"Business."

I feel her stiffen. "Is it about Harrison?"

When I don't answer her, she presses me.

"Massimo, does it have something to do with Harrison? Have you found him?"

"Maybe. We have an address. But it's not confirmed he's there."

I move to my desk and remove a gun from the top drawer. I carry two on me at all times. But when you're walking into an unknown situation, you can never have too much protection. Bianca's eyes track me as I secure a third piece behind my back.

"Then we have to go there. We have to get my money back."

"*We* aren't going anywhere. You're staying here while I pursue this lead."

"You're delusional if you think I'm not coming with you. If Harrison is there, I want to see him face-to-face."

I'm good at picking my battles to win a war. Fighting Bianca will only hold me up.

Whether I like it or not, she's coming with me.

"Fine, but you stay in the fucking car."

IT TAKES us thirty minutes because of roadworks in the city, so by the time we get there, Bianca is chewing her nails and bouncing her knee. Her quest to find Harrison might be over, and an anxious storm is brewing inside her.

"Wait here," I say, pulling up behind Matteo.

"No way," she cries, unlocking her seat belt.

"Listen to me. I don't know what we're walking into, and if bullets start flying, it's going to be hard to protect you. Let me go in first and see what the situation is. Once it's safe, I'll send Matteo out to get you."

"I can take care of myself."

"I don't doubt you can. But we have to do this my way, Bianca, or I'm driving you back to Lair."

Her eyes flare but she finally concedes. She folds her arms and gives me a murderous look. "Fine."

I climb out. I have half a mind to lock her in. But a locked door wouldn't stop her. If she really wanted out of the car, she would blow a hole in the window with the cute little Beretta she carries in her handbag.

I walk over to Matteo where he's standing beside two De Kysa soldiers. He's already figured out a way inside and is waiting for me to give the go-ahead.

"For someone who rips off rich people, he's not overly concerned with security." He nods toward the gate blocking the driveway which is easily scalable. "We've already detected the home security system is off."

Having a tech wizard in our pocket is always useful.

"Who does the house belong to, do we know?" I ask.

"Some overseas oil magnate who rents it out. My guess Harrison is hiding out here until things die down."

I shake my head. We've been scouring the globe and he's been here the whole time.

"Have you seen any sign of him?" I ask.

"No, nothing."

I take in the tall brownstone with the bay windows and prominent front door. Something isn't right.

"You ready for the guys to go in?" Matteo asks.

I give the signal with a nod, and Matteo sends them in. Watching them, I draw in a deep breath through my nose and feel the venom spin through my veins. These are the moments you know you're really alive. When the thrill of the chase is about to end, and you know you're about to win.

Letting out the breath, I stride across the road and follow my men inside the home of Harrison Tork.

It's completely dark, and there is no sign of life.

The house is still, *eerily still*, and when we get to the second floor master bedroom, it becomes wildly apparent why.

Harrison Tork is zip-tied to a chair, his wrists and ankles bound in place, completely naked with a gaping hole in his neck from a gunshot wound. His head is slumped forward, and his eyes stare lifelessly at the floor.

"Well, that's disappointing," Matteo says.

I crouch in front of Harrison and study his wound. He hasn't been dead long.

"He's naked," Dante says. "Lovers disagreement?"

I look at the zip ties. "No, someone wanted something from him and then they shot him."

"You thinking of anyone in particular?" Matteo asks.

"The neck wound. It has Bamcorda written all over it." I rise to my feet. "Tony Vinocelli, the consigliere to Luca Bamcorda, he has a son, Fausto, did a lot of the dirty work for Luca. It's his signature. He liked to aim for the jugular."

"You think Tony Vinocelli is behind this?" Dante asks. "Why would he want Harrison dead?"

"Revenge for stealing from Bianca?" Matteo asks.

"No, they didn't do this for Bianca. They turned their backs on her like scared little mice. No, they did this for the money."

A sudden commotion downstairs tells me Bianca didn't stay in the car.

Of course she didn't.

Now she's screaming blue murder at one of my soldiers.

"Let her up," I call down to him.

I meet her at the top of the stairs, wanting to prepare her for what she is about to see.

"You need to wait," I say, stepping in front of her.

But wild horses aren't going to stop her from getting into

that room. She pushes past me, but stops in the doorway when she sees Harrison is dead.

Her body stiffens and her hands ball into fists at her side, and she swings around to face me.

"Did you do this?" she yells. Her eyes are wild, and her beautiful face is flushed with emotion. "Did you take this from me?"

She's shaking. She's waited for weeks to confront him and get her retribution. But it's a retribution she won't get.

In a burst of emotions, she pulls out her gun and points it at me, but I don't flinch. I'm too damn busy being turned on by my little monster's fire.

Matteo and Dante draw their weapons.

"No need for that," I tell them, my eyes fixed firmly on Bianca. "Miss Bamcorda is simply letting off steam."

If it were anyone else, they would experience the full weight of my wrath for daring to point a gun at me.

But given the chance, I'll punish her in more pleasurable ways. Because if she can cross the line, then I'm going to cross the line and set fucking fire to it.

Tears well in her wild eyes, and her beautiful face reveals the agony she feels. Because after everything she's been through, she needed this.

A lone tear rolls down her smooth cheek.

"Tell me the truth, did you do this? Did you kill Harrison?"

I look her in the eyes. "No, I didn't."

"Why should I believe you?"

"Because I've never lied to you, and I never will."

Her hand starts to shake.

"Look at him," I demand. "I'm not one for theatrics,

Bianca. If I were going to shoot him, I'd do it and be done with it."

Slowly, she lowers her gun and grits her teeth. "Then who did?"

"I don't know for sure yet, but we will find out."

It's a half-truth. My mind tells me it's Fausto's work, but my gut tells me to not put all my eggs in that basket. And until I know for sure, I don't want Bianca doing something impulsive, like hunting down Fausto and shooting him.

"Come on, let me take you home." I offer her my hand, and to my surprise she takes it, and the sudden touch of her skin against mine ignites a protective need in me. I grasp her hand tightly but resist the urge to put my arms around her.

I look at Matteo and Dante. "Ring Damon, tell him to hunt down this asshole's bank records, email, financial records of any kind. If Harrison has a cell phone, don't leave it behind. I want to know who he's been talking to and where he's been."

Matteo nods.

"Dispose of the body and make sure we were never here." Our cleanup crew is meticulous and fast, and will eliminate any fingerprints or evidence that we were ever in the house. "Then call me when you're done. We'll meet up later to forge the plan ahead. Because I want to know who did this, and I want to know today."

SHE'S quiet during the drive back to her apartment in Midtown. She stares out the window, and her hands are still balled into fists on her lap.

"This is just a setback," I say. "You can trust me when I say I will find out who is behind this."

She turns her beautiful face to me. It's tearstained, and her eyes are wet. "I can't trust anyone."

A heavy weight sinks into my chest. Because she's right.

She turns back to stare out the window. "Everything has just changed," she murmurs, lost in thought.

"Yes, it has. But it means we pivot."

The traffic slows because it's peak hour. Outside, horns blare as the traffic into the city gets heavier. But inside the car, it is still and quiet, and I can hear Bianca's gentle breaths as she bites into her lips and reconsiders what Harrison's death means. She's a mix of disappointment and vulnerability, and I want to change that more than I'm prepared to admit to myself.

"Do you think someone else was behind Harrison stealing everything?" she asks, turning back to face me. "Or did they find out what he did and took it from him?"

"We don't know that the money's gone. Damon will let me know within the hour."

"Do you think it'll be there?"

I think for a moment, considering my words very carefully. She's suffered a blow this afternoon, and I don't want to crush her any further.

"Massimo?" she presses.

But I told her I would never lie to her.

"No, I don't think it is. I think someone else is pressing the buttons and Harrison was collateral. Your money is gone."

"Gee, don't hold back."

"Like I said, you can trust me to tell you the truth."

And one day, this will be true, I promise, I think to myself. *But until I fix this, I can't tell you everything.*

She exhales a shaky breath.

"I need to walk it off," she says, suddenly unlocking her seat belt. "I need to think. Stop the car and let me out."

"I'm not letting you out. Not until I know you're okay."

"I'm not okay. I'm so far from okay I'll need a fucking map to get back. That's why I need to walk this off."

"I'm not going to leave you alone." I glance at her. "Let me get you back to your apartment, and we'll talk."

As I pull up to a red light, my phone rings. Matteo.

When I answer it, Bianca opens the car door and climbs out in the middle of the stopped traffic.

"Bianca!" I yell at her. But she slams the door shut.

"Fuck!" I say into the phone, watching Bianca weave in and out of cars until she reaches the sidewalk and rushes off down the street.

"You okay, Massimo?" Matteo sounds confused.

"Fucking Bianca just got out of the car."

"Where are you?"

"I was dropping Bianca home to her apartment in Midtown."

"In Midtown?"

"Yeah, why?"

"Because she doesn't live there."

24

BIANCA

The streets are busy, the crowds heavy, and as I push through the throng of people, I'm happy to disappear into a sea of anonymity and be alone with my thoughts.

My dark, angry thoughts.

I don't know where I'm going. All I know is I needed to get out of the car and walk off the restlessness and disappointment clawing at me. I need space and air to figure out what all of this this means, and what I'm going to do now that Harrison is dead, and I don't have any idea where my money is.

Massimo said we'd go back to my apartment and talk.

But I don't feel like talking.

I feel like walking.

And punching something.

Just when I was taking a giant step forward, it now feels like I've just taken a thousand steps back.

I'm no closer to getting my old life back. This is probably it for me.

I want to cry and scream and yell; instead, I adjust my handbag over my shoulder and keep forging ahead.

I will call Massimo when I get home and find out if Damon has good news. If not, I'm going to the closest gun range, and I'm going to spend my last few dollars on some rounds and unload them into the target.

There are three things I am good at in this life. Spending money. Getting my own way. And shooting shit.

If I can't shoot Harrison in the face, then I'll go shoot pretend Harrison at the shooting range.

I know Massimo will be looking for me. But I need time to figure things out, so I plan to stay low for the next few hours, and I'm pretty sure he won't think of looking for me at a shooting range.

He also doesn't know my Midtown apartment is actually an eight-dollar-a-night motel ten miles in the other direction, else he would've said something when I gave him the phony address. Clearly, whoever planted the bugs in my room hasn't told him where that room is.

Focus, Bianca.

I inhale the late afternoon air.

Someone murdered Harrison.

I can't put into words how shitty it makes me feel.

I know a part of me should be glad he's dead, because he's a lowlife, thieving asshole who destroyed my life.

But there is another part of me, *a gigantic part*, that wanted to confront him myself. To look him in the eye and demand answers.

Would I have killed him?

I've never killed anyone in my life.

But I was prepared to make him my first.

I take the long way back to the motel, and finally arrive about half an hour after I left Massimo back in Midtown.

I unlock the door and pull it open but freeze in the doorway. Because sitting on my bed, looking fifty shades of pissed off, is Massimo. He stands.

"Get your things, you're not staying here."

IT TAKES me ten minutes to gather my things.

The first eight are spent arguing with Massimo about not needing his charity, which he ignored and let me know in no uncertain terms that I was leaving with him, even if it meant he had to throw me over his shoulder and carry me out himself.

Which, if I'm honest, would turn me on if I wasn't so worked up about Harrison.

The last two minutes are spent actually gathering up my belongings and shoving them into my suitcase and overnight bag.

"Is that all of your things?" he asks.

"This is what an IRS raid, a thieving accountant, and two months spent pawning anything of value so you can eat looks like. Welcome to *Down and Outsville*, Massimo. I'm the mayor."

He doesn't say anything, but something dark and tight moves through his expression as he unlocks the trunk of his car. He takes the bags from me and puts them in the back.

By the time we leave the motel, the sun has ducked

behind the skyline, casting the city in a sapphire twilight.

I watch Massimo drive. Like everything he does, it's done with confidence and with a fearlessness I feel drawn to. He's focused, with his eyes fixed firmly on the road, the muscle in his jaw ticking as he grips the wheel, and I realize he is silent because he is pissed about something.

"Are you angry?" I ask.

He shifts gear like a race car driver.

"And here I was thinking I had a great poker face," he says.

"You do. But when you're angry, the little muscle in your jaw ticks."

He glances at me, his face half hidden by shadow, the other side lit up by the city lights. "Is that so?"

God, he's handsome.

He gives me a small smile, then turns his attention back to the road.

"Why didn't you tell me you were living in that shitbox?"

"What does it matter?"

He shifts gear again. "It matters to me."

"Why? It's not your problem."

He doesn't answer and keeps his eyes firmly on the road ahead.

"You lied to me," he says finally. "You told me you were bunking at a friend's apartment in Midtown."

I turn my face from him to look out the window. "Because I didn't want you to know, okay? A girl has her pride."

"You thought I'd think less of you because you were staying in a motel I wouldn't put my worst enemy in?" He glances at me. "Why do you care what I think?"

"Why do you care where I live?"

"Because it's not safe." He shoves the gear stick forward. "And I'm involved now. I can't have you living anywhere unsafe. So no more secrets, little monster. If we're going to get your money back I want you to do two things."

"Which are?"

"Trust me, and don't keep anything from me." He pulls into an underground parking garage.

I can't help but smile. He's being so protective, and after today, it feels nice to have someone so capable in my corner.

Massimo's apartment is in Tribeca and takes up the top floor of the apartment complex.

And it's stunning. Open layout. Exposed brick. Sleek, polished concrete floors. Soft ambient light. Large arched windows stretching from the floor to the ceiling, with the iconic cityscape glittering beyond.

It's the perfect balance between modern design and industrial chic.

Stepping through the steel-framed door, I follow Massimo into the lounge where he drops my bags by the plush sofa and walks over to the bar.

I look around the apartment. It feels warm here. Comfortable. It carries a hint of a woody, earthy scent, mixed with the cold, hard feel of money.

"You live here?" I ask as Massimo opens a bottle of scotch.

"No, I only stay here if I've been working in the city late or if..."

"Or if you want to bring someone home?"

I cast my eye around the stylish loft, wondering how many women have been pleasured by Massimo within these walls. Then wonder how many women screamed his name as he made them come, and I start to feel incredibly inept. He's so experienced, and I'm so... *virginal.*

I run my fingers along the top of the glass table, looking out over the views. "So this is like a fuck pad?"

Massimo cocks an eyebrow and then starts to laugh. "No, I have a room at a hotel nearby for anything like that. As a rule very few people have access to any of my homes."

I watch him pour two drinks. He's relaxed here, less tense.

He hands me a crystal tumbler. "You can stay here until you're on your feet."

I look at him suspiciously. "Why are you being so nice to me?"

"Because I'm a sucker for Mafia princesses who aren't afraid to stand up to me when they think I'm wrong. I like your fire, little monster."

I take a sip of the scotch, which I didn't realize I needed, and end up downing it in one mouthful. It burns like molten lava going down but when the heat spreads through my chest, it makes me feel warm and relaxed and safe.

He walks back to the bar and pours me another, draining his on the way there.

"Come on, I'll give you the tour," he says, passing me the new drink.

He leads me through the loft, and I slowly take it all in.

It's then I suddenly realize I don't want to be alone.

I stop walking, and he notices. He turns around.

"Can I ask one more favor?" I ask.

"Sure."

"Will you stay with me tonight?"

25

MASSIMO

"Will you stay with me tonight?"

I'm not *going* to hell because I already live there.

Every instinct in me screams for me to leave. To say no and get the fuck out before I do something stupid like kiss her.

Because kissing her won't be enough. *You'll end up naked and inside her, driving hard and so fucking deep into her just to hear her moan your name.*

I try to ignore that little voice in the back of my head, but it's telling the truth. Spending one night inside Bianca will never be enough. I've known this since the first night in the back of the car. There is something about her that will always leave me wanting more.

It's the reason I never contacted her after the night we shared in the city. Call it self-preservation. But being involved with a woman long term has never been on my radar, and I know Bianca is the one woman who could change that.

It makes her a threat to my very existence as a free and easy man.

Which I have no interest in giving up.

Yet, the next word out of my mouth isn't goodbye. Or no. Or arrivederci.

No, instead of running toward self-preservation, I go and throw myself right in front of her crosshairs.

"Of course I will."

Yet I don't regret the words once they leave my mouth. Because she gives me a soft smile, and I'm not lying when I say it feels like I've just been shot in the chest.

"I'll take the couch," I say, removing my jacket and throwing it over the back of a lounge chair. I loosen my tie and try not to think of how only a few hours ago she was dancing for me behind the peep glass. But it's impossible. Bianca has a body you don't forget.

"Do you mind if I take a shower?" she asks.

Which is a question that does nothing to stop the images of her beautiful curves replaying in my head.

"This is your home for the time being." I lead her into the bedroom and gesture to the adjoining bathroom. "Make yourself at home. I'll order in some takeout while you shower. Any preference?"

She shakes her head, and I decide I like the way it falls around her face.

As I turn to leave, she says my name. I turn around and she smiles cautiously. "Thank you."

I walk calmly out of the room and straight to the bar and pour myself a triple scotch.

Knowing she's naked in my shower is murder when all I want to do is join her under that stream of hot water and do so many things to her beautiful body. Like lick the water from her delicious curves as I press her against the wet tiles and sink my cock so deep into her from behind.

I drain my scotch and quickly pour another.

I don't think I'll be getting any sleep tonight.

THE STORM HITS the city around two a.m. and I'm woken by a flash of lightning followed by a violent clap of thunder.

My instincts tell me I'm not alone, and I sit up ready to reach for my gun on the coffee table. But that's when I see Bianca standing in the lounge room.

The loft is dark, but there are enough flashes of lightning for me to see her beautiful face and the sweet curves of her body.

Our eyes meet as she walks toward me, and flashes of lightning illuminate the apartment. I swallow slowly, because I don't think I've ever seen anything as sexy as Bianca wearing an oversize band t-shirt. It falls to the top of her thighs, and I can see a hint of her underwear as she walks toward the couch.

She says nothing when she reaches me, she simply pulls back the blanket draped over my body and climbs in beside me, pressing her back to my chest and pulling the blanket over to cover us.

She relaxes against me, and as if it's the most natural

thing in the world, I wrap my arm around her and hold her to me.

"Thank you," she whispers and promptly falls to sleep.

While I lie wide awake beside her, wondering why it feels so good to have her in my arms.

26

BIANCA

I wake up on the couch alone. It takes me a moment to figure out where I am. Then I remember coming to the lounge room in the middle of the night because there was a storm raging outside, and if there's one thing that scares me, it's a thunderstorm.

But it all melted away once I was on the couch and Massimo had his arm around me, and I fell into a deep, restful sleep.

The smell of freshly-brewed coffee and toast wafts through the apartment, and my stomach growls.

Following my nose, I'm greeted by Massimo in the kitchen, making breakfast. He's shirtless and wearing a pair of black pants with a belt, and my mouth immediately goes dry. He doesn't just have abs, he has abs on abs. And every time he moves, they flex and dip, and I can't help but wonder how it would feel to run my tongue along them.

It's not fair that he's so perfect first thing in the morning, while I look like a family of forest creatures have nested in my hair.

"Coffee's hot." Massimo's strong voice doesn't get lost in the spacious apartment. "And breakfast is almost served."

As much as I want to run toward breakfast because it smells so good, I gingerly pad across the Italian tiles to the kitchen, and it almost feels like a walk of shame because last night, I put myself in Massimo's arms and nuzzled into this warm chest, and this morning, I don't know how I feel about that.

I slide onto a stool at the kitchen counter, and he flashes me a grin that sends all kinds of mush through me.

Really, the man is too attractive for his own good.

I let my gaze slide down his ridiculously perfect body and try to figure out why a black pair of pants with a belt and silver belt buckle are so outrageously sexy on a shirtless man. Bare feet too.

"How do you like your coffee?" he asks.

"I don't drink coffee," I reply, trying to shake out the tangles in my hair.

"I'll pretend I didn't hear that." He hands me a cup. "Try it."

I look at the thick, black liquid.

"It will put hair on your chest," Massimo says.

"I don't doubt it," I say. It smells delicious but I've never been a coffee drinker. It gives me too much of a buzz, and I get jittery.

The door buzzer sounds.

"Saved by the bell," I say, sliding off the stool. "I'll get it."

I peer through the peephole. On the other side of the door is Eve and she's carrying a large gold box in her arms.

I open the door. "Eve!"

"Ooh, hello, what are you doing here?" Her eyes gleam with mischief as they sweep over me wearing nothing but an oversized t-shirt. She grins. "Playing sleepovers with my brother? It's about time you two stopped playing cat and mouse and finally did the deed."

"Oh, no it's not like that—"

She waves me off and breezes past me into the apartment. "I've already made up my mind what's happening, and it's way more interesting than *oh no, it's not like that*." She puts the giant gold box onto the kitchen counter. "Hello, gangster brother. Is that coffee fresh?"

Massimo seems unfazed by the tornado that is Eve barreling into his apartment.

"Ignore her," he says to me as he takes a nonchalant sip of coffee. "She keeps forgetting how I am a powerful man who can have her killed."

Eve scoffs and rolls her eyes. "Like you could live without me." She hands him a luxurious looking black envelope. "As requested."

I don't know what is going on, but I get the feeling that Massimo has been up for hours making things happen.

He hands her my cup of coffee. "Bianca doesn't drink it."

"Is she unwell?"

"No, she doesn't like it."

Eve looks confused. "I don't understand."

It's my turn to roll my eyes at their teasing but can't help but laugh when she takes a sip of coffee and sighs dramatically. "God, it's almost as good as sex.

Which I'm hardly a good judge of.

"You know, I expect a gigantic bonus for getting out of bed early on a Sunday morning," she says, taking another appreciative sip of her espresso. "Thankfully, the box was ready to pick up when I got there, and an assistant met me out front so I didn't have to wait around. And in reality, it should be you that's thankful, because waiting around on a Sunday morning before her first cup of coffee could make this girl a little bit surly toward her stepbrother. Mmmm, this coffee is good, I need one of these coffee machines in my apartment." She taps the complicated-looking coffee machine. "Christmas is just around the corner, just saying."

Massimo lifts an eyebrow. "Eve..?"

"Hmmm..?"

"Take a breath," he says.

"I can't, I've got things to do and people to see."

She drains her cup of coffee.

"Anyway, I must be off now. I have a breakfast date, and then I plan to spend the rest of the day in bed with her, so do not ring me. I mean it, Massimo, it's my day off. I don't care if the sky is falling in or a limb has fallen off. Do. Not. Call. Me."

She disappears in the same cloud of sparkling energy as she arrived, and Massimo closes the door behind her.

"I wish I had her energy," I say.

"We all do. She makes me feel like an old man."

"I can't imagine you as an old man."

"Just as I am now but even more handsome."

"And modest, no doubt."

"Modesty is completely overrated."

I look at the gold box in front of me. "So what's all of this about?"

Massimo leans against the marble counter and takes a sip of his coffee. "Go ahead and open it."

I give him a quizzical look. "It's for me?"

He nods, and my heart flutters in my chest.

He bought me a present?

I undo the silky ribbon, lift the top of the box, and immediately gasp. Inside, beneath layers of soft tissue paper, I see a flash of ruby-red silk, and tears spring to my eyes. I carefully part the layers of paper with shaky fingers, and the moment my fingers touch the silk dress, my first tear falls.

"The Bianchon," I whisper, recalling the beautiful gown I'd fondled at Bentley's. I lift my gaze to Massimo. "I don't understand."

He hands me the black envelope and gestures for me to open it. Inside is an invitation.

"The Balboa Charity Ball," I gasp.

"I have to attend and you're going to be my date."

"I am?"

He leans forward and rests his thick forearms on the marble counter. "You're going to show those fair-weather friends of yours how well you've landed on your feet."

I look at the dress again, remembering how delicious the silk felt against my cheek.

It's been weeks—no, months, since I've worn anything so luxurious.

I glance at my bare feet and think about the shoe collection I pawned to pay the rates on a house I didn't even technically own at the time and wonder what I'm going to wear under the ten-thousand-dollar Bianchon masterpiece I'll be wearing.

Maybe I could borrow a pair from Natalie or Eve.

No, I have the tiniest feet in the world. What are the chances either of them wear a size six?

"Why are you staring at your feet?" Massimo asks.

"I don't have any shoes to wear," I say without thinking, then realizing how ungrateful it might sound, I give him a big sunny smile and quickly add, "But I'll find some."

"Where?"

"Excuse me?"

"Where will you find some?"

"I'll buy some."

Walmart. They sell shoes, right?

He does that thing with his penetrating gaze where he studies me as if he's staring into my mind and eavesdropping on the conversation in my head.

A warmth spreads through me.

Followed by the sudden onset of nerves.

The ball will be the first time I see Angelica, Lilah, and Jules face-to-face since the day they dumped me. And what will I tell them? I'm stone-cold broke because not only did my father owe the IRS a bunch of money, but his accountant was a thief who pretended to have my best interests at heart, but then stole everything from under my very nose. Oh yeah, and after pawning all my designer bags and shoes and limited-edition clothes so I could eat, I live in jeans now.

"Hey," Massimo's smooth voice breaks into my overthinking.

I lift my gaze to his, and like magic, all my fear drains away, and I feel calmer. Because Massimo has my back.

"I don't know what to say."

Massimo grins. "Say yes, little monster. Be my date and let's show those assholes exactly who you are."

"And who is that exactly?"

"A fucking queen who doesn't give up."

27

MASSIMO

I blow off my morning meetings to take Bianca to buy shoes.

I'm kind of pissed at Eve for not having the forethought to pick out a pair when I sent her to Bentley's to pick up the dress. But then, that's probably all part of my conniving step-sister's plan. I can see her matchmaking schemes coming from a mile away. She would know I would end up taking Bianca shopping for shoes, and well, here I am proving her right.

When we pull up out the front of Bentley's, Bianca stiffens.

"We can't go in there."

"Why not?"

"Because they banned me, remember?"

"Ah yes, the great scarf heist."

She gives me a dramatic glare. "I'm glad you think it's so funny."

"Relax." I offer her my hand. "You'll be with me."

"Which means what exactly?"

"Which means they will have no choice but to serve you."

Reluctantly, she takes my hand, and we step onto the pavement, and Dante pulls away to park around the back of the building.

As we approach the ornate entrance, the department store still looks locked.

"It's closed," Bianca says, relieved.

But nothing is ever really closed when you're the don of the De Kysa and you know how to pull strings.

George Giulio, the General Manager of Bentley's, greets us at the door. "Mr. De Kysa, Miss Bamcorda, welcome."

Bianca looks at me, then at George, then back to me.

Her eyes are wide, and her face is an open book. *You did this.*

Of course I did. Because even I know Cinderella needs a special pair of shoes to go to the ball.

"It's so nice to meet you, sir," Bianca says to George, taking his hand and shaking it enthusiastically.

"It's a pleasure, Miss Bamcorda."

"Please call me Bianca."

"Alright then, Bianca, shall we find you a pair of shoes for the ball on Friday night?"

We follow George inside the empty store where Bianca's awe continues.

"They opened early for you?" she whispers to me, even though it's so quiet you could hear a pin drop, and her whisper echoes through the store.

"No," I whisper back to her. "They opened early for *you*."

Her eyes sparkle, and something tightens inside my chest when I watch her pillowy pink lips spread into a grateful smile.

"I'd like to personally apologize for your disappointing shopping experience with us yesterday," George says as he walks, his Louis Vuitton shoes clicking on the marble floor as we make our way down the center aisle. "I believe you felt singled out by one of our employees."

"It was a misunderstanding," Bianca says softly.

"Well, the staff member in question has been reprimanded nonetheless and did offer her deepest remorse for the incident."

"That wasn't necessary," Bianca says. "She was having a bad day, I was having a bad day, then we rubbed each other the wrong way in the wrong moment—"

"Then you stole the scarf," I add.

"Then I... wait, no, I didn't." Her eyes dart to George. "I swear on my life, I didn't realize I even put it in my bag."

Bianca glares at me, which I have to admit I like, because I can see the hellfire burning brightly in those big brown eyes.

George smiles. "Of course you didn't, it could happen to the best of us."

Bianca shifts uncomfortably and gives me another glare, and I can't help but grin back at her.

"However, I have asked Anastacia to assist with your shopping this morning," George says and I see Bianca visibly stiffen as a rather cool-and-aloof-looking blonde walks down the aisle toward us.

Her eyes are narrowed on Bianca, but when she sees me,

they flare with interest, and a confident, sexy smile tugs at the corner of her glossy lips.

But I stare right through her as if she wasn't even there.

"Anastacia, I'd like you to meet Bianca, a very good friend of Massimo De Kysa's," George says. "I believe you have something you'd like to say?"

Anastacia bristles but hides it well beneath a façade of professionalism. But it's killing her. Which is very pleasurable to watch.

She folds her hands in front of her as she addresses Bianca. "Of course, I'd like to offer my apologies for yesterday's... *misunderstanding.*"

But Bianca knows a circling shark when she sees one and isn't easily won over by the empty apology. She keeps her expression neutral, but that hellfire is still raging in her eyes.

"Thank you," she says, her gaze burning into Anastacia's cold expression.

The blonde stares back at her.

Jesus, it's like a clash of fire and ice as they stare at one another. Like when molten lava oozes down the mountainside and meets the ocean.

Anastacia breaks first. She plasters on a smile and gestures to the shoe department. "Please, allow me to assist you in finding a pair of shoes for the ball."

When George leaves to attend to another matter, and Anastacia leads Bianca into the shoe department, I take out my phone to ring Matteo for an update on Tony Vinocelli and to check if Damon has been able to locate Harrison's bank records.

Bianca glances at me over her shoulder as she walks away, and I mouth, "Behave."

Because I'm pretty certain leaving those two alone will be like pouring gas on an open flame and hoping no-one gets burned.

She narrows her eyes at me as if to say *I'm not making any promises.*

Which makes me smile again. Which I realize I've been doing a lot lately.

I have to force myself to make my calls because watching Bianca is proving to be enjoyable. I won't lie. She is a distraction. I like her fire. I know her confidence is rocked, but it will be a cold day in hell before she shows Anastacia how shaky it is. Which again, I admire.

I find myself wanting to be around her, and as much as I know it's a bad idea, sometimes I just can't talk myself out of it.

I want to blow off the whole day just to hang out with her.

But it's not my choice.

I walk away from them so I'm just out of earshot and make my call.

Matteo answers on the second ring. "Boss?"

"Any update from Damon about Harrison's financial records?" I say into the phone, careful to keep my voice down so it doesn't echo through the empty store.

"Not yet, but he would've worked on this through the night."

"I want to know the moment he finds something useful."

"Of course. What about the Vinocelli? You decided how you want it to play out?"

"We don't make a move until we hear from Damon. I don't want to go in with guns blazing and start a goddamn war only to find out they have nothing to do with any of this."

"I'll give Damon a nudge."

"Good, I want an update by the time we meet this afternoon."

Matteo sounds surprised. "You don't want to meet earlier?"

I glance over at Bianca. I'm not ready to call it quits on our morning together even though I know I should.

"No, I've got an important meeting."

"More important than moving forward with—"

I cut him off. "Yes, what I have to do is more important than any of it."

Matteo barely hides the suspicion in his tone. "Okay, I'll get onto Damon before then."

I end the call and look over to Bianca, and a warm sensation spreads through me.

I smile, but it quickly fades, and I have to remind myself that this feeling is fleeting and not to get too attached to it.

Because when Bianca learns the truth, she won't ever want to see me again.

28

BIANCA

Anastacia walks behind me as I slowly stroll through the rows of designer shoes, and I can feel her resentment walking beside us like an evil twin.

I decide to ignore her and enjoy the landscape of designer shoes in front of me. After all, I'm in my happy place, and I intend to enjoy it.

But it's hard to do when I can feel her cool gaze burning a hole in the back of my skull.

"You don't like me much," I say.

"What I think of you doesn't really matter," she says, a tight smile on her face.

"Well, you're absolutely right about that," I say, picking up a glorious Thomas Monroe shoe with a death-defying seven inch heel and studying it.

"You used to come in with your friends. Two blondes and a brunette."

My eyes flit to hers. "So?"

"It was sad, really. Another spoilt princess spending daddy's money on her friends so she could keep them."

"Excuse me?"

"We could all tell they were using you."

"They weren't using me—"

"But then, we see that all the time around here. Sometimes we feel bad, other times we laugh about it." A cruel gleam in her cold blue eyes tells me which category I fell into. "Money makes people so tasteless. Your friends seemed, I don't know... *off*."

This ice maiden doesn't know how right she is. But it will be a frosty day in hell before I let on.

I turn away from her to put the Thomas Monroe down. "I think I preferred it when you weren't talking."

She scoffs. "I suppose you're expecting another apology."

"Not if it's as fake as the first one." I select a pair of Betty Saville stilettos with a four-inch heel and hand them to her. "I'll try these in a six."

Feeling the sting of Anastacia's accurate description of my friends, when she leaves to find the shoes in my size, I walk over to the elegant chaise lounge by a row of Keeley Jones handbags, and sit down.

Thinking about the way my friends treated me still makes me feel small. Hell, the heels on the Thomas Monroes felt taller than me. I know there is no way she could know about what happened with my friends. *About the lunch date from hell.* But it's like her smugness is clairvoyant, and she knows I'm friendless and vulnerable and at my lowest.

So when she returns with the shoes and tries to sit beside

me I stop her with a look and a raised eyebrow. "You can't help me if you're sitting up here." I look at the floor and then back to her. "You'll need to get on your knees."

Our eyes lock. She hates me as much as I hate the last three months of my life, and if her eyes had bullets then I'd be machine gunned to death. But they don't, and I'll die of old age before I look away.

Her jaw tightens so much I think her teeth might shatter. But she slowly lowers herself to the ground by my feet, nonetheless.

Now, in my previous life—the one that didn't have me living in a dive motel and selling my belongings to a pawn dealer for bill money—I would be enjoying this moment immensely.

But sitting here watching her sink to her knees to help me slide on these delectable Betty Saville shoes is not nearly as satisfying as I thought it would be.

In fact, it kind of feels shitty.

After all, I don't know what cross she is bearing. Maybe her closest friends dumped her at the same time as someone stole everything from her, and it's made her angry as shit.

I should probably give her the benefit of the doubt.

"Look, I'm sorry we got off on the wrong foot," I say, and when I recognize the lame pun, I laugh. But she looks up at me with a blank expression and says nothing, so I push on. "Perhaps we could put it down to we were both having a bad day and move on."

But again there is silence.

"It seems pointless to keep—"

"You know, that's the good thing about working here and meeting all the people with money," she says, cutting me off.

"You can tell who has money and class…" She looks up at me. "And who only has the money."

I lift an eyebrow. "Meaning?"

"Meaning a pig in sheep's clothing is still just a pig."

I stare at her. Mouth agape.

"Are you seriously calling me a classless pig in sheep's clothing? For starters, the saying is a wolf in sheep's clothing, and secondly, fuck you—"

"Oh, I wouldn't dream of saying such a thing." She looks up at me through her long Velour lashes. "I was just making conversation since you seem so intent on talking."

She glances over at Massimo, and a wicked smile curls on her red lips.

"Now *he* has money and class. The woman he ends up with will be an elegant masterpiece. She'll have to be if she wants to keep him. A man like that doesn't come along more than once in a lifetime."

"You do realize I'm going with him to the ball on Friday, right?"

"Oh, I'm sorry, I thought George said you and Mr. De Kysa were just friends." She hisses back a grimace. "Just as well you're thinking about buying the Betty Savilles. I mean, some girls need all the help they can get, right?"

And just like that I don't care what cross she is bearing.

"Oh, will you look at that, you need a pedicure," she says as she slips the shoes onto my feet.

Yep, she could fall into a big tub of *I don't give a fuck* and sink right to the bottom with that big ole cross attached to her, and I wouldn't care.

And while we're at it, the benefit of the doubt can go to hell too.

I'm ready to punch her into next week.

But suddenly the clouds part, and bright biblical rays shoot down from heaven, and Anastacia and all her nastiness just slips away when I look down to see the Betty Saville masterpieces on my feet.

The shoes are perfect. Pointed toe. Four inch heels. Crusted in Swarovski crystals in an ombre pattern of red to gold. Not only do they glitter like a hundred little suns, but they're comfortable to walk in, too.

Wearing them is like slipping back into my old life for a few minutes and remembering how lucky I was to wear couture footwear back then. Its bittersweet. My life was rich and opulent and I didn't even realize how fortunate I was.

Anastacia is forgotten as I walk over to the full length mirror and study them from every angle. I want to cry, they look so good.

When I glance over to Massimo, I see he's watching me with a strange expression on his face. It's not a scowl, or a smile, or even pensive. It's... *regret?*

I glance back at the reflection in the mirror and again feel that flutter of appreciation for the shoes, but when I turn back to Massimo he has resumed his usual stony-faced expression.

"I'll take them."

I return to the chaise lounge to take them off.

"It must really kill you to do this," I say, as I hand them to Anastacia.

"Not really. You'll leave with the shoes, but we'll still laugh about this when you're gone. Poor little rich girl with more money than class." She gives me a smug smile, then leans forward and whispers, "Only this time I'll get a big fat commission." She stands and plants the phoniest of phony smiles on her face and says, "Let me pop those in a bag for you."

Emotion burns through me like a firestorm as I watch her saunter off to get a Bentley's bag.

George comes over, looking none the wiser. "How did we go? Did you find what you are looking for?"

I shake off Anastacia's ectoplasm, determined to show George my appreciation and to shield him from the fact that he has Satan working for him.

"Yes," I say with a grin. "I found the perfect pair of shoes. I'm very grateful, thank you."

His smile broadens. "Well, looking after our very special clients is important to everyone at Bentley's."

Not everyone.

Speak of the devil. Anastacia returns with a big Bentley's bag containing my new shoes. She hands them over, the fake smile still plastered on her face.

Massimo joins us, and I turn back to George. "I am so grateful for what you've done for me today. And I just had the most wonderful discussion with Anastacia who felt terrible about the misunderstanding yesterday. And because of it, she's decided to donate the entire commission she earned today to the Christmas for the Children charity here in New York City. Every single dime of it."

I grin triumphantly. While Anastacia's smile slips right off her heavily made up face.

"That's the Bentley spirit," George says to Anastacia, impressed.

She won't be able to back out now without looking bad.

I feel Massimo's curious gaze on me. But I don't look at

him. Instead, I mentally do the sum in my head. I know for a fact Bentley's pays its sales assistants a twenty-five percent commission. The shoes are five thousand dollars. I smile to myself. The Christmas for the Children charity coffers are going to swell by twelve hundred dollars thanks to Anastacia's generosity.

I'll make sure of it.

I wink at her and she almost explodes trying to keep that tight smile on her face.

After saying goodbye to George, Massimo takes my arm and leads me outside. "So much for behaving."

"I underestimated how much effort that would require," I reply as we walk toward the car.

"Want to tell me what that was all about?"

"Someone needed to put her manners back in for her."

He opens the car door for me. "I have a feeling someone has needed to do that her whole life, but why did it have to be you?"

I give him a wicked grin. "Because she found the wrong button and kept pushing it."

Massimo is strangely quiet during the drive back to his apartment. Gone are the relaxed shoulders and the easy-going nature of a man who likes to tease me.

No, in his place is a man with something on his mind.

Something big enough to affect his mood completely.

"Is everything okay?" I ask.

"Why do you ask?"

"You've gone quiet. You seem tense." Then it hits me. "Oh, is it the shoes. Were they too much? I didn't even think about asking you if the price was too much, because I was blinded by all the bling. That happens, you know. Getting visually drunk on all the shiny things. I think it's a real affliction. If they cost too much, we can always take them back—"

"The shoes are perfect." He smiles but it doesn't reach his eyes. "You are going to look beautiful on Friday night."

He gives me another smile that doesn't hit.

Something isn't adding up. But I decide to let it go. He's a busy man. He's probably put off doing some important stuff, and now he's refocusing on what he has to do for the rest of the day.

When he lets us into his apartment, I turn around and come face to face with his chest. He's close enough for me to feel the heat of his body swim around me. And his scent, God, his scent, it's like a hit of smack sending a wakeup call to every pleasure neuron in my brain.

"Thank you for this morning," I say, trying not to outwardly show how being this close to him affects me. "I don't know what to say."

He looks down at me, his face unreadable, but I can feel something, something dark and warm emanating from him. He's in two minds about something. I'd even go as far as to say the decision is torturing him.

"I have to go," he says.

I hate that he's leaving, and I can't keep the surprise out of my tone. "Are you coming back?"

He pauses at the door. "Not tonight."

My stomach drops. But I don't show it. I plaster on a smile.

"Thanks for today."

He smiles but it's sad and those rigid shoulders are back. "I'll see you soon."

I nod, trying not to feel the disappointment coiling in my chest.

"Massimo," I call out to him, and he stops and turns around, and I see it on his face. Something is hurting him. "Are you sure this is what you want? Me being your date on Friday night?

This time his smile does reach his eyes.

"Nothing will bring me more pleasure than having you on my arm, little monster."

And without another word he turns, and leaves.

29

BIANCA

That night I meet Eve at Lair.

We're in her office, and I'm dressed and ready for my first dance for the mysterious client who Eve has confirmed has booked me twice a week for the next few months.

"So who is he?" I ask her.

She gives me a pointed look. "I can't tell you that."

"Why not?"

"Because some of our clients like to remain anonymous and he is one of them."

"But you know who he is, right?"

"Of course."

"He's not some creep, is he?"

Her eyes go round. "No! He's a good guy."

I eye her suspiciously. For her to react so vehemently to the question, she must know him better than she's letting on.

"You know, it might help me to know a little bit about him so I can ensure he enjoys the performance," I suggest.

"Nice try, but I'm not telling you anything other than he's not a creep and he's only interested in seeing you dance."

For a split second, I wonder if its Massimo, and a shiver of excitement travels up my spine.

But then my good sense steps in. He doesn't even know I'm doing this.

Or does he?

"Massimo still doesn't know about me dancing in the peep show, right?"

"Where did that question come from?" She looks surprised. Then she frowns. "Oh, you think your mysterious client is Massimo?" She laughs as if it's a ridiculous idea.

"Okay, okay, it was a reach," I say. "But it's got me intrigued why this client wants to remain anonymous."

"Don't overthink it."

"I can't help it. That's my default factory setting."

"I know it is." She leaves her desk to stand in front of me and puts her hands on my shoulders. "Go in there and dance your little black heart out, okay Twinkle Toes."

"I'm nervous."

"You've got this." She smiles and its comforting. "Don't dance for whoever is on the other side of the glass. Dance for yourself."

I'M nervous as I step into the peep room. But the moment George Michael's "Freeek!" starts to play, my nerves fall away, and I get lost in the moment. It's like I'm being taken over by the music and my body begins to move with its own natural rhythm.

It's a hyper-sexual song. Throbbing with heavy beats and a wanton pulse that weaves its way through my body.

I let go of Bianca and become who the mysterious stranger paid to see.

Miss Hellfire.

I'm wearing thigh-highs and a PVC bikini, with a tuxedo jacket with tails over the top, and I feel sexy and powerful and in control.

I'm dancing completely unrehearsed, but it works because the music is writing the choreography with my body.

Eve told me to forget whoever is on the other side of the glass. But I can't, because I can feel a pair of eyes on me, and their gaze is warm and tortured and very familiar. I know that sounds crazy, but it's true.

Its him. Massimo.

I could be wrong—or maybe its wishful thinking. All I know is it feels exciting to think it's him sitting in the dark watching me.

When I rip the jacket off and throw it at the glass, I fling my head around and drop to my knees. I crawl. I arch my back and shake my ass. I lose myself in the music. All the while those eyes are on me. Watching. Needing. Wanting.

And it fans the flames in me.

I want it to be him.

To be sitting there in a heightened state of arousal.

The tension builds. Their physical need grows. Their entire being lights up with hormonal chemistry.

Is that what is happening on the other side of the glass?

Everything gets just a little bit harder and a little bit hotter.

Is my dancing doing that to him?

And when they finally come and the serotonin and the oxytocin surge through their grey matter, it will literally blow their minds.

Oh God.

The more I think of him watching me, the more turned on I get. My skin feels like it's on fire. Sweat drips between my cleavage. My body hums and my need takes over.

"Freeek!" changes to Madonna's "Justify My Love" which has a slower, dreamer beat, but it's equally as sexual. I spend most of it on my knees letting the music and lyrics consume me. Miss Hellfire reigns and Bianca Bamcorda is gone, and it's the most free I've felt in a long time.

Madonna finishes, and the peep room falls into darkness.

Nine minutes and twenty-six seconds, and I'm done.

And five hundred dollars richer.

But this wasn't just about the money.

This is about me breaking free and knowing I can be whoever the hell I want to be.

30

BIANCA

Massimo doesn't come back to the apartment all week, and I don't see him at work at all, although he does call in the evenings to check on me. But the conversations are stilted and strange, like we're strangers.

Like he's distancing himself from me.

Even when I dance for the mysterious client for a second time during the week, I can't feel the warmth of his gaze on me, and I start to think I have it all wrong.

That maybe it is wishful thinking after all, and he isn't the stranger behind the glass.

By the time Friday arrives, I'm convinced I've gotten it so wrong and this attraction to him is completely one-sided. Which makes me feel lousy and stupid.

But I'm still going to the ball, and I plan to look fabulous.

Now it's four o'clock on Friday afternoon, and I'm nervously pacing the kitchen. I have less than three hours to get myself glammed up, which probably seems like a lot of time for someone to get ready. But I'm out of practice.

I stare at my pitiful supply of makeup scattered on the kitchen counter.

Okay, I can work with this.

I'm not worried about the makeup. I can do a full face in the dark with my eyes shut. And I can certainly make a two-dollar pencil look like a thirty-dollar pencil.

What I can't do, is hair.

Never have.

Never will.

Because I have so much of it, and I get overwhelmed. I'm all fingers and too clumsy, not to mention too impatient to master hairstyling.

In the past few months, I've made do with a quick brush and a ponytail, and it suits me just fine.

But a quick brush and a ponytail isn't going to work tonight.

I need to bring the magic.

A ten-thousand-dollar Bianchon gown and a pair of five-thousand-dollar heels tell me I have to.

Rummaging through my toiletry bag, I hit pay dirt.

"Yes!" I say, holding up the packet of bobby pins.

Coupled with a YouTube video on how to create an up style, I am going to create magic.

Except an hour later, I have to concede that I won't.

I stare at my reflection in Massimo's gleaming bathroom.

Admitting defeat, I pull up a number on my phone.

"I know you have plans this afternoon but this is an emergency."

An hour later, the door buzzer goes. By now, I'm showered and moisturized, and my hair is hanging in damp strands over my naked shoulders.

I answer the door wearing a tank top and yoga pants.

"I've brought reinforcements," Eve says, breezing into the apartment with Natalie not far behind her.

"I'm the one who can actually do hair," Natalie says. "This one doesn't have a clue."

"Hence the pixie cut," Eve says as she dumps a bottle of champagne on the counter.

"I thought you said you could do hair?" I say, watching her untwist the foiled top of the champagne bottle.

"I lied. Well, it was a little white lie. I knew Natalie would be able to help, and well, I'm here for moral support. Oh, and I brought the champagne."

"What if I wasn't available?" Natalie asks.

Eve shrugs and gives me a mischievous grin. "Then I was going to improvise."

She pops the cork and goes looking for glasses.

Natalie takes my hand. "Okay, princess, let's get you ready for the ball."

We congregate in Massimo's bathroom where the light is best. Natalie sits me on a stool in front of the mirror and dries and straightens my hair while Eve sits on the edge of the bath with a glass of champagne in her hand.

"So tell me, are you and my stepbrother keeping it casual? Or are you falling in love with him?"

That's one of the things I love about Eve. She doesn't hold back.

"I told you, it's not like that, we're just friends."

"A man who gets his moody stepsister out of bed on a Sunday morning to pick up a dress he knows you were admiring, then takes you shoe shopping all morning, is not just after friendship."

I look at her in the mirror. "He isn't?"

She shakes her head. "You know, for a Mafia princess you can be pretty naïve."

"I second that," Natalie says. "I've seen you take a drunk asshole by his metaphorical balls and force him to show you some respect. You're street-smart and ballsy, but when it comes to this kind of shit... Eve is right, you're clueless."

"Thanks," I say sarcastically.

Do I tell them?

I hesitate long enough for Natalie to pick up on it. "Is there something you're not telling us?"

I decide not to say anything. Instead, I turn my attention to Eve.

"I'm sorry I interrupted your afternoon plans."

"Oh don't be." She waves me off. "We had a liquid lunch date and fell into bed almost immediately, so I was already well and truly laid by the time you called. Three orgasms for her and three for me. I was about done. I needed a break."

"I know what you mean," Natalie says. "When my husband comes home from touring with his band I have to leave the bed just so I can get some rest."

Eve lifts her glass of champagne. "Here's to our significant others and all the lovely orgasms they give us."

"I'm a virgin," I blurt out.

The laughing stops and Natalie snags the brush in my hair. Both of my friends look at me.

"Well, I'll be goddamned," Eve says, astonished.

"I second that," Natalie adds.

I wait for them to laugh or to tease me. But they don't.

"Good on you, princess." Eve holds up her champagne again. "Cheers to that."

Natalie gives me a warm smile in the mirror. "Tell me, how can a twenty-something hottie like you still be a virgin? Are you holding out for marriage?"

"No, my father was."

She gives me a confused look.

"My father was old school. He wanted me to marry well to build an alliance. He said a powerful man doesn't want what other men can have."

"So he kept an eye on you and made sure you didn't have any fun?" Natalie looks astounded. "What about high-school boyfriends?"

"I went to an all-girls boarding school."

"And college?"

I shake my head. "No, my father didn't allow me to go to college."

I reach for my glass of champagne on the vanity and gulp down half of it, my cheeks flaming with embarrassment.

"Well, I think that's pretty cool, I mean, if you still want to be one," Eve says.

I laugh. "No, I don't want to be one. That's the thing. I'm so ready to not be one."

"But..?"

"When my dad died, my life got complicated real quick. I was too busy picking up the pieces to jump on someone and ask them to take my virginity."

Eve's eyes widen. "My God, does Massimo know?"

"Yes. He knows."

Is that why he hasn't made a move to touch me?

My phone rings, but I can't move to reach it because Natalie has a handful of my hair and is twisting it up and pinning it in place with a million bobby pins.

So Eve picks it up.

"Speak of the devil," she says before answering it. "Hello, Cinderella can't come to the phone right now because her very beautiful and very talented fairy godmothers are busy making sure she is going to be the most beautiful woman at the ball tonight."

I can't hear what he says, but Eve replies with, "You know, Prince Charming is supposed to come to Cinderella's door to pick her up. Not send a car to do it."

Which isn't technically true.

"Fine, I'll pass it on. But you and I need to talk about what women expect on a date. What do you mean it's not a date? She's wearing a ten-thousand-dollar Bianchon gown and Betty Saville heels. Fine. Seven o'clock. She'll be ready."

She hangs up and sighs. "Prince Charming is going to meet you there."

I look at her through the mirror. "See, it's not a date. He said it himself."

"Yes, but that's going to change the moment Cinderella arrives at the ball. Trust me. It might not be a date now, but by the end of the night, it will be."

31

MASSIMO

"Are you out of your goddamn mind?"

My brother does his best to keep his voice even on the other end of the line. But he's failing.

"It's under control," I assure him.

I've just told him I'm attending the Balboa Ball tonight with Bianca as my date.

"No, it's not under control. You lost control the moment you hired her. Now you're taking her on a date?"

"You're reading too much into it," I say calmly. "It's not a date."

A fleeting memory of Bianca's warm body pressed against mine fans the flame that hasn't diminished since I woke up with her in my arms on Sunday morning.

It's a flame I've tried to dampen over the past week. I've pulled back because there are things I need to make right. Things she needs to know.

But you still watched her dance, that nagging voice in my head reminds me. *Because there's that part of you that can't pull back completely.*

"If it's not a date then what is it?" Nico asks.

"Let the Vinocelli see Bianca is with me. I want to show them she is under the protection of the De Kysa."

My brother grunts, still not convinced I'm doing the right thing but satisfied enough to know that attending a highly publicized event with Bianca on my arm will let the Vinocelli know they fucked with the wrong person.

"And if it isn't the Vinocelli who are behind the accountant's death?"

"Then this will help smoke out who is behind it." They will start their scrambling. Make mistakes. Try to launder the money through the wrong channels or open their mouths to the wrong person. Either way, they will react, and I will find them.

"And what happens when you find her money?"

"I give it back and move on."

"That's it? Just like that you'll be done with her?"

"There won't be a reason for us to work together anymore."

I think about her dancing behind the peep glass and how I'll miss watching her. I know the standing date for two days a week in the peep room is wrong. But it's the only secret I plan to keep from her.

All the others will come out in due course.

And then I won't have a choice about seeing Bianca again. Because she will be done with me for good.

~

The afternoon vanishes, and it's time to leave for the Balboa Ball. I change into the spare suit I keep in my office and meet Dante at the back entrance.

By the time we arrive at The Met, there is a line of cars pulling up to the entrance. When I climb out, flashes of light from the paparazzi ignite in the twilight, and I realize I made a mistake by not picking Bianca up. I should be arriving with her so the paparazzi capture us together, and I make a mental note to stick close to her tonight so we don't miss out on any other opportunities to be seen together. I want to make sure the Vinocelli see us. Let them know she is with me. Let them squirm knowing that I will be coming for them the moment I get confirmation it was Fausto who murdered Harrison.

But I've already overstepped the line with Bianca. I need to pull back and establish clearer lines in the sand. This is not a date.

Inside, I'm met by a waiter with a glass of champagne, which I accept, then move into the main ballroom. The ball is well underway. Music plays. People in gowns and tuxedoes dance arm in arm. Chandeliers glitter, and the din of conversation hangs in the air. I barely get inside before I'm met by an elderly socialite who is dripping in jewels and won't let me pass until I say hello to her homely looking daughter, who looks like she'd rather be eating a plate full of razorblades than be here.

Further along, I meet two actors I know well, one whose pool house was the location of a very satisfying encounter I had with three models one night—long before I became the don. And long before I started to feel dissatisfied by such encounters.

We make small talk before I excuse myself to find the bar. I've finished my champagne but need a scotch to numb the strange sensation in my chest.

I'm almost at the bar when I feel her enter the room. I can't explain how or why it makes me turn around. But I do, and there she is, walking into the ballroom. She pauses on the step to scan the room for me and my heart stops. I can't swallow. I can't take a breath. All I can do is stare at the most beautiful vision I've ever seen.

She looks phenomenal.

The dress fits perfectly over her beautiful curves and her raven hair is swept up into a messy bun, with stray curls falling around her beautiful face.

And those ruby-red lips.

God, how I ache to taste them again.

She sees me and smiles, and that smile lights up my chest.

Like I'm being pulled by a magnet, I cross the room toward her and she meets me halfway, parting the sea of people when they see the beautiful woman in red.

"I was worried I wouldn't find you," she says when she reaches me.

"There was no chance I wouldn't find you," I say, sweeping another appreciative gaze over her. "You look stunning."

She gives me a beaming smile that has the same effect on me as the first one.

"Can I get you a drink?" I ask.

She shakes her head. "It took two fairy godmothers to get me into this dress. I'm not sure how I will go about peeing without their help."

I can't help but chuckle. "How about a dance then?" I ask.

"Sure, but I warn you, I still have my training wheels on with these Betty Saville shoes I'm wearing. It might be like dancing with a newborn giraffe. I'm a bit out of practice."

I take her hand and lead her to the dance floor. "Then lean on me. I won't let you fall."

I pull her into my arms, and she relaxes against me as we move in time to the music. She feels soft and warm, and the intoxicating scent of her skin sends me falling deeper and deeper toward this being a date more than a plan to smoke out the Vinocelli. No matter how many lines in the sand I've tried to set, holding her in my arms is setting fire to them.

"You're a very good dancer," she says softly.

"So are you," I say, my voice gravelly because her body pressed against mine is doing things to me. I feel her stiffen at my slipup, wondering if I'm her mysterious client. Our eyes meet and I can see her searching them. *Yes, it's me who watches you in the peep room and it's my favorite part of the week.*

"No training wheels needed," I add, and she relaxes.

The music is upbeat, but we dance slowly, as if there is no one else in the room. And in that moment, there isn't because all I can see, feel, and smell is her, and I don't need anything else.

It's Bianca who brings the moment to an end, whispering in my ear, "Massimo? I don't want to break the spell, but I need food."

I grin and guide her off the dance floor and over to the canapes table and watch with amusement as she loads a tiny plate with an array of canapes.

When she catches me watching her, she looks uncertain. "What?"

"I'm enjoying the smile on your face."

Her smile widens. "Want to know a secret?"

"Yes."

"I'm having a wonderful time."

"You seem surprised."

Her smile widens. "Two weeks ago, I was living in a dive motel and eating microwaved noodles. Now I'm at the most glamorous event of the year, dining on exquisite canapes while wearing a Bianchon gown and dancing with the most handsome man in the room. Life doesn't stop surprising the hell out of me."

I cock an eyebrow. "You think I'm handsome?"

"You know you are. So do all the women in this room. Look at them, they keep looking."

"It's not just the women, it's the men too. But none of them are looking at me. They're looking at you."

She looks up at me, her big eyes gleaming in the chandelier light of the ballroom.

I move closer.

She moves closer.

She has a drop of mascarpone on her lip and I glide my thumb across it before licking it off my thumb. She watches me and shivers, and I know I'm going to kiss her.

Except I don't get a chance to, because in that moment, three women walk over and interrupt what I've been aching to do for weeks.

32

BIANCA

My fair-weather friends have the worst timing in the world.

I haven't seen them in months, and in that very magic moment, they decide to show up.

I want to kill them.

I don't know what's worse, them breaking up with me during my darkest hour, or them interrupting this moment with Massimo.

Right now, both feel equally as painful.

As usual, Angelica is the first to speak.

"Massimo De Kysa," she coos, her over-plumped lips gleaming with pink gloss. "And Bianca, how delightful to see you."

I bristle, and Massimo notices. He plants his palm against the small of my back. A gesture that clearly says, *I've got you.*

Angelica looks at him through heavy lashes. "I don't think we've had the pleasure to meet in person."

"I'm afraid if we have, then I have forgotten," Massimo says with a tight jaw.

She extends a hand for him to take, but he ignores it, leaving her hanging. Embarrassed, she quickly tucks her hair behind her ear.

"It's good to see you, Bianca," Jules says, looking awkward.

"We saw that dress at Bentley's," Lilah adds. "And we both mentioned how amazing it would look on you, didn't we Jules."

"Oh yes, we did. And we were right. You look stunning."

I had wondered how I would feel when I finally saw my friends again. Would the wound be as fresh as it was that day in the restaurant when they so cruelly deserted me, or would I forgive them and pursue some kind of reconnection with them?

Surprisingly, I feel nothing. The truth is, looking at my friends in their designer gowns and five-hundred-dollar hairstyles with their fake smiles and insincere words, I no longer ache for their friendship. In fact, standing here, I wonder what the hell I ever had in common with them.

You were just like them once, says the little voice in my head.

And I'm sorry.

I really, really am.

Massimo takes my hand, and his grip is tight and possessive. "If you will excuse us, Bianca and I were just heading for the dance floor."

He doesn't say goodbye. He simply dismisses them and

whisks me away.

"That was brutal," I say, as we reach the dance floor, and he takes me in his arms once again. "Are they staring at us?"

"Like three birds on a wire." He holds me close. "You feel okay?"

"That was satisfying to say the least. Angelica has a crush on you."

"She does?"

"Yes, and it will kill her seeing you dance with me."

His eyes fill with dark mischief. "Then this is really going to kill her."

He takes my face in his hands and crushes his lips to mine. The world spins around and around until it's gone, and it's just Massimo and I on that dance floor, with his mouth on mine and his tongue exploring my mouth.

I forget to breathe. To stand. To exist. All I am aware of is the heat of the kiss and the desperate need for more of him coursing through my body.

His mouth is commanding, his lips sweet with champagne and lust and him. And it sparks a fire in me. A need so searing hot I start to wonder if you can come from kissing alone. And if it's possible, then this man is the one to do it.

When he breaks off the kiss, I stare up at him absolutely kiss drunk.

"Is she still looking?" he asks.

"Who?"

"Angel, Angela, whatever the hell her name is."

I don't take my eyes off him to look. "I don't care."

A flush of warmth spreads through my body under Massimo's hot gaze.

I think he's going to kiss me again when his phone

begins to vibrate in his jacket pocket. A look of dissatisfaction crosses his face.

"You're not going to answer it?" I ask.

"No. I'm going to kiss you instead."

He leans down and his lips brush mine and I melt into him. And again, the world and everything in it washes away.

Except his phone. It starts to vibrate again.

We both realize it must be important, and the kiss is abandoned.

"Answer it," I say. "I'm going to freshen up in the ladies' room."

He is about to disagree but when he pulls his phone out of his pocket and sees the name on the screen, he nods. "I need to take this."

I leave him to take his call and weave through the crowd of glamorous dresses and designer suits to make my way to the ladies' restroom.

Inside, I check my reflection in the mirror, noting my flushed cheeks and the sparkle in my eyes. I think about Massimo's kisses, and my stomach flutters.

I look at the slightly smeared lipstick, and my insides turn, remembering the feel of those soft but commanding lips ruining my lipstick.

"If you keep throwing yourself at him that way you'll run out of lipstick by the end of the night," comes a voice from behind me.

Angelica steps into view, and I watch her in the mirror as she throws daggers at me with her cold eyes.

I ignore her and keep fixing my lips.

"What, cat got your tongue? Or did Massimo swallow it when you were pawing him on the dance floor?"

Realizing she isn't going to let up until she says what she came in here to say, I turn around and face her. "Jealous?"

"Jealous of you? Please." She scoffs. "Tell me, how many times did you have to get on your knees and blow Massimo De Kysa so he'd buy you that dress?"

"How do you know he bought this dress for me?"

"Word around town is you're stone-cold broke." She grins. *She actually grins.* "There's no way you could afford a Bianchon. Unless you're putting that mouth to good use."

I cock an eyebrow. "Just because that's your currency doesn't mean it's mine."

Her face darkens. Then she remembers. "Oh, that's right, you're a virgin." And she laughs at me.

Oddly, in that moment, I think about Natalie and Eve's reactions when I told them, and how it didn't make them see me as anything but their equal. Not like Angelica, who's always thought she was so much better than me because she was more worldly and experienced and had a rich, ambitious husband with an insatiable sexual appetite.

"You know what I've come to realize, Angelica?"

"Pray tell." She sighs dramatically.

"You're not worth it."

She bristles. Because she can see she isn't getting to me.

"You did me a favor when you ended our friendship. Oh it, hurt. But it allowed me the chance to see that my life is actually better without you in it."

Her eyes narrow. "You think you're something special now because you're on his arm tonight. You can't possibly think walking in on the arm of the most prestigious bachelor in the city is going to fix what your father did. We can still smell the stench of who you really are no matter how many pretty dresses you put on. And I don't know what game you're playing at with Massimo De Kysa, but it doesn't change the fact that you're just not good enough."

Wow.

Like, really wow.

I don't know what to say, I'm so stunned.

So I do the only thing I can think of... I yawn.

As if her words didn't sting like a scorpion's tail and simply rolled off my back.

Then I smile. With lips that have just been so exquisitely kissed by Massimo. They broaden into a brighter, bigger, better smile because I realize Angelica can't hurt me anymore.

Let her drown in her own venom.

"I'm sorry, I do that when I'm bored," I say, turning my back on her to continue fixing my lipstick in the mirror. "Fly away, little bird, I don't have time for people who think they're too good for me."

I feel her dark energy tighten around us. "You can talk, ignoring us out there as if you're too good for us because you're horny for Don Massimo."

I drop my lipstick into my tote and turn around.

"You want to know why I ignored you?" I say, towering over her because somehow she seems smaller and less of a threat. "It's because you dumped me at the first sign of bad weather, and if you don't stand by me in my worst hours, then you sure as hell don't get to stand by me during my best."

Without another word, I leave the restroom knowing I'm done with her for good.

And boy it feels good.

33

MASSIMO

I can see by the look on her face that something happened in the bathroom. Her cheeks are flushed and she's walking faster back to me.

"You okay?" I ask.

She flashes me a big grin. But she lies. "Couldn't be better."

I don't ask her what happened in the ladies' room. Because I have a feeling she wants it left in the past. But there is a fierceness about her. A change. Like she's just found a missing piece to her puzzle and feels powerful, strong enough, to make it to the next step without something holding her back anymore.

I take her hand. "Wanna get out of here?"

"That depends."

"On what?"

"Are you going to feed me?"

"Yes, I am."

"Right answer," she says with a dazzling smile.

I give her my arm. "Then let me take you to the best food in town."

~

"Fat Mikey," Bianca reads the name on the side of the food truck.

"Home to the best Italian sandwiches in New York City," I say.

"Oh my God, that's exactly what I want," she says, clutching my arm as we walk up to the truck. "I'm starving."

"Then we've definitely come to the right place. These sandwiches will keep you satisfied until morning."

She cocks an eyebrow, and I cock one back, then step up to the serving window.

"Two Fat Sals," I tell the server.

"What's a Fat Sal?" Bianca asks.

"The best sandwich in the world, is what it is. Delicate prosciutto with lashings of smoked mozzarella, homemade ricotta spread, the plumpest sun-dried tomatoes you've ever seen, fresh basil, all served on a bed of peppery arugula."

"I can't tell you how turned on I am right now."

"If I knew that's what turned you on, I would've talked food to you a lot sooner."

I know I'm walking a thin line but I can't help it with Bianca. She makes me want to take risks, and unfortunately, in my line of business, that is a giant mistake.

But there is a simmering attraction buzzing just beneath the surface that neither of us can deny. Oh, we've been dancing around it. Hell, I've been in flat out denial. But tonight, all those walls are slowly crumbling around us.

And I should be doing everything I can to stop it. Because this is only going to end in heartbreak.

Yet, here I am, taking her to one of my favorite places in the city to eat. Where I can blend in with other diners. Although, right now, blending in is the last thing we're doing in our attire.

I hand Bianca her sandwich, and we walk over to the water's edge. I watch her take a bite and see her eyes roll back in pleasure. My body buzzes in response. What I would give to be the one to make her eyes roll back like that.

Then she starts moaning as she takes another mouthful, and fuck, I feel those moans right along the length of my cock.

I clear my throat. Trying to vanquish thoughts of what I could do to make her moan that way. "Good?"

"You're right, these are the best sandwiches," she says around a mouthful.

"So is this where you take all your dates?" she asks. "Or am I special?"

You're special, I agree before I can shove the thought away.

"I don't date," I say instead.

"Oh, that's right." She takes another bite, and a dollop of ricotta sits on her lips, and I almost groan because of the ache I feel to lick it off.

The reckless part of me is tempted. To say to hell with it, and take this one moment in a sea of moments, and just kiss her again.

I kissed her earlier to prove a point to her nasty friends. I didn't do it to show them Bianca was better than them, because she does that naturally; no, I just wanted to piss them off because of the way they treated her.

Now, if I kiss her, it would be because I want her to be mine for the night, and I can't do that to her.

Every moment for the next fifteen is torture, her moans and licking lips going straight to my groin. I'm almost relieved when we have both finished our sandwiches.

She's quiet on the drive home.

I park the Audi in the parking garage and ride the elevator with her to the loft. But at the door, I stop.

"This is where I have to tell you good night."

She looks surprised. "You don't want to come in."

The way she says it tells me she wants me to come in for more than a nightcap.

And fuck, I want to do that more than I want to breathe.

But tonight, I saw her shed her vulnerability, and I don't want to be responsible for taking that away from her when she finds out I'm not the nice guy she thinks I am.

She takes my hand. "I had a great time tonight, and I'm not ready for it to end. I'd really like you to come inside and spend the rest of it with me."

Jesus.

I am so fucking tempted.

But I won't do that to her.

No matter how hard it is to say no.

In a surge of unexpected emotion, I'm hijacked by a need to unburden my soul and come clean. To let her know why she really doesn't want me to come inside. "Bianca, there's something you need to know—"

She puts her finger across my lips and looks up at me with big eyes. "Stop talking."

She kisses me and I can't fight her sweet lips. She's so soft and delicious, and I'm barely hanging on by a fucking thread.

And thank God for small mercies because my phone rings, forcing me to bring the kiss to an end.

I should ignore it, but I don't, because it's the only thing standing between me and kissing her all the way to the bedroom and ripping that gown from her body and spending the night worshipping those luscious curves.

I answer my phone, and Matteo begins updating me on something that could've waited until morning. If he wasn't saving me from making a grave mistake, I would be pissed.

I hang up and return my focus to Bianca.

"It's probably a good thing," she says, her eyes sparkling. "I had a great night tonight, Massimo. Thank you for my Cinderella moment."

"You're welcome, but I should go."

There is so much I want to say to her in this moment.

I fucked up.

You don't need to dance for me in the peep show.

You should run as far as you can from me.

But I say none of it. Instead, I brush a kiss to her soft cheek.

"Good night, little monster."

And using all my strength, I walk away.

34

BIANCA

The next day, I'm sitting in the office with Eve when Natalie puts her head in the doorway.

"You've got a visitor," she says to me with an unimpressed look on her face.

"Who?"

"I don't know, someone who looks like you. But you know, different."

"Did she give you a name?"

"What am I, your secretary?"

Leaving my desk, I follow her downstairs to the club, but when I see who is waiting for me at the bar, I stop suddenly. Natalie notices and turns around.

"What's wrong? It's not who you wanted to see?"

"It's Jules," I say softly.

"The best friend who broke up with you in your hour of need?"

"The one and only." I can't believe she has the nerve to be here.

"Want me to throw her out and make sure her ass hits the sidewalk with a hard thud?"

Yes.

"No, it'll be fine. But thank you."

When I approach the bar where she is sitting, Jules swings around. Her hair is down, and Natalie is right, she does look like me.

"What do you want, Jules?" I ask, fully aware that Natalie is listening from behind the bar as she prepares limes and other garnishes for tonight's drinks. I get the feeling she's waiting for things to turn sour so she can throw Jules out.

"To say I'm sorry," Jules says with a sad expression. "To beg your forgiveness. To tell you I miss you, and I have ever since—"

"You ditched me when I needed me the most."

She nods sadly. "I deserve that."

"You do." I fold my arms. "But as you can see, I survived. Landed on my feet."

"Yes, you did. And I'm glad, really, Bianca, I'm so grateful." She sighs, and I realize I've been missing her more than I was prepared to admit. She was more than my best friend. She was the sister I never had. "I miss you, and I wanted to talk to you. See if I could repair the damage I've done. Can I take you to dinner tonight?"

I hesitate. Since my father's death and the fallout that followed, I've managed to build a solid wall around my heart. A wall with a sophisticated alarm system that's currently ringing loudly in my ears.

She ditched you.

The hurt part of me tells me to call it quits on the friendship once and for all. But the old part of me, the one that loved Jules like a sister, tells me I should hear her out for old times' sake.

"Sure, send me the time and place," I say.

"Do you still have the same number?"

I nod, full of mixed feelings.

Jules gives me a soft, warm smile, and it looks genuine. "Thank you, Bianca."

I watch her walk away, my feelings still divided.

Natalie comes to stand behind me as I watch Jules disappear out the door. "You sure it's a good idea meeting her for dinner? You might open old wounds."

"Probably, but I know I'll regret it if I don't at least hear her out."

"Does your gut tell you she's on the level? Or do you think she's up to something?"

"She seemed genuine." I turn away from the door to look at Natalie. She has her arms folded and looks concerned. She doesn't think this is a good idea. "I'll be fine."

Natalie shakes her head.

"You're too nice, princess. If it were me, I'd punch her in the nose."

I MEET Jules for dinner at a cute restaurant in the heart of Manhattan. Because at the end of the day, Jules and I had something a lot deeper than what I had with Lilah and Angelica.

She's sitting at a small table toward the back of the

restaurant, reading the menu. As I make my way over to her, delicious aromas waft in the air, and the soft din of dinner conversations follow me.

She looks up as I approach the table and smiles.

"Thanks for meeting me. I wasn't sure if you would come," she says.

I take a seat across from her. "I almost didn't."

I'm frosty, but it's because that wall around my heart is still buzzing in alarm.

"I ordered a bottle of wine." Again she smiles, but it's cautious. "You look lovely."

The server appears, and we place our orders. But there is a cloud of tension hanging over us, and I'm sure he can feel it.

When he leaves, I put down my menu. "Cut the small talk, Jules. What am I doing here?"

"Like I said, I wanted to say I'm sorry."

"I don't hear from you in months, and the moment you find out I'm spending time with Massimo De Kysa you come running."

"That's not how it is, I swear to you." She looks down at her napkin. "The truth is, it never sat right with me what Angelica told us to do."

"What do you mean?"

"She told Lilah and I to break off our friendship with you. She said the aftermath of Bella De Kysa's kidnapping and your father's death would affect all of us in a really bad way. I got scared. I spent a lot of time in your home, saw a lot of things, knew a lot of the game players, and it scared me. I knew how things could turn on a dime and I got frightened."

"About what?"

"About being involved with the Bamcorda. About a war taking place and being caught in the middle. I was trying to pick up the pieces of my own life after—"

"Your famous boyfriend's wife found out about the two of you and created a shitstorm in the press. Yeah, I remember what was going on in your life even when mine was falling apart. I was there for you—"

"And I'll regret it for the rest of my life that I wasn't there for you." She reaches for my hand across the table. "But if you give me the chance, I will be here for you. Let me be your best friend again."

I pull my hand away. "You've got a long way to go before I'd ever consider you a friend, let alone a best friend."

She nods. "I understand."

Our meals arrive, but I can barely eat. The air between us is strained.

"So tell me about Massimo De Kysa. You two were looking very cozy at the gala the other night."

"We're just friends," I lie.

"He doesn't look at you like a friend. He looks at you like he wants to eat you." She takes a sip of her wine. "And you look at him like you want to be eaten."

I can't help it. I laugh. "Hardly."

"I could think of worse things."

"What about you?" I ask, changing the subject. Because I don't want to share anything about Massimo with her. "Are you still dating that Greek tycoon?"

She grins over her glass of wine. "Gregor. Yes, and he's the most perfect man ever. How did you know about him?"

"I saw it on one of the gossip pages a few weeks ago."

When I say it, I suddenly realize I haven't looked at any of the online gossip pages since.

Because none of that matters to you anymore.

"You'd love him, Bianca," Jules gushes. "He's sweet and kind and—"

"Loaded." The word slips out.

Jules's eyes narrow for a split second. "It's not like that."

"Of course, I didn't mean to imply anything."

She relaxes. "I think I'm in love with him."

My eyes dart to hers. "Really, that's wonderful."

Jules had the worst upbringing. A drunk mom and an even drunker father. Everyone thought their murder-suicide was a tragedy. But not Jules. She confided in me once that she was relieved her father did it because she hated her parents toxic relationship and what they used to do to each other when fueled by alcohol. It was a loveless childhood. So to hear she's finally found someone makes me... happy?

I'm surprised because it's true. I'm really happy for her.

Is it possible I can forgive her?

As if reading my mind, she reaches for my hand again, and this time, I don't pull it away.

"I'm going to prove to you that you can trust me again," she says. "Whatever it takes, I'll show you that I'd do anything for you."

35

BIANCA

I leave dinner and take a cab back to Lair because I have a nine p.m. peep show with the mysterious client. It's eight o'clock when I arrive, and the club is starting to fill up. Natalie and Elsa are being slammed behind the bar, so I step in to help.

"Your date didn't go well then," Natalie says, brushing past me to grab a bottle of tequila.

"It went okay," I reply, shoveling ice into two glasses. "I'm still in two minds."

"Well, you know where to find me if you need someone to bounce her out of your life."

Natalie moves away to pour the shots of tequila, and Elsa steps in beside me to use the soda tap. "Thanks for helping out."

"The new girl didn't work out?" I ask, sliding two

whiskeys and ice across the bar to the customer, a famous country music singer. She hands me her card to pay for the drinks.

"You didn't hear?" Elsa says, running a customer's card through the card machine. "Massimo fired her this afternoon."

"He fired her, why?"

"He didn't fire her," Natalie says, walking past to get some limes. "She quit."

Elsa leans close so only I can hear. "Apparently she hit on him in his office. Took her clothes off and everything."

"Wait, what? I've only been gone a couple of hours."

"She's been lusting after him for weeks," Elsa adds. "Finally made her play for him."

Natalie leans in too. "Crashed and burned, though."

We all return to our customers, but I'm stunned by the possessiveness I feel when I imagine the new girl taking off her clothes and offering Massimo whatever it was she was offering him. So the moment it gets quiet in the bar, I head for his office.

He's sitting behind his desk and I lean against the door-frame, watching him. *God, he's so handsome.*

"If you linger in that doorway much longer, I'm going to have to start charging you rent," he says, not looking up.

I walk in and approach his desk. But I don't say anything. I'm too busy admiring the way he looks. He's discarded his suit jacket over the back of the chair, and his white shirt is open enough that I can see the top of the tattoos on his chest. His long lashes fan his high cheekbones as he reads whatever it is in front of him on the desk.

"Can I help you with something, little monster?"

Goose bumps spread across my skin.

Yes, I want you to kiss me again.

"Just thought I'd pop my head in to say hello before my —er, before I head home."

He looks up, and his black eyes focus on me. Something moves through his expression, but I can't make it out. It almost feels like he knows I'm lying to him.

Is that because he knows I'm dancing in the peep show in thirty minutes?

And does he know that because he is my mysterious client?

In my heart, I *know* it's him.

"I heard what happened," I say.

He cocks an eyebrow. "What happened?"

"With the new girl. Is it true?"

Damn, why did that come out sounding so jealous?

He picks up on it, and sits back in his chair. "Is what true?"

"That she took off her clothes and propositioned you?"

A small smile tugs at the corner of his lips. "There was some removal of clothes."

It's a poor choice of words, because in my head, I see both of them removing clothes and making out, and it drives me crazy with jealousy. It's so irrational and ridiculous, yet tell that to my mind. Maybe Natalie and Elsa got it wrong, and something happened. Which sends another bout of insanity into my brain.

"And did anything happen?" I ask.

I can't keep the possessiveness out of my tone, and Massimo can tell, and I think he likes it. He rises to his feet.

"She offered me something I wasn't interested in," he says.

He walks around his desk, moving like a hunter stalking his prey, and I know I want him to catch me and devour me wildly. I'm in a perpetual state of arousal around him, and I'm done with holding back.

I want him to slide everything off his desk with one swipe of his arm like they do on TV and then fuck me on it.

I want to know what he sounds like when he fucks.

I want to see his cock and feel it break me open.

Dear God, I'm so turned on, I can't hide it.

It's like the lock has been broken, the dam holding my emotions at bay collapsing under the sheer weight of them. I don't want to hold back anymore. But I need to know if he wants me.

"Is there something you want to tell me, little monster?"

His growly voice is my own personal aphrodisiac.

"Yes, last night I invited you in, and you turned me down, and now hot young girls are taking their clothes off in front of you, and it makes me think I made this all up in my head. That this thing between you and me isn't real, that I made it up."

He walks toward me, and I back up until the back of my thighs hit his desk. I look away because I feel like my feelings are exposed enough, and he doesn't need to see the confirmation of my feelings for him in my eyes.

He lifts my chin. "Every part of me wanted to spend the rest of the evening with you last night. You have to believe me when I say walking away was hard. I wanted to turn around and come back the moment I left the building."

"I wish you had."

He leans closer until all I can see is his face and those full kissable lips.

"You want to know why I walked away?" he asks as the tips of his fingers roam my face and his gaze warms my cheeks.

"Yes, I want to know why you don't want me."

"Oh, I want you, little monster. I want you so badly I'm barely holding on."

"But?"

"You deserve better than this," he says, his gentle fingers caressing my jaw.

Our lips are close. I lick mine in anticipation, aching for him to kiss me.

I can see the battle in his eyes.

"But I want you," I whisper.

The muscle in his jaw ticks, and if it's possible, his eyes darken further. He's fighting a good battle, but he's losing.

"But it can't happen," he says.

Shit. He's rejecting me again.

The hurt sinks into me like a weight in water.

"Bianca, I have to tell you something."

I push him away. "No, I don't want to hear it."

I try to move away but he stops me. "You need to hear this."

"No, I need you to leave me alone. You've made it clear."

"Nothing is clear until you hear me out."

"Let go of me."

With perfectly bad timing, Matteo walks in. "Fuck, sorry," he says, shielding his eyes.

Massimo closes his eyes and lets out a rough breath.

"I can come back at a better time," Matteo says.

"No, I have to be somewhere." My cheeks are warm. Hell, my whole body is on fire.

And I can't get out of there quick enough.

36

MASSIMO

I keep telling myself to not attend tonight's peep show.

That she won't know I'm not there, and she'll still get paid.

That I need to put an end to this and tell her everything.

But at nine p.m., I slip into the peep room unnoticed and take my seat. A bottle of Macallan sits on the table, and my first glass is already in my hand by the time the lights appear behind the peep glass.

Anticipation lights up my chest, and my heart kicks hard against my ribs as the slow beat of EZI's "Maraschino Love" fills the room.

Bianca appears, dressed in a black dress that barely reaches the top of her thighs and a pair of thigh-high boots that make me instantly hard.

Fuck.

Those boots.

Those legs.

That body.

I'm in so much trouble.

I drain my glass and pour another one, giving myself permission to sit back and enjoy the show.

She dances like a temptress, sensually moving those perfect curves in synchronicity with the song, and my body begins to hum as I watch.

Unable to take my eyes off her on the other side of the glass, I lean back in the chair. I've never jerked off while watching a performance in my club. I prefer any gratification to be taken in the privacy of my home.

Besides, a man is most vulnerable when he is mid-orgasm and I'm not making myself vulnerable in a dark room without any protection. I can see the headlines now. *Don De Kysa assassinated while fucking his own hand at his club.*

What a great fucking legacy that'd be.

Except, right now, my cock is fucking begging for it.

Watching Bianca run her hands all over her delicious body has me so fucking wound up I could burst.

I grip the end of the arm rest to stop myself from reaching inside my zipper.

But I have to adjust myself... just once.

Ok, twice.

Three times... *fuck.*

I begin to rub my cock through my suit pants.

She's got me so hard I can't help myself.

On the other side of the glass, she sits on a chair with her legs slightly parted as she trails the back of her fingers down the center of her body, from her cleavage down to her flat belly. Her thighs part further, and I can't tear my eyes off the soft damp shadow on her satin panties.

She's fucking wet.

This is turning her on.

Fuck.

My cock cries for me to pump it.

When her fingers reach the top of her panties and she dips them beneath so I can see the outline of her finger slide through her pussy, I can't hold back. I grind my palm against my cock, mesmerized as she drags her free hand over a perfect pink nipple and crushes her teeth into her cushiony lip in pleasure.

God, I want to touch her.

Taste her.

The throbbing becomes too much.

Growling in submission, I unzip my pants and wrap my fingers around my cock. I start to pump slowly using the precum pooling in the head to lube each slow, torturous stroke.

"Are you watching me, lover?"

Bianca's voice fills the room, and it's like a shot of pure ecstasy to my brain.

Yes.

"Do you like what you see?"

Yes.

She starts to rub herself faster, her body growing restless, her breathing coming quicker.

"I like you watching me," she moans. But it's barely a whisper. Like she's right beside me, whispering in my ear.

Heat soars through my body. I have to unbutton my shirt.

"Do you want to fuck me?"

God, yes.

She moans and I know she's close to coming.

I let out a groan.

Because so am I.

Through heavy lids, I watch her rise from the chair and walk to the glass where she slides to her knees, her fingers in her panties, her other hand pressed against the glass.

"You want to watch me come, lover?" she moans in a voice laced in desperation and lust.

Yes. Yes. Fuck me, yes.

Her fingers work feverishly beneath her tiny red panties. While my hand runs up and down my cock, harder, faster.

My toes curl. I start to pant. There is so much pressure building, I think I'll break apart when I come.

Her moans get louder.

Christ, she looks amazing.

"Are you going to come, lover?" she asks.

Yes.

She presses her palm to the glass and looks up through her long lashes. "Come in me."

Fuck.

Me.

My orgasm tears out of me, and it's a violent tide of pleasure and need and desire as streams of cum hit my abs. On the other side of the glass, Bianca arches her back, her hand still pressed firmly on the glass, the other in her panties, and she comes. *And fuck she looks incredible as she's coming.* Her face is mesmerizing, and I can't rip my gaze from her as I pump and pump and pump the release out of me.

I'm coming so hard it's going to kill me.

My head falls back as ecstasy sweeps me away on a mindless ride to nowhere.

And just like that, it's over. The music stops, and the lights disappear behind the glass, signaling the performance is over. But I can still feel her there, waiting for me in the darkness.

I grab a cocktail napkin from the table, and quickly clean the mess from my abs, and rebutton my shirt and rezip my pants.

Shoving the napkin into my pocket, I press the *Request Participation* button on the table.

I want her, and I'm done holding back.

A soft whirling sound enters the room, and the glass separating me from safety begins to lower slowly. Anticipation rages through me, my body craving the release only she can give me.

Bianca is still on her knees, her thighs parted enough for me to see a flash of those panties I'm desperate to remove.

Her expression is hot and wicked, and her red lips curve into a mischievous smile that tells me she is done holding back too.

Our eyes lock.

"Get over here," I demand.

I might have just come, but I'm still hard, and I'm not going to have any problem coming again if it means I'm with her.

She eases off the stage and walks toward me, and I can't tear my eyes off her. Excitement zaps through every nerve ending as she slides those delectable thighs either side of my hips and sits on my lap. My cock throbs, instantly ready for her.

"I knew it was you," she says, placing her palms on my chest.

And without wasting another second, she kisses me, and I know I'm done for.

Her kiss is sensual but urgent, and with every stroke of her tongue, her need intensifies, mirroring my own desperate need.

She reaches for my zipper, but I stop her. "Not here."

She rips her lips from mine and sits back, her brows pulling in. "Seriously, you're turning me down again?"

I lift my hand and run my knuckles down her smooth cheek. "Not a chance, little monster. But we're not doing it here." I trail my fingers down her neck and across her cleavage, and she shivers beneath my touch. "Let me take you home. Let me make love to you in my bed."

I pull her face to mine and kiss her hard so she knows I'm all in. There's no more hesitation. But I've got to do right by her.

I'm not taking her virginity in a peep room of a sex club.

And the way she kisses me back tells me she appreciates it.

THE DRIVE back to my apartment is torturous, and Bianca doesn't help things by rubbing my thigh tantalizingly close to my straining cock. I can barely keep my eyes on the road, and I break every speed limit to get home before my little monster makes me come a second time.

I skid to a stop once inside the parking garage, and we almost run to the elevator.

When the elevator doors close, I grab her and kiss her hard. I push her up against the mirrored walls, desperate to rip her clothes from her body and barely holding myself back from doing so.

The elevator ride, which is usually fast, feels painfully slow as I kiss Bianca until we're so high with lust we can barely stand up.

When the doors open, we tumble into the apartment, shedding clothes as we head toward the bedroom.

It's then that it hits me.

I'm going to have to take this slow.

I need to pull this back a bit.

Take my time.

Get her ready.

Make this something for her to look back on and not regret.

Because I'm under no illusions that this is forever; as much as my heart may protest at the thought at giving her up, I know I will have to one day. Because once Bianca knows the truth, she will hate me and won't want anything to do with me.

But I can give her this now.

And damn if I won't make it special.

37

BIANCA

I'm nervous but excited and so damn ready.

We stand at the end of the bed, and he kisses me gently. There is no pressure here. No need for nerves. I am safe, I can feel it in every kiss, in every stroke of his tender fingertips against my skin.

We remove our remaining clothes as the moon rises higher in the night sky, and it feels natural and right.

Massimo's body is strong and muscular. A thrill zips through me when I see his cock. It looks heavy and thick, the shaft roped with veins, the head wide and shiny.

He kisses his way along my jaw and whispers, "Touch me."

I do as he says and reach for him, brushing my fingers across the deep grooves of his abdominals, which flex and dip beneath my touch.

"Lower, baby," he rasps in my ear.

My fingers trail lower to where his cock rests against his lower abs. Thick and heavy, it feels warm and rutted with veins.

He groans in my ear. "That's it, you're doing good."

He wraps my fingers around the shaft and guides my hand to start stroking. "Mmm, feel that, feel how hard you make me."

Another groan. Another whisper of fingers along my skin. I whimper, positively dripping with the need for him.

"I want you inside me," I say between kisses.

He brushes his lips across the shell of my ear. "In time, little monster."

He eases me onto the bed and stands above me. His cock is thick and heavy between his thighs as he reaches for a condom and rips open the packet.

"Put it on me," he says, handing it to me.

I've never touched a condom before. Not even in health class when they got the students to roll one on a banana. My fingers shake, but I manage to secure it over the smooth head.

"That's it, now roll it down my cock," he says, his voice like smooth whiskey.

I stroke the sheath down his length, feeling the ridges and smooth planes beneath my palm.

He crawls onto the bed and excitement surges through me. This is it. This is me losing my virginity.

He kneels between my legs and eases down. "Lift your knees."

I do as he says, and when he buries his face between my thighs, his tongue grazes my pussy, and dear God, who knew how good that was going to feel.

He licks and strokes, and I arch my back as raw pleasure flies through me.

"You're so fucking perfect," he murmurs.

I begin to shake.

The moment his tongue reaches the summit of my clit, my body jerks, my back arches, and I explode. Between my thighs, he is a god. Masterful and genius, and very giving. As in, he gives me two very powerful orgasms that flush though me from head to toe.

As the second one recedes, he pushes up on his powerful arms and looks down at me. "Are you ready?"

Affection warms his expression and suddenly, I'm not nervous anymore.

"More than ready," I say.

He takes his heavy cock in his hand and places it where his tongue has just been. He rubs the thick head through the wetness, where I'm still swollen and sensitive, and I jerk beneath his touch.

He leans down with his palms either side of my face and looks at me with so much affection I feel myself fall.

"I've got you," he whispers, and without any further hesitation, he pushes his cock inside me.

The sting is immediate, and I bite back the pain. Tears form in the corner of my eyes and then spill down my cheek.

He pauses, giving me a moment for my body to adjust. "You okay?"

I nod between the palms of his hands. "It's perfect."

One more push, and he breaks me. I cry out, and he plants his mouth onto mine and kisses me through the pain.

He starts to rock into me with more rhythm, and I start to move with him.

He kisses a tear from my cheek. "You're doing good, little monster."

I'm not going to come. Not again. But I feel loved and taken care of, and exactly where I want to be.

"You're so beautiful," he moans. He's taking it slow, but I can see the struggle on his face. He's trying not to let go and thrust too hard. He's also trying not come. Which makes me feel warm and excited because I'm doing that to him. Massimo De Kysa is inside me and I'm putting that look on his face.

"I always knew it would be like this with you. So perfect. Oh God... so fucking perfect." He kisses me hard, and his hands find mine and drags them up to rest by my head. He clasps them tight as his hips gather speed.

The pain has lessened, and we move together in perfect harmony. Slow and deep. Hard but gentle. And when he comes, it's not violent or rampant. He clasps my hands and drives his cock deeper, and I feel it throb as he releases into me.

He sinks onto me, blanketing me with his warm body, and I melt boneless into the mattress, wrapping my arms around his broad back.

We lie together in silence, and I feel the rapid pounding of his heart. He's still inside me, and I've never felt closer to another human being than I do right now.

When he finally eases out of me, I feel the loss of his warm body and know I want to do it again as soon as my body is ready.

With my head sunk into the pillow, I watch him leave the bed and disappear into the bathroom. I hear the sound of water running, then the tap switches off, and when he returns, the condom is gone and he's holding a damp wash cloth.

He kneels between my legs and tenderly places the cloth against my heated skin.

"Did I hurt you?" he asks.

I shake my head. "No, it was perfect."

"But it's tender?"

"A little."

He's being gentle with me. Despite knowing those hands are capable of great brutality, right now they're being tender and loving and taking great care of me.

"Better?" he asks.

I nod. "Thank you."

He disposes of the cloth and comes back to bed, securing me in his arms. I melt into him, feeling the most content I've ever felt in my entire life.

Until my stomach rumbles. Loudly.

He chuckles. "Sex is hungry work."

"Apparently," I say, embarrassed, nuzzling my face into his warm chest.

"I'd better feed you, then."

He pulls on a pair of sweatpants that sit low on his hips and show off the sexy V that men have. He's not wearing underwear, and the outline of his heavy cock is clearly visible. I slip on one of his shirts and follow him out of the bedroom, feeling the rawness between my legs with every step I take. My virginity is gone, and it was Massimo who took it. I don't know what any of this means, but I know it's exciting and new and exactly what I need.

In the kitchen, I sit at the counter and watch Massimo prepare us dinner. Spaghetti with Napoli sauce. From scratch. No frozen meals. No takeaway. This Mafia don likes to cook.

If there's one thing I could never get tired of, it's watching Massimo in the kitchen cooking me a meal. I absorb it all. The muscular back. The well-defined shoulders. The tattoos crawling across his broad chest and down his powerful arms. He doesn't have a clue how sexy he is as he thinly slices the garlic and chops onion, celery, and carrot.

He catches me watching him and smiles.

"What?" I ask.

"I like you watching me."

I grin. "Cook me dinner every night and I'll happily sit here watching you."

Our conversation is easy as he boils spaghetti and stirs his sauce. He pours me a wine, and taking a sip, it is as sweet as berries and spreads warmth throughout my body.

We talk while sipping our wine and by the time he dishes up the meal, I've drunk two glasses, and am feeling warm, and flushed, and so damn happy.

"Come here," Massimo says, patting the counter by the two bowls of spaghetti.

He lifts me up, and plonks me on the cool marble, and parts my thighs to stand between them. He picks up a bowl and fork, and I watch him twirl pasta onto the fork, feeling the warmth from his shirtless torso and enjoying it way too much.

He holds up the fork full of pasta, and I open my mouth. As I close my lips over the fork, my eyes roll to the back of my head because it tastes so good. I can't help but groan, and Massimo smiles.

"Oh my God, that tastes like heaven."

"It's good?"

"It's more than good. It's delicious."

He feeds me another mouthful, and again, it's a hit of pure dopamine. I moan, wanting to devour the entire bowl of food.

"I like to hear you moan," he says, his voice rough.

The food is out of this world but not so good I don't notice his cock getting heavier and harder in his sweatpants.

"Sex and food are now my two favorite things," I say as he lines up another mouthful.

A dollop of Napoli sauce slides down the corner of my mouth, and Massimo licks it from my chin.

I swallow my mouthful, and his lips travel up my chin to meet mine in a searing kiss.

He's standing between my parted legs, his erection obvious in his sweatpants, and my pussy throbs. It's instinctual. I open my legs wider, wanting to get closer to it.

The kiss deepens, and the bowl of spaghetti is forgotten. He pulls me against him, and the heat of his skin wraps around me. He removes my shirt and growls at the sight of my erect nipples. He takes one in his mouth while he palms the other breast, the sensation going straight to my clit, and I start to wonder if I'm going to come from the sensation.

He switches nipples and begins to suckle, and I drop my head back and wrap my legs around his hips. When he pulls back, I see the wild hunger on his face, and it excites me beyond measure.

"I've never wanted anyone as much as I want you," he says, his voice deep and gravelly and laden with need. "I want to make love to you until neither of us can walk, and even then it still won't be enough."

"Then take me to the bedroom and show me what that looks like," I say, feeling swept up and wanting more.

With a rough growl, he lifts me up into his powerful arms and carries me like I weigh nothing. He walks us with purpose to the bedroom like he's going to give me orgasms for the rest of the evening.

And laying me down on his warm bed, he crawls across my body and proceeds to do just that.

38

MASSIMO

I make love to her again, taking my time to get her body ready for me by making her come with my face between her thighs and my tongue on her clit, before I slide my cock inside and rock slowly in and out of her beautiful body.

And God it feels good.

Like nothing I've ever known.

Her tightness. Her sweetness. Her soft little whimpers that make me want to hold her in my arms and never let go.

She's warm and supple, and as much as I want to spend hours inside her, I don't want to hurt her, so I let go, exploding inside her with a deep, heavy growl as my orgasm spreads through me like a warm rush of water.

Afterward, I pull her into my arms and hold her against my chest and know deep down in my gut that I am doomed.

~

THE PHONE CALL comes just as the first ray of sunlight breaches the horizon. It buzzes me out of a dreamless sleep. Bianca stirs against me, and I groan at my erection that is demanding attention.

I glance at the time on my phone as I answer Matteo's call, seeing it's 6:12 a.m.

"This better be important," I growl.

Bianca moves away from me in her sleep, but I pull her back and hold her against my chest, not ready to let her go. I close my eyes, enjoying her warmth, briefly thinking about what I am going to do to her when I hang up the phone.

She might be too sore and sensitive, but there are other ways we can pleasure each other. Christ, just the thought of her hot little mouth on my cock sends a rapacious thrill into my groin. I'm going to feast on her pussy until she is writhing in pleasure on the bed beneath me.

Matteo's voice pulls me back to the present. "I just had a call from one of my contacts at the police department. Tony Vinocelli and his sons are dead."

My eyes flick open. "What the fuck happened?"

"I don't know yet. But something big is going down. The detectives are just arriving on scene. I'm in a car a few doors down. There are so many cops and ambulances, the street is lit up like the Fourth of July."

Suddenly, my day is looking very different and far less pleasurable than spending hours in bed with Bianca.

I untangle myself from her luscious body, trying not to disturb her, and pull on my pants while I'm talking to Matteo. "Who are the lead detectives?"

"Domic and Ford."

"Good." Both of them are friends of the De Kysa. I don't

call on them often, but I will be calling on them today. "I'm on my way."

"You want me to stay here and lay low?"

"Yes, but call Dante. I want a couple of men posted outside my door while Bianca is staying here."

"You think Vinocelli's demise has something to do with Bianca?"

"I have forty-two million reasons to think it does."

I hang up and dress quickly. There's no time to shower. Later, when I'm home, I'll shower with Bianca and take her against the wet tiles of the shower. Again, my body protests leaving her.

On my way out, I pause by the bed to watch her.

I don't know what any of this means—the murders, her missing money, my feelings for her—but I know she's my priority now, and I won't stop until she's safe and those responsible for ruining her life are forced to face her retribution.

I lean down and brush a strand of hair from her face.

"Is everything okay?" she murmurs sleepily, her long lashes fanning her cheeks.

"It's more than okay," I reply, thinking how beautiful she is.

"What was the phone call?"

"Nothing, just business. I have to go tend to it, but I'll be back soon. Rest up." My lips brush her ear. "You're going to need it."

She smiles softly and disappears into sleep again.

Pulling on my suit jacket, I head for the door.

It hurts leaving her, but I need to figure out how the pieces in this puzzle fit together.

First Harrison and now the Vinocelli.

This all started when Bianca asked me to help her find her money.

And my gut tells me the person who has it wants to stop her from finding it.

THERE ARE five dead bodies inside the Vinocelli compound. I'm standing beside the body of one of Tony's bodyguards. He was sitting at the table when he was gunned down—a bullet to the back of his skull. Now, his face is slumped against the table, and there's blood and brains in his nearby coffee.

A second bodyguard lies dead only a few feet away on the kitchen floor, blood pooling on the white tiles beneath his head.

"Tony is upstairs," Domic says. "I can take you up there but then you really gotta let forensics do their stuff."

Domic and Ford weren't exactly thrilled to let Matteo and me into their crime scene. But they granted us ten minutes to walk the scene with them.

Matteo and I follow Domic up the winding staircase to the landing and down the hallway to where Tony Vinocelli lies dead in his bedroom doorway. Dressed in nothing but his robe and a pair of bed shorts, he's on his stomach, head turned to the side, and his lifeless eyes staring out at nothing.

"He took two bullets to the chest," Domic explains.

"What's your theory?" Matteo asks him.

"Too early to tell exactly, but it's not a professional hit."

"It's too sloppy for a professional hit," I say, looking at the two bullet holes splintered into the doorjamb and another stuck in the bulkhead above the door. "They were startled by Tony."

Domic nods. "I think the suspect walked up the stairs, and encountered Tony in the doorway, and just started firing."

"Tony was coming out of his room when he was shot," I say.

"Yes, but I don't think this started downstairs. I think it started in the pool house."

"Then let's see the pool house," I say, turning around to walk down the stairs.

We have to pass through the dining room again to access the door leading outside.

We take the pathway leading from the main house to the pool area, lit by a row of solar lights. Halfway along, Giulio Vinocelli, Tony's oldest son, lies dead on the ground.

He's on his back, arms at his side, two bright red stains spread across his shirt. Inches from his right hand is a gun.

"He had his gun in his hand," I note.

"I think he heard what was happening in the pool house and went to inspect it when the suspect ambushed him here." Domic points to a shattered tree branch in the magnolia tree along the path. "Again, the suspect fired off a couple of shots before hitting Giulio. Whoever they are, they have experience with guns but not enough to be a hired gun."

"This is personal," I say, standing over Giulio's lifeless body. His eyes are half open and staring up into a new dawn, early morning light slanting across his face.

"You want to see personal? Follow me."

We leave Giulio and follow Domic as he leads us into the pool house where Fausto Vinocelli lies dead amongst a sea of broken glass. He has three bullet wounds to the chest and one to the face. When he fell, he crashed through the glass coffee table.

"He's been shot more times than the others," I say.

"Looks like overkill. Makes me think he was the target."

But I disagree. I think they were all the target, and as Matteo and I leave the crime scene and head back into the city, an unease tightens in my gut.

"What's the theory?" Matteo asks.

"Someone is cleaning house. I think they killed Harrison to keep him quiet because he knew their identity. They killed him in a way that would throw suspicion on the Vinocelli by using Fausto's signature shot. It was a good plan. Throw heat onto gangsters well-known to law enforcement, while they disappeared with all the money. But then Bianca asked me for help, and when they found out about it, they panicked and killed the Vinocelli—who didn't even realize they were caught up in this scenario."

I don't know any of this for certain. But I'm rarely wrong.

And my gut tells me Bianca is next on their list.

"Dead?"

I see the color drain from Bianca's face as the news of the Vinocelli massacre sinks in.

"Yes. Someone shot them."

We're standing in the kitchen, and she eases down on the

stool by the counter. She looks dazed and scared, and when she lifts her watery gaze to me, I see the terror in her eyes.

And damn if I don't want to fix that.

"Who did this?" she whispers.

"You don't need to worry."

"Don't do that," she snaps. "Don't start lying to me. You think whoever killed Harrison and the Vinocelli is after me, don't you? I can see it on your face, Massimo."

I want to lie to her because I don't want to frighten her. But she deserves the truth. "Yes."

"Why?"

"Because you're looking for your money and they don't want you to."

"How can you be sure?"

"Because they killed Harrison when you came to me for help. Now they've killed the Vinocelli. It's a message. Stop looking."

I walk around the counter and pull her into my arms. I hold her against my chest, and I can feel the rapid beat of her heart, and I know I will stop at nothing to make this right.

I lean back and take her face in my hands. "I'm going to keep you safe. Do you trust me?"

She nods. "Yes."

"Good. Now I need you to pack a bag."

"Where are we going?"

"Misty Lake Mountain. I have a cabin there, and you'll be safe."

39

BIANCA

Misty Lake Mountain is as picturesque as it sounds. Miles and miles of alpine forests. Low cloud cover. A stunning lake that's so still it looks like glass. For the most part, we're on even road, but when we turn off onto rockier terrain, Massimo navigates it with ease.

As I take in the sweeping views and foggy mountain beauty, I try not to let my fear get the better of me. But it's hard not to, considering the way Massimo hustled me out of the city. He thinks someone is going to kill me, and damn if that doesn't frighten a girl.

I'm silent for most of the drive. Too stuck in my own head to make interesting conversation.

"Tell me a happy memory," Massimo says as we drive along the isolated mountain road.

I turn away from the window to look at him. "What?"

"I want to know one of your happy memories," he prompts.

He's trying to take me to some happy place and I kind of love him for it.

"Come on, humor me," he coaxes. "When you think of a happy memory, what is the first thing that comes to mind?"

I don't hesitate. "My mom."

"What was she like?"

"The belle of the ball. Always immaculately dressed. Not a hair out of place. Nails perfect. Makeup flawless. Never without her signature scent." If I close my eyes and try hard enough, I can still smell her signature perfume. Soft and delicate with light floral notes. "She was a lot of fun. She had this smile that could light up a room, and this infectious laugh, that no matter how annoyed or angry or upset you were, if you heard that laugh, you couldn't help yourself, you'd start laughing too."

"She sounds like an incredible woman."

"She was. I remember wanting to be just like her when I grew up. I used to love sitting next to her when she was doing her makeup. She had one of those three-mirrored dressers where you can see your face from different angles, and I would sit there and watch her, and we would talk and laugh, and she'd tell me little stories about growing up, or about the people she would meet. Her and my father were always going to fancy parties and rubbing shoulders with famous people, and she would wow them all. But in those intimate moments in front of the mirror when it was just her and me, it felt like I was her whole world and none of the glamour and celebrity encounters meant anything to her. It was those moments she loved the best, she said. Hanging with her favorite girl. After she was finished doing her makeup, she'd paint my lips with lip gloss. I remember how cool and soft her fingers were on my chin when she painted on the gloss. Then she would laugh and tell me that every girl should have a good lip gloss in her purse." I sigh. The nostalgia feels heavy in my chest. "Gosh, I haven't thought about that in years. Not since she died."

It's bittersweet remembering my mom. She meant so much to me, and my memories of her make me happy. But to know I will never see that smile in person again breaks my heart.

"How old were you when she died?"

"I was twelve."

"That's a young age to lose your mom."

"My father came home late one night and found her floating in the pool. I was asleep upstairs, so I couldn't shed any light on what happened. Talk about feeling guilty. For years I carried that around, the giant *what if I could have saved her*."

"You were just a kid asleep in your bed. No guilt required."

"Tell that to twelve-year-old Bianca. I blamed myself. Especially because her death remained unsolved."

"I heard they had various theories but couldn't make one stick."

"For a while, they thought her death was the result of foul play. But when the toxicology reports came back showing high levels of alcohol in her system, they theorized she'd consumed a bottle of wine at the pool's edge and then slipped on a wet step. She hit her head and fell into the pool. But she didn't drown. The blunt force trauma she sustained in the fall was what killed her."

"So why didn't they rule it an accident?"

"Two things. The odd angle her of her head. It was as if someone had placed it on the step of the pool, so her face was just out of the water."

"Odd," Massimo says, his brows pulled together. "What was the other reason?"

"The antique locket she never took off went missing. It was silver with a big ruby on the front of the pendant. It was the second thing that stopped them from ruling it accidental."

"Maybe it slipped off during the fall."

"They drained the pool." I can still see my father standing on the edge of the pool, looking out at the sweeping view of New York City beyond the gates, his shoulders slumped and tears streaming down his face as the pool was drained and searched. "They never found it."

"Was it worth anything?"

"It was a family heirloom, so it was sentimental to my mom. That's why she never took it off. It had been handed down through seven generations. But I later found out the necklace was insured for three hundred thousand dollars. Although my father never collected on it. He said it would be tasteless."

"Is it possible someone stole it? Perhaps they heard it was worth three hundred thousand dollars and decided they wanted it. It would be easily sold on the black market."

"When the police couldn't do anything more, my father almost went insane looking for that necklace. He put out feelers all over the world, all over the internet. But the necklace never showed up, and her death remains unsolved." I stare out the window at the mountainside dense with trees and low cloud cover. "My father was never the same again. I suppose I wasn't either."

At the time, it was too much to understand. I was a young girl on the precipice of adolescence, at an age when I needed my mom the most. My father didn't know what to do with me, so he put me in the charge of the housekeeper and threw money and things at me to make up for his absence, not knowing what else to do. If I cried, I got jewelry. If he felt bad for missing a school event or something important—which was always—I got a trip away, or clothes, or makeup, or anything of monetary value that showed how much he loved me. It's no wonder I became a spoilt brat when the teenage hormones kicked in. Buying things kept the pain at bay. Just far enough away for me to pretend it wasn't even there. People die. But expensive things are forever.

Now when I look back, it's with shame. And it's taken losing everything to shed that suffocating skin of privilege and entitlement, and for me to be able to see it.

I turn my head to look at Massimo. "I know who I am, and I don't want to be her anymore."

"What do you mean?"

"You said it yourself. I'm a spoilt Mafia princess." I let out a shaky breath. "And I don't want to be her."

"I shouldn't have called you that."

"No, you were right. I *am* a spoilt brat."

"There are more layers to you than you give yourself credit for. If you think you're just a spoilt brat, then you are not who you think you are."

"You're just saying that to be nice."

"I don't do nice very well, little monster."

I can't help but smile. Massimo has the crazy ability to make every situation better, and in that moment, there is so much I want to tell him. That I am so grateful for him and for what he's done for me in these last few months. That the last ten years of my life seem so shallow and vapid, and that despite all the shit that's gone down in the last year, these last few weeks with him have been the happiest in my life.

But I don't get a chance, because up ahead, a beat-up red truck is parked on the shoulder, and Massimo turns off the road to pull up behind it.

"What's going on?" I ask.

But Massimo is annoyingly vague. "Grab your things."

I do as he says and climb out, grabbing my overnight bag from the back seat.

A huge man climbs out of the red truck. And when I say he's huge, I mean he's massive, with muscles for miles. He's wearing a lumberjack shirt and jeans, and has long, messy hair tangling around a weathered-but-handsome face.

He greets Massimo as if they're old friends.

"Bianca, this is Axel. He and his wife Lauren live on the mountain."

"It's nice to meet you," I say, still in the dark about what is happening.

He gives me a friendly nod. "Ma'am."

"From this point onward, we'll be using Axel's truck," Massimo explains. "Everybody knows everybody on the mountain so we want to blend in as much as we can."

Axel and Massimo swap keys.

"I'll keep the Escalade in my garage until you need it back," Axel says. "And if you need anything, you know where to find me."

Massimo and I climb into the old truck, which is a stark contrast to the well-appointed interior of the Escalade, and Massimo starts the engine. It clunks and thuds and finally comes alive with a deep rumble. Axel drives away, and Massimo pulls onto the road, and we're off again, heading toward our secret location.

"So who was that guy?" I ask.

"Axel and I used to know each other a long time ago. He's ex-military and used to work as a bodyguard."

"He's very dark and mysterious."

"He's just cautious. A few years back he was done for murder."

"Wait, what?"

"He was accused of murdering his client. He was innocent, but when his affair with his client came to light, well, the press had a field day. The prosecutors followed. He went to prison for it."

"But they found him innocent eventually, right? Otherwise, how is he out?"

"He escaped prison and lived on the lam for a long time. Came out here because it's easy to disappear on the mountain. But then he went and kidnapped Lauren, his now wife, to save her from her fiancé, and the police found him."

"Hold on, back up. He kidnapped Lauren?"

"It's a long story but an interesting one. Short version, he saved Lauren from a violent fiancé, and they fell in love. To have a future together, he went to the police only to find out they'd found evidence to dispute his guilty verdict, and he was released."

"And then he married Lauren?"

"Yes."

"I like that story." I smile to myself. "He came here to hide away from the world but found his person instead."

"I suppose," Massimo says in a tone that tells me he doesn't care for the romantic side of the story.

"You're not very romantic," I say.

"I've never needed to be," he replies. "But I disagree with your observation. I can be very romantic."

"Oh really?"

"I'm bringing you to the mountains, aren't I?" he deadpans.

"Because you think some psychopath wants to kill me. But I suppose you *are* protecting me, and I admit that I find that very romantic. So I stand corrected. Massimo De Kysa, you are a romantic."

He gives me a dark grin. "Wait till we get inside the cabin and I show you just how romantic I can be."

The wicked lure in his voice tells me there will be little romance but a lot of orgasms. Which is fine by me. Driving these bumpy roads in a truck with no suspension has kind of got me aroused.

Massimo turns onto a secluded driveway and follows the muddy path deeper into the pine forest, eventually pulling up in front of a charming little cabin.

"Wow," I say, climbing out. "It's beautiful."

The stone and timber cabin sits in the small clearing amongst the tall pines. There's a small porch, a stone chimney, and a stack of firewood piled up to the windows.

I collect my bag from the back of the truck and follow Massimo up the front steps.

We pause on the little porch so Massimo can punch a sequence of numbers into the digital lock, which seems completely out of place for the rustic cabin. Heavy locks retract, and he pushes the front door open.

Inside, the little cabin reveals its full country charm. Timber floors. A large stone fireplace that takes up one wall. Arched windows looking out onto a sweeping view of the valley below. Comfortable-looking couches and recliner chairs set in front of the fireplace.

Massimo closes the door behind us, and I hear the clunk of a heavy lock sliding into place.

"That sounded serious," I say.

"This whole place is rigged for safety. Follow me."

He leads me to the first room off the short hallway. Inside is a desk set up with several monitors and other surveillance equipment.

It's then I realize that despite looking like your normal weekend cabin on the outside, it's far from that. There's not one degree in the three-hundred-and-sixty-degree scope of the property that is not visible to the cameras.

"There are also twenty sensors set up outside that will alert us if anyone approaches the cabin." He gestures to a monitor showing a series of little green lights all in a row. "If something triggers the sensor, the light will turn red, and an alarm will sound."

"Do animals and birds set off the sensors?"

"No, they're designed to detect certain sizes. A bird or a rodent won't set it off. But someone walking through the woods will." He indicates one of the monitors. "Every entry into the house is alarmed. But if for any reason we get separated, and you're in danger, you're to run to this room. It's a panic room. And if anyone breaches the cabin, you come in here and hit this button." He points to the red button on a panel of buttons by the door. "No one will be able to get through it."

To prove his point, he hits it, and a thick, sturdy door shoots out from the door cavity and slams shut. He taps it to show me how impenetrable it is, then points to another button on the panel.

"This button here will alert the police to the break in. And this one will alert Axel."

"Axel?"

"He'll get here a lot quicker than the police. And he's a lot deadlier."

He pauses, and I see affection in his eyes. He can see I'm terrified, and it hurts him. "I'll keep you safe, Bianca. You have my word."

I shiver, and he notices. Up until now, I've put on a brave face. But this fortress with its booby-trapped backyard makes my situation all the more real, and I'm not ashamed to admit that I'm scared.

"Last week, I was worried because someone took all my money," I say. "Now I'm worried someone wants to take my life."

40

MASSIMO

When I realized Bianca was in danger, I was caught between sending her into hiding with my best soldiers and staying behind to find who is behind this or taking her to the mountains and protecting her myself.

I chose the latter because no one can protect her as well as me. I'd die before I let anyone get to her. And that has never been as true as it is now, standing here in front of her and seeing the fear in her beautiful eyes.

I don't understand the meaning behind these feelings of protectiveness toward her. But I do know I won't stop until that look of fear is gone from her face.

I pull her into my arms and kiss her because kissing Bianca is becoming my favorite pastime, *and* the most natural thing to do when I'm feeling so protective of her.

We take a shower in the cabin's rustic bathroom where the stone shower cubicle is big enough for two.

We kiss under the steady stream, lost in each other as fingers whisper across flesh. Her wet body feels like heaven against mine, her heady kisses sending me further and further toward a beckoning unknown.

When she slides to her knees, I have to brace myself against the stone wall as her delectable mouth finds my engorged cock.

I'm falling hard, and I don't even give a fuck.

This angel fucking my cock with her beautiful mouth has me thinking things that a man who wants to remain single doesn't think. Like a future full of nights fucking only her. Of mornings waking up in her arms. Of giving her my name. Of babies. Fuck, the thought of making her pregnant makes my cock even harder.

I push my fingers through her hair and tighten them against her scalp. For someone who has little experience, my little monster certainly knows how to torture me with her exquisite tongue. She hollows her cheeks, and glides her mouth back up again, and I'm seeing stars. My balls send me a warning, they're heavy and tight, ready for release.

"Bianca... it's too good... I'm going to come..."

But she only pulls away long enough to look up at me through long lashes and says, "I want to taste all of you, Massimo, come in my mouth."

I groan. It's too much to hold back.

Her words.

The sight of her on her knees in front of me.

The way she looks at me through those thick lashes.

Come in my mouth.

My cock explodes on her tongue, my release pumping out of me with a delicious violence, and my little monster takes it all. Pump after pump, I grip her hair and groan. My knees weaken, and I slump against the wet tiles.

Mind fucking blown.

I help her to her feet and kiss her.

"Was that okay?" she asks, her lashes wet with droplets of water.

"Baby, that was more than okay." I kiss her again. "Now, let's get dried off so I can show you my appreciation."

SHE LIES on her stomach on the bed. I lean down to kiss her cheek and trail my lips over her shoulder and down her back. Her skin is smooth and warm, her body luscious and soft. I kneel behind her and run my hand over her juicy ass and lift her hips to expose her beautiful pink pussy. Despite coming in her mouth less than half an hour ago, I'm hard, and aching to be inside her.

I reach for a condom, but she stops me.

"I'm on the pill to help with my period," she says. "And I know you're clean."

"Are you sure?"

"I want to feel all of you, Massimo. Every naked inch. And then I want you to come inside me."

Christ, when she says shit like that, what am I meant to do?

I don't hesitate. I take my cock in my hand and enter her with one smooth thrust, my eyes rolling into the back of my head as her pussy swallows my cock and wraps tightly around it.

I didn't think heaven existed. But I'm pretty sure that's where I am right now.

She's so wet and tight.

So fucking tight.

I grip her hips and begin to pump slowly. Nice and easy. I don't want to come too soon. I want to give her plenty of orgasms before I take my own.

I pull out and rub the engorged head through her wet pussy, rubbing it hard against her exposed clit until her legs start to shake and her moans come quicker.

She grips the sheet with shaking fingers and starts to come.

As she cries out, I shove my cock inside her and thrust hard, driving deep into her. She clenches around me, almost making me see stars as her pussy convulses around me.

She collapses onto the bed, and I roll her onto her back. She opens her thighs for me, and I thrust right back into heaven.

She gasps, and her eyelids flutter and then close. Her back arches and she moans, and it is soft and feminine, and makes me surge harder and deeper into her just so I can hear it again. She cries out, and my heart shatters as I fall irrevocably and unexpectedly in love with her.

I can't hold back. It feels too good. I'll give her more orgasms later because stopping myself from coming right now is like trying to stop a wave from crashing on a shore. I explode into her, and the release is like nothing I've ever known. It breaks open my brain and everything goes white as a moan is torn out of me.

I fall against her, wrecked by an orgasm so bright and violent I'm never going to be the fucking same again.

I WAKE up to the sound of rain on the roof. On the bedside table, the alarm clock reads 9:32 p.m.

Bianca is in my arms, and I feel at peace.

My phone rings and the name John Doe appears on the screen.

Nico's alias.

I answer it quickly so I don't wake Bianca. She stirs against my chest but settles back to sleep, her soft breath grazing my neck.

"Yeah?" I say as quietly as I can.

"I just landed. I'll drive up to the mountain tomorrow. You sure you still want to go through with this?"

I swallow thickly as the heavy weight of anticipation stirs in my chest.

"I don't have a choice," I reply. "It's the only way."

After I hang up, I lie still, listening to the rain, my body heavy with regret. I secure my arm tighter around Bianca's warm body and stare up at the ceiling.

Just when I've found real happiness, tomorrow, it will all be over.

41

BIANCA

We wake up to more rain, and it's hard to leave the bed, especially when Massimo is determined to keep me there. His body is warm as he holds me in his arms and kisses the back of my neck and down my shoulder. He's hard, I can feel him pressed against the back of my thigh, and I know I won't be leaving the bed until he's given me another delicious orgasm.

No words are needed. Our bodies do all the talking. His hips gravitate toward mine. Fingertips whisper across skin. Lips graze flesh. He rolls me onto my back and pushes deep into me with a sleepy groan.

He blankets my body with the warmth of his own and slowly rocks in and out of me. He pushes his hands through my hair and seals his mouth over mine.

I open wider to him and secure my legs around his

narrow hips as he strokes into my body, his groans driving me closer to falling off the cliff.

"Open your eyes, Bianca. Watch us fucking."

I open my eyes and watch his impressive cock stroking in and out of my body. He's long and thick, and it drives me wild watching something so big disappear inside.

My body tenses, and from out of the foggy depths of sleep, my orgasm skyrockets. Raw pleasure streams through me, and I cry out. "Massimo...oh God..."

My legs tighten around him, my body clenching and throbbing against this cock. It's all he needs to follow.

He nuzzles his face into my throat, his groans coming louder. "Oh fuck, little monster... what the fuck have you done to me..." He jerks to a sudden stop and grips the pillow beside me as he shudders and groans.

When his breathing evens, he lifts his head. He's still sleepy and soft in the face, and I don't think I've seen him look more handsome than he does now.

"Hey," he says, pushing up on his big arms so I have no choice but to see his flexing biceps. His skin is golden in this light. Flawless and utter perfection like the rest of him.

"Hey, yourself," I reply, reaching up to lace my fingers around the nape of his neck.

"I think this mountain air is driving me to distraction. At the very least it's making me lazy."

"Yeah, how so?"

"I don't want to do anything but fuck you."

His cock is still inside me, still hard and thick, and I clench it in appreciation.

He hisses in a rough breath. "That kind of behavior will get you punished."

I clench again to let him know I'm here for all the punishment he can deliver.

Which he delivers with pleasurable torture for the following hour, bringing me to the cusp of coming but not letting me fall, over and over again, until finally letting me plunge into a full body orgasm like I've never experienced. I unravel beneath him, blinded by ecstasy as pleasure spreads through me, then sink into a boneless heap on the bed.

When he leaves the bed to take a shower, I sink into the mattress and try not to read into a future that may never happen.

But I already know I'm done for.

Because I've already fallen in love with him.

WHILE MASSIMO FIXES us breakfast in the kitchen, I have a long shower, taking the time to wash my hair and relax under the stream of warm water, losing myself in fantasies I know I shouldn't entertain but can't help.

Maybe we could move to this mountain and whittle away the days by fucking until we're both too exhausted to stand.

I'm sore thanks to a combination of Massimo's size and the amount of sex we're having, and I can't say I hate it. There is nothing about this that makes me regret what is happening.

Except for the whole invisible serial killer who wants me dead.

But I know Massimo won't let him get to me.

I know he'd die trying to stop anyone from hurting me.

And if I'm honest, I feel like it's always been this way with us. Like there has always been something bigger drawing us together like magnets. A bond decided before we met. A promise. *A destiny*.

I turn off the faucet and dry off, trying not to lose my head over images of lazy days on the mountain in bed with Massimo and forgetting the outside world exists.

When I pull on my jeans, my phone rings. Reaching for it, I can see it's Jules.

I ignore it and finish getting dressed. But she rings back immediately, and when I ignore that call, she rings again.

Something's wrong.

When she rings a fourth time, I pick up.

"Jules, what's wrong?"

"Bianca, wherever you are, you have to get out of there." She sounds breathless.

"Why, what's going on?"

"Is Massimo with you?"

"He's in the other room. What is this all about? Why do you sound panicked?"

"Listen to me," she rushes. "I've found out what happened to your money. It was Massimo who took it."

I let out a humorless laugh. "What are you talking about?"

"I told you I was going to prove to you how much our friendship means to me, so I've been doing some digging. But I'll explain all of it later, right now you need to get away from Massimo. It was him who paid Harrison to rip you off."

An uneasiness begins to tingle in the base of my spine.

"That can't be true," I say. "Massimo would never hurt me like that."

My heart couldn't bear it.

"Remember what your dad always used to say?" Jules says. "Never trust a De Kysa."

As soon as she says it, I remember how my father would get worked up about Nico marrying Bella instead of me, and he would beat his fist against his desk or the kitchen counter and growl, *"Never trust a De Kysa, Bianca."*

"What reason would he have to do it?"

"To flush out your allies. Look, we don't have time. I'll explain it all later. Right now, all you need to know is that it was him, Bianca, and it's been him all along. Him and Nico."

"Nico?"

"Yes, Nico is alive."

"No—"

My phone pings with a message. It's a photo of a man wearing a baseball cap and a beard. Those eyes. So much like his brothers. It's a blurry image but it's clearly Nico.

"I don't understand. This can't be real."

"It is real. I took that photo at a gas station this morning. He is on his way to the cabin—"

"Massimo wouldn't hurt me."

"They've brainwashed you, Bianca. You need to listen to me, your life depends on it. Massimo killed Harrison and the Vinocelli. He didn't take you to the cabin to protect you, he's taken you there to dispose of you. You have to believe me."

I feel beyond dazed. She sounds scared. What Jules is saying makes sense when it shouldn't. I don't want to believe her, but there's that broken part of me that wonders if she's right and questions if Massimo is responsible for me losing everything. After all, we were rivals and in the aftermath of my father's death, it would make sense he would want to know if the Bamcorda were secretly rebuilding and getting ready to retaliate.

Nausea twists in my stomach. Is my luck so bad that while I was falling in love, he was planning my demise? The crime channels are full of stories about cruel criminals who prey on the vulnerable. And if I was anything when I turned up at Massimo's club it was vulnerable.

I'm so confused I can barely breathe.

"What do I do?" I whisper in utter disbelief.

It feels as though my heart is actually breaking.

"You need to get out of there. Don't collect your things. Don't talk to him. I mean it, Bianca, you can't tell him any of this. He'll tell you he's in love with you just to confuse you. Then Nico will turn up and it will all be over."

"Has he got my money?"

She sounds surprised. "Of course he does."

All this time and he had my money.

All.

This.

Time.

"I need you to focus, honey," Jules says. "I need to get you safe. Can you get the car keys?"

I nod, so lost in my pain I forget she can't see me.

"Bianca, can you get the car keys?"

"Yes," I reply, my voice small.

"Good. Do it now. I'll meet you in town. And Bianca—"

"Yes?"

"If you have to shoot him, do it."

She ends the call, and I stand there breaking apart from the inside. A powerful sob lurches inside me and I let the tears fall. I let myself feel every agonizing piece of his betrayal before I quickly wipe away the tears and reach for my gun.

Massimo is on the phone in the kitchen when I walk in. When he sees my gun aimed at him, he excuses himself from the call and hangs up.

"What are you doing?"

"Is Nico alive?"

"You're not going to shoot me."

I pull the trigger, and the wall behind his right shoulder splinters as the bullet smashes into it. "That was your only warning."

He reluctantly holds up his hands.

He's not afraid. He's pissed.

I grit my teeth. "I repeat, is Nico alive?"

"You know I can't answer that," he says.

Which means yes.

Which means Jules was telling the truth.

Which means she was probably right about Massimo being behind Harrison taking my money.

I was wrong when I thought I had hit rock bottom. I just hit it with a violent thud.

My next words burst out of me in a wave of unchecked emotion.

"Did you put Harrison up to it?"

Massimo's brow lifts, then drops, and it's enough to tell me I'm right.

My knees go weak, and I start to shake. "Why?"

"Put the gun down, and I'll tell you everything."

And there's the verbal confirmation that he was behind this, and it goes through me like a bullet.

"You did this to me?" I choke.

"No."

"Tell me the truth. Did you tell Harrison to steal my money?"

"Bianca—"

"Did you?" I cry.

"Yes."

It's another blow. And I think I actually feel my heart break.

"Why?"

"Bianca, put down the gun."

My tears breach my lids and drip down my cheeks. "How could you do this to me?"

"It's not what you think."

"Then how is it?"

"We don't live in a world where trust and betrayal breaks hearts or makes us cry, Bianca. You and me, we live in a world where broken trust and betrayal gets you killed. I did what I did to stop a war from brewing."

My chin quivers. This hurts so bad. "There was no war brewing."

"How was I to know? Nico had just killed your father and a lot of Bamcorda soldiers. We waited. We watched. We thought the Bamcorda went underground to regroup. Then Nico was shot, and in the fallout I was forced to make quick decisions."

"And stealing from me was one of them?"

"Things were different when I put the pieces in place. I didn't know you like I do now."

"You knew me the night of Nico's engagement... when you stole my first..." I can't even finish the sentence because it hurts so much.

"A lot had happened since then. Both sides had suffered." He looks pained, I'll give him that. But it only hurts me more. "It wasn't personal."

"Well, it was very fucking personal to me."

"It was necessary. If a war was coming, I needed to see it before it got here."

"That doesn't even make sense."

"The Bamcorda had scattered. Surveillance only scratched the surface. I needed to know who were still aligned with the Bamcorda name."

"So you took everything from me?"

"If you take everything from someone, you watch who they turn to and who helps them. It will show you who their true alliances are. Tell you who you need to watch."

"There wasn't going to be any retaliation. You know why, because everyone abandoned me. They were too afraid of the fucking De Kysa to do a goddamn thing to help."

"How was I to know that? I couldn't take the chance."

Standing here, I feel as broken as I ever have, and I don't know how I'm ever going to keep going. But I know I will.

Just not with Massimo.

I let my arm drop.

"I wish I'd never come looking for you." Pain spirals through me like venom in my blood. "No, I wish I'd never met you."

Massimo found me when I was at my most vulnerable and lured me in. But the real crime, *the real cruelty*, was him making me fall in love with him.

He takes a step forward, and I put my hand out to stop him because I don't want him close to me. Because I'm not going to be drawn into his alluring orbit ever again.

"I deserve your hate," he says. "But you don't know the full story."

"I know enough. You killed Harrison and then you killed the Vinocelli."

"I put things in place, but I didn't kill Harrison and I had nothing to do with what happened to Tony and his sons."

"You're lying."

"I told you I would never lie to you—"

"Yet that's all you've done."

"No, it's not."

"You betrayed me. Do you expect me to believe you now?"

I turn away from him.

"Don't leave," he begs.

I swing around.

"Why shouldn't I?" I cry.

"Because I fucking love you," he yells.

He'll tell you he's in love with you just to confuse you.

I point my gun at him again. Because how fucking dare he.

"Don't you dare say that to me." More tears prick my eyes. "Don't you fucking dare."

I think about the last few months with Masimo and the thought of them being a lie is unbearable.

Never trust a De Kysa.

Massimo reaches for me. "Bianca..."

I aim my gun at him again.

"You stay away from me, or I swear to God I will shoot you."

I don't shoot him.

Instead, I steal his car keys and flee the mountain.

42

MASSIMO

"It's not what you think."

I can't believe I said that to her. I sounded like an asshole who's been caught with his pants down.

I call Nico. "Bianca just fled."

"What happened?"

"She found out about the plan."

"I knew this was going to blow up in your face the moment you hired her."

"Your *told you sos* will have to wait. We need to find her."

"I'm ten minutes away."

I hang up from my brother. I had asked him to the mountain to talk to Bianca. If I wanted a future with her, then she needed to know that my brother was still alive. And that's what I want—a future with her. Because I wasn't lying when I told her I am in love with her.

I've never been in love, but I know this is how it feels. It has to be.

I'm batshit crazy for her.

Nico and I had fought about it. He thought it was a colossal mistake, but I told him I wanted to marry Bianca and that meant revealing the truth about him still being alive.

No secrets.

I remember the promise we gave each other.

And I'd meant it. I had every intention of coming clean and telling her. But I wanted to find her money first.

Now I feel gutted. Seeing her face crack with the pain of knowing what I did to her is killing me.

What I told her is all true. I approached Harrison to embezzle her money because I wanted to see who she turned to in her hour of need.

I wasn't expecting it to be me.

But then she showed up wanting my help, and I thought it would make it easier to keep an eye on her and whoever she was aligned with.

I tried to keep her at arm's length.

Tried to control my emotions.

But the truth is, the moment she stepped into my club, I knew I was in trouble. Because I hadn't forgotten that stolen kiss or how soft and supple she felt to touch.

And I wasn't counting on it to cut as deep when I realized she was completely alone. And as soon as I realized she had no alliances and was trying to heal from her devastating circumstances, I tried to contact Harrison.

Only I couldn't find him.

He had vanished.

Finding him dead and zip-tied to a chair in his apartment in Soho came as a surprise.

Not to mention a worry.

It was then I realized I had lost control of the situation, and the Vinocelli massacre only drove that realization home.

Because it meant someone else had joined the game.

An unknown ghost.

Now she hates me, and she has every right to.

But I need to push that aside and focus on finding her.

Because the unknown player is still out there, and I have a feeling Bianca is playing right into their hands.

"I'LL HAVE the location of the truck for you in a minute," Axel says on the other end of the phone. "It has a tracking device attached to it."

I listen to him tapping on a keyboard. The seconds tick over slowly. I'm anxious; I need to find Bianca before whoever else is looking for her does.

"Okay, I found the truck's location. It's heading down the mountain toward town."

"Okay, thanks."

"Wait, she might dump it though. Let me grab her location using her phone."

"You can do that?"

"There's not a lot I can't do. But hacking into the system is going to take a few minutes."

"Okay, do that and call me back."

I pace the floorboards, feeling helpless.

Feeling like an asshole.

I hear the sound of tires on the gravel outside and stalk over to the window, hoping against hope that it's Bianca. But it's not. It's my brother.

I run my palm over the back of my head.

I fucked up.

I always knew this day would come. I just didn't realize it was going to hurt this much.

The door opens and Nico appears. "What a fucking mess." He steps inside. "Have you heard from her?"

I shake my head. "But Axel is tracking her phone. Once he gets a lock on it he will call me back."

"Then what?"

"Then we go get her."

43

BIANCA

I swipe tears from my face as I drive down the mountain. Heartbreak numbs my body, but it doesn't stop the tears from flowing, and I know it's only a matter of time before the agony sets in.

The roads are almost empty, but occasionally I see another car traveling in the opposite direction, and I wonder if Nico is in any of them. On his way to the cabin to help Massimo get rid of the last piece of the puzzle. *Me.*

My fingers grip the steering wheel so tight they are white-knuckled.

It's almost too crazy to believe. But crazy is what I've been the entire time since my father died.

Crazy to think I could force the enemy to help me.

Crazy to think it was a good idea to fall in love with him.

A fresh wave of tears stream down my cheeks, bringing

the sting of betrayal with it when I think about how I gave Massimo my heart and he ground it up like minced meat.

Heartbreak is a funny thing. During the drive down the mountain, I move out of the first stage of shock and dive headfirst into the second stage of anger.

I have half a mind to turn the truck around and storm back to the cabin to give Massimo a bit more of my mind. But I don't think my heart could take seeing him right now.

Instead, I drive on until I reach Main Street where I park the truck and walk over to the gas station like Jules told me to. She's waiting for me in the parking lot. The black Mercedes.

The moment I slide in, the weight of leaving Massimo and the truth of what he has done to me hits me like a wall of water and I burst into tears again.

Jules starts the engine. "Don't cry, Bianca. You're safe now."

I HAVE SO many questions but don't feel like talking, so I stare out the window at the misty alpine landscape as Jules drives us the rest of the way down the mountain.

Somehow, I manage to fall asleep, lulled into a dreamless state by the forward motion of the car and the long winding roads. When I wake up, I'm surprised to see we're just out of New York City.

I sit up but wince because of the kink in my neck.

"Sorry," I say. "I didn't mean to fall asleep."

"That's okay, you must've needed it. I don't imagine you

got a lot of sleep while hiding away in a cabin with Massimo De Kysa."

I don't know if there is something in her tone that makes me feel on edge, or if it's the fact that she's right, I didn't get much sleep while we were in the cabin because of all the sex, and thinking about that hurts.

But there is a strange tingling sensation working its way through me.

It could be because I just woke up, but it feels like something in the car has changed. Jules is razor focused on the road. Maybe she's tired too, but her mood seems low.

"How far away are we from your new apartment?" I ask.

"About twenty minutes, why?"

I don't want to poke a tired bear, but I really can't wait twenty minutes. "I really need to pee."

She looks annoyed but pulls into a gas station a few miles down the road.

She waits in the car while I run to the restroom. Inside, I empty my bladder and feel the sting of this morning's love-making, and a warm rush of tears surges through me. But I fight them off because I know once I start crying again, I might implode with the pain, and I don't want to do that in a gas station off the I-95. So I pull my shit together, splash water over my face, and ignore the reflection in the mirror with the drawn features and sad eyes.

Never trust a De Kysa.

Back on the road, Jules is still quiet.

"Is everything okay?" I ask.

She pulls her eyes off the road and gives me a smile. "Of course, why wouldn't it be?"

"You've gone quiet. I thought you might be pissed at me."

"Maybe I'm tired, did you consider that?" She frowns and turns back to the road. "It's not always about you, Bianca."

I feel the sting of her words. "I know, I'm sorry. But if something is wrong, I want you to tell me."

The tension in the car seems to thicken, and I don't understand why. I want to know what happened to the woman I had dinner with the other night. The one who was apologetic and seeking forgiveness. She's gone, replaced by someone tense and agitated.

My sixth sense is screaming at me to press further.

Your life depends on it, I hear it whisper.

But I don't. I keep quiet as we drive past familiar landscapes.

I expect her to turn left and head toward Tribeca, but she doesn't, she keeps driving straight ahead.

Eventually, she pulls into the parking lot near the waterfront and kills the engine. She climbs out and walks off. I sit there stunned, trying to work out what just happened.

After a couple of minutes, I climb out and follow her, wondering how I offended her. She's in the gazebo overlooking the water, leaning against the railing. A crooked smile slides across her face as she waits for me to step into the gazebo.

"Jules, what's going on?" I ask. "Why are you so angry at me? And why are we here? I don't understand what just happened."

The strange feeling returns, snaking its way through me.

It is my friend standing in front of me. But something is very off about her.

"You know, I imagined how this would play out in a lot of

different ways. It was important for me to get it right, especially after all the planning."

My brows pull together in a frown. "I'm confused. What planning?"

"But then I waded through all the memories of when I felt so belittled and humiliated by you, and I remembered that night all those years ago when I confessed how I truly felt about you. That I was in love with you. And then I tried to kiss you, and you turned away and laughed it off, telling me I was drunk." She blows out a slow breath to steady her emotions. Then she scoffs. "I tell you that I am in love with you. That I want to be with you and what do you do? You laugh at me. Just like you always did."

"What are you talking about? I never laughed at you."

And I didn't. I knew what it felt like to be laughed at. I knew what it was like to be humiliated. I might have been a bitch back then, but I never laughed at anyone. My father taught me how deep that hurt could cut, and I wasn't ever going to pollute someone else's veins with that kind of pain.

"Oh, you didn't laugh at my face. But I knew you laughed behind my back."

"I didn't, I swear to God. Jules, what is going on?"

She starts to laugh. "Are you really that dumb? Bitch, it was me. I have your money. I killed Harrison."

I stare at her, utterly disbelieving. "Jules, you're not making any sense. Why would you kill Harrison?"

Is my friend suddenly some kind of criminal mastermind?

"You learn a lot when your best friend gives you the key to the Bamcorda Mafia. All those years of playing tagalong, staying over in the mansion, going on family dinners while your father talked business. You watch and absorb it all. How all the big players play, what their roles are, what their strengths are, what their weak links are. I was invisible, but I heard and saw everything. Harrison, now he was easy pickings. When I found out he'd stolen your money, I knew my chance had finally come."

"How did you know he'd stolen my money?"

"The day at the restaurant when your card wouldn't work. It didn't take a genius to work out he'd run off with all your money. Only I figured it out before you, because you're so dumb when it comes to the simplest of things."

Of all the things that could hurt me right now, being called dumb somehow manages to make it to the top of the list.

"I knew where to find him. I'd spent enough time around him at your father's house to know the first thing he'd buy would be a whole new wardrobe of those custom suits he loved so much. And there was only one place he'd ever go to get them. So I made sure I ran into him. He was cautious at first, of course, but when he realized I didn't know anything about your missing money, he relaxed, and let's just say his male urges made him easier to manipulate. Side note, he was filthy dirty, and I was only too happy to give it to him that way as long as he did what I told him to do."

"You slept with him so you could steal my money from him?"

"Forty-two million dollars is a lot of compensation for having to do the shit he wanted me to do to him." She scoffs. "He confessed to me about Massimo paying him to hide your money. So I convinced him to double-cross Massimo and run away with me and all your millions. Told him I'd give him all the dirty sex he wanted, and the fool was only too quick to agree." She cocks an eyebrow. "See, I know what the boys like, and I know how to give it to them."

"But you killed him."

"Because I wasn't going to share all that money with him. Of course, I had to get a bit heavy-handed with him. Force him at gun point to send the money to an offshore bank account." Her grin is pure evil. "Then *click, click, boom*, he was one less thing to worry about, and I was forty-two million dollars richer."

I can only stare at her, momentarily speechless. Who even is this psychopath standing in front of me?

"You made it look like a hit," I say numbly.

"Of course I did. I'd been around Tony Vincelli and his dumbass boys long enough to know how it would go down. You know, for supposedly tough Mafia men, those boys have loose lips. The shit I'd hear when I was at your house. No wonder the Bamcorda empire fell so easily. You had too many stupid people in high places."

More pieces click into place. "You killed them too."

"I thought about blowing them up and being done with it. But truth be told, after Harrison, I kind of developed a taste for it. Who would've thought all those sessions at the gun range with you would prove so useful? Not to mention deliciously addictive." She inhales with a look of deep satisfaction, and then exhales with a moan, like she's just inhaled the enticing aroma of a good meal. "There's nothing like the rush of mowing someone down with a Beretta. Even better if you have two."

My God, she's more insane than I thought.

"But how did you even pull it off? Tony Vinocelli was a zealot for security."

"One thing your father taught me... every stronghold has a weak point, and if you find that weakness, then you'll find your way inside. Fausto was my ticket in. It wasn't hard to turn his head. I was a familiar face. Someone he'd thought about banging but never tried, so when I approached him and offered him his wildest fantasies on a plate, he didn't think twice. We met in the same hotel room for weeks before he finally invited me to spend the night in the pool house in the family estate."

The look of displeasure on her face turns to disgust. "Tony Vinocelli had crazy security surrounding his home but only had two bodyguards inside. Crazy, arrogant fool. So I killed Fausto first. Then I ran into Giulio on my way into the main house and shot him too. The bodyguards were at the dining table playing cards and didn't bat an eyelid when the ditzy brunette Fausto was banging came inside looking for a glass of water. The first one didn't see it coming, but the second one did, even managed to pull his gun, which was a rush, but I shot him in the chest before he could pull a round off."

I have no words. I can only stare at her.

"I found Tony coming out of his bedroom. He'd heard the noise downstairs. When he saw me, he looked so confused. Almost as if he couldn't believe it was a woman who was going to end his life. Do you know what his last words were? *Not you.* That's what he said. And I have to admit it was a little insulting. I mean, why not me? So I shot him twice in the chest and down he went."

By the gleam in her eye, I can see the enjoyment she feels as she recalls the massacre.

"You know, there's nothing quite like the stillness of a house when all the people inside it are dead." She sighs. "It's something that's always intrigued me."

"Always?"

Jesus, how many times has she done this?

Then it clicks.

"You killed your parents," I gasp. "It wasn't a murder-suicide."

The pleasure drops from her face. "Do you know what my father used to do to me while my mother was sleeping off another bender? He took from me what he no longer wanted to take from her, and she didn't protect me like she was supposed to. I told her once, and she slapped me across the face. What else was I meant to do? They both deserved to die."

Okay, somewhere in my slightly empathetic mind, I can see her point of view. After all, a lot of people have wished for revenge on those who have hurt them. But whatever darkness grew in her during those years didn't die with her parents. It grew more powerful. To a point where she could kill five people in one night.

"You enjoyed it. Killing Harrison. The Vinocelli murders."

"Of course I did. Consider it payment for services rendered. Do you know how tiresome it was to endure Fausto's clumsy lovemaking? It felt good to finally be able to shoot him in the face because I couldn't endure one more grope from the disgusting pig."

Massimo told me Fausto was shot four times. Now I know why.

"Besides, I couldn't afford to have any loose ends."

"Yet here we are, or is that why you lured me out of the cabin? You obviously plan to kill me too."

Her eyes gleam with psychotic excitement. "I knew I'd have to take you out eventually. If you're one thing, you're persistent. I knew you'd come looking for your money." Her cruel lips twist. "But I didn't count on you going to Massimo. Oh, I knew you had a good set of balls on you, but not the giant ones you needed to turn to the enemy for help. I admit, I didn't see that coming." She tilts her head. "And if I'm really honest, I admire that. Actually, I always respected that about you. Your resilience. But unfortunately for you, it's interfered with the rest of my plans."

The cold ache of betrayal tightens in my throat. "Which are?"

"Live your life, only better. You didn't deserve what was handed to you on a silver platter. But I do. I paid my dues. All those years I endured being your poor, *not-quite-good-enough* friend. I'm owed this."

I feel my chin quiver as the reality of what is happening sets in. The hurt is enormous and so gut-wrenching I can barely breathe.

"You did this because you wanted to be rich?"

"I did this because I want to be you," she spits. "You're a spoilt fucking bitch who didn't deserve any of it."

Her words gut me like a knife, and I can barely get the words around the cold lump in my throat.

"What are you going to do?"

"I'm going to enjoy every moment of watching you die. And then I'm going to help Massimo get over your death."

"Massimo won't fall for it."

"Of course he will. I'll be there when he needs comforting. It won't take long; I'm sure a man like him has a strong sex drive. He'll want to forget the pain of losing you. I'll make sure he does."

I don't know what hurts more.

The fact my friend stole all my money because she resents me, or because she wants to kill me so she can actually *be* me.

The fact she wants to steal Massimo is the cherry on top of this shitstorm sundae.

Anger tears up my spine and burns at the nape of my neck. She'll get her thieving hands on my man over my dead body.

I pull out my gun and point it at her.

But the last thing I want to do is shoot someone who used to be my best friend, and my hand shakes slightly.

Her eyes narrow. "I'd think twice about that if I were you."

"But that's the thing, you aren't me and you never will be. Even with all my money, even with all my belongings, hell even with Massimo, you will never be me." She wants to play this game, then game on, bitch. "You'll always be plain little mousey Jules who only ever got what she got because she was my friend."

Her expression sharpens to pure hatred. But she shakes it off, revealing the ace up her sleeve.

"You think I didn't expect you to point a gun at my face?"

Fear tingles at the base of my spine.

She tilts her head. "Did you check to make sure it's loaded?"

I hide my unease well, but I'm feeling it like a full-blown anxiety attack. "It's always loaded."

"I know. When you went to the bathroom at the gas station I looked."

Fuck.

She doesn't have to say it. I already know.

She emptied the clip when I used the restroom.

I drop my aim. I don't need to check to see I'm right, but I do anyway.

The clip is empty.

I raise my face to look at her. It's something my father taught me. Don't bow your head to the enemy. Look them right in the face so you can see what they have planned as it's coming.

"So how is this going to play out?" I ask, sounding braver than I am.

An impending doom has settled on my shoulders, acknowledging I might be dead by the time this is done.

Which becomes very apparent when Jules produces her own gun from the pocket of her hoodie.

Double fuck.

"You die, and I barely get away with my life."

"No one will believe you," I say, with more calmness than I feel.

"I think we've already established that I'm a good actress. I'll say we came here to talk. You were upset over your breakup. Your boyfriend had stolen your money and I was comforting you. *It was a tweaker, officer. He shot at us. Poor*

Bianca." She sobs, then just as quick, her face clears and the hatred returns to her expression.

"And you think you'll be happy even with me dead?" I shake my head. "You can't escape what you are."

"But that's where you're wrong, Bianca. I can be whoever I want to be, and I've decided I want to be you. So I'll be living your life. Spending your money. *Fucking your man*."

"I don't think so." The voice comes from out of nowhere.

Massimo.

I swing around, and there he is, cautiously walking toward us, Nico beside him. Both with their guns drawn.

I've never been so relieved in my life.

"Don't come any closer, Massimo," Jules warns.

"Or what, you'll shoot us all?" he growls.

Clearly not realizing that killing everyone is kind of her thing.

"If I have to," she says, her eyes sharp. "But I'll start with her."

She aims at me, and I know she's going to fire. I feel it in my bones. So does Massimo, because he launches himself in front of me as he fires off a shot and shoots Jules in the arm.

The world slows. Massimo falls. Jules falls. I drop to the ground where Massimo is clutching his shoulder. Nico kicks Jules's gun across the gazebo and aims his gun at her, ready to fire.

"No!" I cry, and Nico looks at me, his eyes as black as black. "She has to live."

"Why?"

Jules is lying on the ground, wounded but not in enough pain that she can't flash me an evil smile that says, *I know you won't let them kill me because somewhere deep down you still care for me.*

"Because she has my money." My eyes lock on hers. "When I get it back, then you can kill her."

Her grin fades.

I turn to Massimo and help him into a seated position.

"Let me see how bad the wound is."

He tries to get up, but his feet slide against the gazebo floor, and I have to help him over to the barbecue table.

I open his shirt and frown when I see the bullet wound to his shoulder. Blood spills down, covering the tattoos on his chest.

"It's just a flesh wound," he says, downplaying it. Because it's not a flesh wound at all. The bullet has lodged in his shoulder.

"Nice shot," I say, inspecting the wound. "Shooting her in the arm so she'd drop the gun."

"Not really. I was aiming for her head."

I feel the searing heat of his eyes on my face, but I can't look at him.

"I meant what I said back at the cabin," he says. "I'm in love with you."

"Don't," I warn.

"But it's true, Bianca. I'm so in love with you that nothing else even matters anymore."

"And I'm not opposed to jamming my finger in that wound to make you shut up."

I still can't make eye contact, and instead, I keep studying his wound. Although I'm not even sure what to do with it.

"Do you love me?" His voice is rough.

So rough it makes me finally look at him.

And just like I thought it would, it hurts. "How can you even ask me that right now?"

"Because I think you need to know that now more than ever. If we're to get past this, then you need to know if you love me or not."

"Get past this? You didn't steal my lunch out of the fridge or wreck my car, Massimo. You had someone ruin my life."

"Yes, I had Harrison take your money. But it was only supposed to be for a couple of weeks. Enough time to for you to reach out to your allies. By the time you arrived at Lair asking me for help, your money should have been returned weeks earlier."

"But it wasn't, was it? Because Jules got her hands on Harrison and convinced him to double-cross you."

"And she will pay for it," he growls.

"In prison," I tell him.

I'm vaguely aware of Nico making phone calls behind us.

"Can we at least talk about everything before you make your mind up about me?" he asks.

"You need to get to the hospital."

"I won't be going to the hospital as much as she won't be going to jail."

"What do you mean?" I ask alarmed. "You need medical attention, and she needs to be locked in a cell for the rest of her sorry life."

"In a few minutes, Matteo and Dante will be here. Along with some very mean men who will force Jules to hand over your money before they dispose of her."

"No, I don't want that. She has to live."

"Why?"

"Because I want her to pay for what she did. And dying

will be too easy. I want her to be locked up in a cell knowing I'm out here living the life she so desperately wanted. And I'm going to make the most of it, Massimo. I'm going to do all the things I've wanted to do. I'm going to live free and happy."

"Is there any room in this free and happy life for me?"

My heart aches as I look at him. I want to kiss him and tell him that of course there is, that I don't want to take another step without him walking beside me. That waking up without him lying next to me is going to hurt.

But I don't know if I'll ever be able forgive him.

Two sets of headlights appear behind him before I have a chance to answer.

I hear the opening and closing of car doors before a man in a suit appears and walks over to us. It's Matteo. I recognize him from Harrison's house. He's joined by Dante, Massimo's driver.

"Where will you take Massimo?" I ask Matteo.

"We have a doctor with their own discreet surgery." He looks at the bullet wound. But Massimo's gaze is fixed firmly on mine.

"Dante will take you home," Massimo says.

Looking into his tortured eyes, I feel that sharp pain barrel through me again. "Promise me she goes to jail, Massimo. Don't let them kill her. If you grant me this, we can talk. But I'm going to need some time."

He nods reluctantly and turns to Dante who has joined us. "Make sure she gets home safe."

Dante nods at his boss. "You got it."

He gestures for me to follow. But before I can take a step away, Massimo grabs my hand. "I love you."

And before I can stop myself, the words slip from my lips. "I love you too."

He lets my hand go, and I begin to walk away with Dante.

But fuck it.

I'm not done with Jules.

I stomp back to where Nico and some rather rough-looking men are holding her. She's on her feet now and gives me another one of her smug smiles, and I punch her so hard in the face I manage to dislodge a tooth. *And probably break one of my own knuckles.*

But, man, it's liberating.

When she falls the ground, I lean down so we are eye level. "That's for making me sell all my Gucci."

44

BIANCA

I'm already in the car when I hear the gunshot.

Dante tries to stop me, but I'm out the door so fast, lightning couldn't catch me.

I run through the parking lot and up the stairs of the gazebo where Jules lies dead on the floor, a bullet wound beneath her chin seeping blood onto the floorboards, and a gun lying by her left hand.

"No!" I scream, running toward her.

Massimo and Nico swing around, and Massimo grabs me, but I fling him off and drop down beside Jules. Her eyes are half-lidded, staring upward, and blood spatter pools on her cheeks. What is left of her mouth is open, and her shattered teeth are glazed with blood.

"Who did this?" I cry.

"She grabbed my gun," one of Massimo's men says. I've never seen him before. He's young, and he's gone gray in the face, and I don't know if it's because he's never shot anyone before or if he's telling the truth, and Jules grabbed his gun and shot herself, and now he's in hot water with his boss.

I rise to my feet and turn to Massimo. "Is that true? Did she do this, or did you have him kill her because that's what you wanted?"

Despite the pain of the bullet in his shoulder, he puts his hands on my arms. "She grabbed his gun, Bianca. She didn't want to go to jail. She was desperate, and when she saw the opportunity, she took it. You have my word."

I shake him off. "I'm sorry, but your word means very little to me right now."

"I can't make you believe me. But it's the truth. I made you a promise that I'd let her live, and I was going to do it your way."

He looks pained, and I know it's more than his shoulder that's hurting. But I can't let that break through the wall I've very suddenly erected around my heart. Let him hurt. Let him know how it feels to hurt right down to his bones.

"I know I have to do everything your way now," he says. "And I will. But you need to go home and let us take care of her."

"Don't make her disappear," I say, the enormity of the situation seeping through the thin veil of shock. "At least let her have a funeral."

He nods and despite my hurt telling me not to, I believe him.

Dante drives me back to Massimo's loft. But I don't stay. I quickly stuff all of my belongings into my overnight bag and leave fifteen minutes later. Any longer, and I'd fall in a tearful heap on the floor, driving myself crazy with memories of what has gone down in the last twelve hours.

I need to keep moving forward and get away from Massimo.

Outside, I hail a cab and give him the address of the only person I want to see right now.

When I arrive, the front door opens, and Eve ushers me inside, pulling me into a hug.

"Are you okay?"

I dump my bags at the bottom of the stairs.

"I'll be fine."

"Of course you will be. Come on, I'll open a bottle of wine, and you can tell me what my dumbass stepbrother did."

It's just after midnight when a loud banging on the door wakes us.

"Okay, okay, geez," Eve exclaims on the way to the door. "I have neighbors, you know."

I follow her down the stairs, tying my robe as I reach the door behind her.

She opens it and a very unkempt and emotional Massimo is on the other side, swaying where he stands.

One arm is in a sling and he's holding a half-empty bottle of scotch.

"What are you doing here?" she asks.

But his glazed eyes are fixed firmly on me.

"I need to talk to you," he says, his words slightly slurred.

"You need to know how much I fucking love you, and I'm not going to let you leave me."

I fold my arms. "Is that right?"

"Yeah, that's right. You and me, we're meant to be together. We make sense. My world is fucked up and dark, but you being in it makes it all worth it."

"And what, you think you can come around here half-cut on scotch and tell me that after what you did?"

"Yes, yes, I do. Because here I am, Bianca, standing in front of you, telling you that you're the best fucking thing to ever happen to me."

"Seriously, Massimo, I'm sure the neighbors don't appreciate your declarations of love at twelve thirty at night," Eve interjects.

But Massimo doesn't care.

"Fuck the neighbors." But he pushes inside and before I realize it, my shoulder blades are against the wall, and he has me pinned with those dark and stormy eyes and an expression that warns of more bad weather to come. "I can't wait until tomorrow or the next day or whenever the fuck you think you want to talk to me again. I need to know now."

"You need to know what?"

"If you don't want me anymore."

He looks tortured, and I can hear the pain and desperation in his voice, and it hits me right where my heart lies broken in my chest.

"Massimo—"

He grabs my face and presses his forehead to mine. "Is it over, Bianca? Have I lost you?"

His breath is sweet like scotch and sugar, his lips close

enough to kiss. And I'd be lying if I said I wasn't aching to feel them on mine.

"Tell me I haven't lost you," he begs.

I can barely breathe, let alone swallow.

"Go home, Massimo. I don't want to do this anymore."

45

BIANCA

My money reappears in my account three days later.

Eve says I can stay with her as long as I like, but I move into a hotel until I can buy a more permanent home, because I need to do this by myself. No help from no one. No relying on anyone but me.

Two weeks later, I enroll in college to study business and start attending classes, making friends.

I join a gym, and volunteer at an animal shelter once a week, and help out at a community kitchen every second weekend, determined to give something back to the community. And once a week, Eve, Natalie, and I meet for dinner or cocktails, and Massimo's name is absolutely, one hundred percent banned from the table.

I've heard from him only once since that night at Eve's when I told him it was over. He rang me the next day and begged me to see him. But I couldn't. The wound was too raw and I needed space to heal. But it's been radio silence since then, and that's fine by me. I don't want to hear about how I've been replaced, or how he's over me. And I will cut out my own tongue before I ask either of my friends for information about him.

It doesn't stop me from wondering about him though. Especially at night when I lie alone in my bed, with my head churning and my imagination running away on me. Wondering who he is with. Wondering if it hurts him as much as it hurts me to be apart.

My numbness over losing Massimo is gone, replaced by a physical longing that I doubt will ever go away. It's a cold ache buried in my chest where my heart used to live. I miss his touch. His kisses. The way he would roll over in bed and secure me in his arms and hold me against his warm chest.

Some nights I go to bed and pray I will forget about him and wake up feeling happy and content because I never met Massimo De Kysa. But the next day, I always wake up to his ghost, and I'm reminded of what has been done and what I have lost, and the agony starts all over again.

I love him.

Painfully so.

But he hurt me more than I thought anyone could, and that is an amazing power for someone to have over you.

In his absence, I've created a well-structured routine to get through each day without falling apart.

I visit the gym. Go to school. Stop into my local coffee shop to study. Climb into bed at night and cry myself to sleep.

Rinse and repeat.

Oh, I am strong, and I will survive, and I will buy my own flowers and hold my own hand and all of that super-powerful stuff like the songs suggest. Because the new me is strong and independent, and she knows how valuable her self-worth is.

But I miss him.

I miss *us*, and everything that was, and everything that could have been.

And that's the tragedy.

What could've been.

When we were together, it felt like we could take on anything and win.

Except him stealing my money and ruining my life.

So I move forward, but life becomes stuck on repeat while Massimo remains silent, and I start to wonder if I really meant anything to him at all.

Then life becomes unstuck on day twenty-nine of my new life while I'm sitting in a coffee shop near campus, reading some study notes from my commerce class. I'm sitting at a table in the corner nook where the light is dim, and I'm far enough away from the other tables that I can't hear any conversation. It's a perfect table to study. Little distraction and lots of privacy. Apart from the waitress bringing me my tea, I get left alone.

So it's a surprise when a man wearing a baseball cap and sunglasses slides into the chair across from me.

I'm about to tell him to go away when he takes off his sunglasses, and my words get caught in my throat.

Nico.

For a moment, all I can do is stare.

But then it hits me.

Exactly who I'm sitting across from.

He's not just Massimo's dead brother. He's the man who killed my father.

I get up to leave, but Nico stops me with a tone that is both a warning and a threat. "I wouldn't do that if I were you. The best thing you can do right now is listen."

I want to tell him to go to hell. But a bigger part of me wants to know why he is here.

"Fine, say what you've come to say. But I swear to God, Nico, if you try anything stupid—"

"Like what?"

"Like hurting me."

"Why the fuck would I want to hurt you? My brother is in love with you."

"Don't say that."

"It's true. And if I laid one finger on you, he'd break all of mine. But I don't have a reason to hurt you, do I?"

"I'm not blabbing, if that's what you mean. Your secret is safe."

He studies my face with those ink-black eyes. "Why would you keep quiet about it?"

"Because this bullshit rivalry between the Bamcorda and the De Kysa has already caused too much pain, and I don't want to be a part of it anymore."

"What do you want?"

"To live in peace. To be able to come to my local coffee shop and not be accosted by some *supposedly dead Mafia don* who insists on talking to me."

"We don't have to be enemies, Bianca."

"You're not seriously suggesting that we can be friends."

"At least friendly."

"Hmmmmm. Let's see, you killed my father, and your brother stole all my money. Sorry, but I can't see the appeal of being friends."

"Yes, I killed your father, and if I had to do it all over again, I would. He kidnapped my wife. He put his hands on her, beat her, was going to rape her—"

"Stop."

"He had her strung up. He repeatedly hurt her. Put a gun at her head and was about to pull the trigger."

"I said stop," I snap.

I can't stand what my father did.

But forgiving Nico for taking his life is a mountain too high for me to climb right now.

He was my *father*.

Nico remains as cool as a cucumber. "Tell me, what would you have done in my position?"

It's a fair question, and one I've considered every day since it happened. But sitting here across from Nico now, it feels too hard to tell him the truth.

I would have done the same.

I don't want to admit it because that would mean showing forgiveness, and I don't know if I can.

"Did Massimo send you?" I ask.

"My brother doesn't need me to do his bidding."

"Yet, here you are."

"Massimo doesn't know I'm here. He's out of the country."

That explains why I haven't seen or heard from him. He's vacationing overseas. Getting on with his life after sending a nuclear bomb into mine.

"What do you want, Nico?"

"To leave this city, and go back to my wife and child who are waiting for me on our island home, where I can take lunchtime naps in the sun and drink sweet berry wine and forget about this damn city and all its ugliness. But I can't do that, not until you and my brother work out whatever there is to work out."

"Nothing. That's what there is to work out. Nothing at all."

"Wrong answer. You look miserable."

"Thanks. That beard isn't exactly working for you, either."

He ignores me. "And I don't know what you've done to my brother, but I think you broke him."

"What do you mean?"

"He seems determined to win you back, no matter what."

"And yet you're here, and he isn't."

"There are things in play that I can't explain."

"You're speaking in riddles. What do you mean I broke him?"

"He's different. Like a damn piece of him broke off when you walked away. He didn't take your money to hurt you. He took it to protect the De Kysa and everyone in it."

"I know," I say. Because I get it. It was a smart move. Wound the enemy to see who shows up to help them. "But he should've come clean about it before I pulled a gun on him and forced it out of his mouth."

"Do you know why I was on my way to visit you both in the cabin?"

Jules said Nico was on his way to kill me, or to help Massimo dispose of my body. But we've established what a lying psychopath my ex-best friend was and how she manipulated the truth to suit her narrative.

And surprisingly, I never circled back to ask why Nico was on his way to the cabin.

"No, I don't," I say, wondering why it never occurred to me to ask.

Because you were too preoccupied with the bomb that had just gone off in your life.

"He called me. Told me he was going to tell you everything. About the money. About me."

"And you were okay with him telling me about you?"

"Fuck no. But I knew once he'd made up his mind there was no way to change it. He was determined to make things right with you. He said if he was to have a future with you then you needed to know the truth."

"A future with me?" I whisper. "He told you that?"

"He did. He was adamant that was the end goal for him. He asked me to the cabin to talk to you. To tell you what happened with your father, as if he could somehow broker some kind of peace between us." For the first time since sitting down, Nico's expression softens. "My brother is an idealist. He wanted everything wrapped up in a bow. For him to be with you, he needed you and I to be right with each other."

I don't know what to say.

Is there really an existence where things would be okay between Nico and me?

"Massimo will want to talk to you someday soon." He stands and puts his sunglasses back on. "I suggest you listen."

He turns to leave, but when I speak, he stops.

"I'm sorry for what my father did to Bella," I say.

His jaw tightens. "I wouldn't be standing here if I thought otherwise."

Then, walking away, Nico disappears out of view and back into oblivion.

46

BIANCA

Day thirty-three of my new life, and it's been raining. At lunchtime, having finished my classes, I find myself walking across the rain-soaked campus to my car when a man steps out in front of me.

I look up, straight into a pair of obsidian black eyes, and my heart squeezes to a stop.

"Massimo."

He's wearing a winter coat over his impeccable suit. His hair is a little longer than normal, but it looks good. *Too good.*

"What are you doing here?" I barely get the words around the cold lump in my throat.

A cold wind blows across the quad and tangles in his hair, and I itch to reach up and touch it. Instead, I tighten my arms around my waist.

"I've missed you," he says, and I can see the quiet agony on his face. His Adam's apple bobs in his throat as he swallows. He looks just as handsome as I remember, but in the flesh, he is devastating, and my body aches for him.

All I can do is stare and absorb every inch of his handsome face with a longing in my chest. Those heavily lashed eyes. The high cheekbones that seem too perfect. The dark hair softening the sharp lines of his jaw.

But those lips, the ones I've spent hours kissing, seem so distant to me now. So untouchable it hurts.

"Clearly. Nice tan by the way. Where were you vacationing, somewhere tropical, or just far enough away from New York City to forget about me?"

"I wasn't on vacation, Bianca."

"No, what was it then?" I can't keep the sharp edge out of my voice because damn, where has he been? I didn't expect him to keep trying to call me forever. But I didn't expect him to give up so easily and flee the country either.

"Can we go somewhere to talk?" he asks.

I want to tell him to go to hell. But my heart is tired of being hurt and wants to hear what he has to say.

So I nod and follow him to his car. Dante isn't with him, so he climbs into the driver's seat while I climb in the passenger side.

Inside, it smells like him, which only hurts more.

"It's good to see you," he says.

I nod. But I can't look at him, because if I do, I know I'll cry. "It's good to see you too. How is your shoulder?"

"Healing."

"Are you still in pain?"

"Not from that."

It's weird that things are so cold and stilted between us when once they burned so hot and wild. But the air is thick with unspoken feelings, and it feels like it's going to snap any minute, and I won't be able to contain my hurt any longer.

Yet, somehow I manage to speak with absolute calmness. "You hurt me."

"I know. And if I could go back and change it I would."

"I know we weren't friends, but I always thought that night when you kissed me... I thought it meant something."

"It did. More than you could ever know."

"Yet it didn't stop you from turning my life upside down for your own benefit."

I finally look at him, and his expression is pained. "I couldn't let it stop me from doing what I needed to do. But that doesn't mean that night wasn't something special to me." He's quiet for a moment, then adds, "You know the things I have to do because of who I am. The choices I have to make. Sometimes those choices are ones I don't want to make and taking your money was one of them. The intention wasn't to hurt you. I paid Harrison a lot of money for a new life. In return, he was instructed to put your money elsewhere for a period of two weeks. Then he was supposed to return it and vanish. But then you showed up, and I realized he had double-crossed me. None of this was designed to hurt you."

"Why didn't you tell me?" I ask.

"At first, I was trying to work out what the situation was. Were you using our previous encounter to infiltrate the De Kysa—"

"I would never do something like that," I cry, a little too passionately.

"And I know that now." His brows pull together. "When I

realized you were asking for help because you truly needed it, I knew I had to do something."

"You didn't help me because you're a good person. You helped me because you felt guilty."

"Yes, I felt guilty. When I realized what had happened and what it had done to you, it fucking did me in. It set me on a path I never saw coming. It led me to you. To falling in love with you. The plan was easier to carry out when you were just a memory. But then you came along, and all I wanted to do was be around you, and it confused the fuck out of me. I wanted to tell you the truth, but the thought of hurting you made me a coward."

It's hard not to think about all the things we did together, all the conversations and moments I felt vulnerable around him. And all the while, this black cloud was hanging over us and I didn't even know a thing about it. "I feel so stupid."

"You deserved better, and I didn't give it to you. But if you give me a chance, I'll make sure you never feel that way again."

My heart is begging me to surrender. But my head is a stubborn beast.

"Where have you been?" I ask quietly.

He reaches across to open the glove compartment, and I'm engulfed in his scent, which only makes me ache for him more.

He removes a black box from inside and hands it to me. "Open it."

I open the box, and inside is an antique silver locket. A ruby gleams in the silver.

I gasp. "It looks like my mother's."

"It is your mother's."

I turn to look at him. "I don't understand. It was lost the night she died."

"It's where I've been all this time. Finding out what happened that night."

All I can do is stare at him.

"You wouldn't see me. You wouldn't let me explain. I couldn't wait around and do nothing, I had to do something to show you how much you mean to me." I can hear the regret in his usually confident voice. "I took from you, and it hurt you. I wanted to give you something no one else could. *Answers*."

"So you went looking for my mom's necklace."

"I knew how much your mother's death affected you. I thought if I could find out what happened and get the necklace back, at least I could end the pain for you. I knew it was a long shot. It's been a decade. But I had to at least try."

"But the police tried to find it. So did my father."

"The police investigation was flawed. They had several murders that month, and a mobster's wife who more than likely died an accidental death was not on their list of priorities. And your father was overcome with emotion. He wasn't clearheaded. He missed leads."

I touch the gleaming ruby, remembering the last time I saw it around my mother's neck. It was the evening she died.

"How did you find it?" I ask.

"I found a picture of it and started circulating it through various networks aligned with the De Kysa. It was sold on the black market a few months after your mother's death."

"Who had it?"

"You had a gardener, Bert."

"Yes," I say. "He was kind and lovely. He wouldn't hurt my mom."

"No, but he recognized an opportunity when he saw it. He found your mom, but she was already dead."

I frown, thinking back to the kindly old man who was quiet and gentle. It's blurry, but I can remember how upset he'd been after her death. He retired a few months later. "The police interviewed him. Just like they interviewed everyone. But he didn't know anything and was never a suspect."

"But he did know something. Your mom's death was an accident. She slipped and fell. Hit her head. He saw it happen. He tried to save her, but she was dead. When he realized he couldn't help her, his desperation kicked in, and he stole the necklace."

"You spoke with him?"

"No, he passed away a couple of years ago. But I spoke with his wife."

"Did she say why he did it?"

"He wanted to help out his family. He figured your mom was dead, and your dad was rich. It was a temptation born out of desperation. His wife was sick. They had a child with a disability. Money was tight. Life was a struggle."

I touch the necklace again. "So he stole it because he needed the money."

"He was desperate to fix a complicated situation. Good people can do things they never thought they would do when they're backed into a corner."

I know that kind of desperation.

"Is she better?"

"Who?"

"The wife. You said she was sick."

"Yes, the money from the necklace allowed her the medication and treatment she needed."

It's hard to hate Bert for being desperate enough to steal the necklace when it meant he could save his wife.

For a second, I can see his thoughts. Feel his desperation. My mom was dead. His wife still had a chance.

"That explains the unusual placement of her face on the pool step," I say.

Massimo nods. "He couldn't leave her floating face down. Despite her being dead, he wanted to keep her face out of the water."

We sit in silence as the information settles over me. I inhale a deep breath and feel the calm slide through my body. A heavy weight has been lifted.

"You did this for me?" I whisper.

"Yes, and I will spend the rest of my life doing anything and everything for you. Because I love you."

He speaks with so much conviction it's hard not to believe him.

But I can't reply, because I know if I open my mouth to speak, my voice will crack. And once it cracks, the tears will follow, and I'll be reduced to a blubbering mess when I had been so sure I would never shed another tear in front of him ever again.

A new war takes up inside of me.

Leave and never look back.

Forgive him and move forward.

I'm being pulled toward the latter by an aching heart that wants to end this suffering.

I look at Massimo.

I can't stand it. Being without him. Not waking up next to him. Looking at him and seeing the pain on his tortured face and knowing I can end it all.

I grab his face and press my lips to his, and God it feels good. The release from the pain. The untethering from heartbreak. I'm immediately swept up in his scent and the warmth of his lips on mine, and I know this is the way forward. He groans and pushes his fingers through my hair.

Tears fall from my closed eyes and slide down my cheek. His kissing is sweet agony. But oh so beautiful.

I pull back. "I think you'd better take me home now."

47

MASSIMO

We kiss like we're possessed, shedding our clothes like a trail of breadcrumbs as we stumble toward the bedroom.

It's been almost two months since I've made love to her, and I can't wait another minute to be inside her. Once we're naked and on the bed, I push into her sweet pussy and my eyes roll to the back of my head.

"Fuck, nothing feels as good as this," I groan, overwhelmed by the rush of pleasure surging through me.

She moans beneath me, and I know there's not a snowflake's chance in hell that I'm going to last. Not when she feels so soft and supple and warm, and when she moans like that, I feel it all the way down the length of my cock.

I've got two months of pent-up desire for her begging for release.

She wraps her legs around my waist, and the move pulls me in deeper, and it takes everything not to come. I grip the bedsheet and bite back the urge, determined to get her there before me. My little monster has similar ideas, because she lifts her hips to meet each thrust and chases her own release beneath me. She stops suddenly, and her pussy clenches tightly around my cock, throbbing against my engorged length as she comes. She cries out, and I can't hold back. The cries. The clenching. The soft warmth. It's too much, and my release roars out of me with blinding ecstasy.

I collapse against her and bury my face in her neck, and the smell of her skin and the warmth of her body lulls me into a peacefulness where it is just her and I who exist.

Rolling onto my side, I pull her with me and secure my arms around her.

Outside, the rain has stopped, and the sun has burned through the cloud, sending warm rays of light into the room.

Everything feels right. Which is in stark contrast to the last six weeks.

I'm not too proud to admit I was lost without her. Driven to the point of almost-madness in her absence.

At night, her face would come to me, and my body would ache with longing, and my heart would harden beneath the grief. I fucked my hand so many times I lost count, and every time, I told myself I was fucking her memory out my head. But I'm a liar. I would come and she would still be there, that beautiful face haunting my memories.

Finding her mother's necklace and figuring out the truth of the night she died was the only thing I could do to keep me sane. I was like a dog with a bone. Determined and tenacious. Because she needed answers, and I needed her.

I also needed to keep busy or my obsession for her would start to kill me from the inside.

It made me focused.

It made me determined.

And it made me realize how much she meant to me.

Now I know with emphatic truth that Bianca is the only woman for me.

My little monster.

And I'm never letting her go again.

48

BIANCA

I wake up alone in the bed and see the golden shades of dusk splashed across the wall. The bed is still warm where Massimo has been, and when I slide my palm across the empty space, I know without doubt that I am where I belong.

I climb out and find him on the terrace, looking out at the cityscape. Stepping into the crisp afternoon, there's a freshness in the air that reminds me the hot summer is behind us and the cool days of fall are well and truly here.

Massimo turns around. He's wearing sweatpants and a long-sleeved shirt, but he's got bare feet. His hair is mussed up from me running my hands through it when he was driving hard and deep into me, and there is a softness about him, like he's just woken up and is sleepy and content.

He smiles, and like it always does when he looks at me

with that smile, my stomach flutters with a million butterflies.

"Hey, you," I say, and he opens his arms and pulls me into his chest. He's all kinds of warm, and I melt into him.

"You looked too peaceful to disturb, so I let you sleep," he says.

"I needed it. I haven't slept well these past few weeks."

In response, he presses a kiss into my hair and secures his strong arms tighter around me.

The sun is gone, and its dying rays have painted the sky in red and gold. Below, the city hums, but up here it is peaceful and quiet, and in Massimo's arms, I feel safe and content.

"I missed you," he says, his gaze looking out at the bleeding sky. "There were a lot of times I dialed your number but stopped myself hitting the call button because I wanted to give you the space you wanted. But it killed me. Every day without you was a new death."

"There were a lot of times I wanted to say to hell with it and call you too. I missed you so much." I take a deep breath, feeling secure in his arms. I turn in them and look into his handsome face. I brush my lips against his jaw and feel his heart skip.

"I was worried about you and how you felt after everything Jules did. I knew it would hurt you, and I felt so powerless because I knew I couldn't do anything to ease that pain."

He's right. The weeks following Jules's death were crushing. I've seen dead bodies before, but looking into her unseeing eyes had gutted me. Even after everything she did. Even knowing how much she resented me and how she wanted to take my life and live it as her own, I was still gutted by the loss of my friend.

And I can't lie, my pain was only compounded by Massimo's absence.

"I've never felt so alone in my life," I say softly, pushing the memory away because it hurts.

But it's too late, a lone tear escapes and slides down my cheek, but he swipes it away with the gentle brush of his thumb. "You're not alone. You're a part of the De Kysa now."

Another tear falls, followed by another, and then another. But they're grateful tears, because right now, I feel more loved than I've ever felt in my life. All because of the way Massimo is looking at me.

His big hands slide around my jaw to cup my face. He brushes his lips against mine and kisses away my salty tears. "You belong with me. And my heart belongs to you if you want it."

"What are you saying?"

"I'm saying, be my wife."

"What?" I stare up at him with genuine surprise. "You said you never wanted to get married."

"Apparently, I was wrong because I want to marry *you*." His thumb brushes over my damp cheek. "And if these past weeks without you have taught me something, it's that I want to marry you more than I want anything else."

I stare at him dumbly. "You said you'd never intentionally set fire to your life by getting married."

Amusement twitches on his perfect lips as he cocks an eyebrow at me. "Are you overthinking this?"

"Of course I am. Because it's a big deal and I don't want you to regret your decision."

An unmistakable seriousness sweeps through his expression.

"You know I don't do anything I'm not completely committed to doing." His thumb slides to my lips. "And I am completely committed to this."

He kisses me, and it's deep and loving and powerful, and I feel it from the top of my head right down to my toes.

My God, I've missed this.

Bianca De Kysa.

It has a nice ring to it.

I'm not a Bamcorda anymore.

This is who I am.

He breaks off the kiss to look at me with such affection my toes curl.

"My brother took his wife away from this life. But I'm asking you to join me in it. Walk into the fire with me." He presses his forehead to mine. "What do you say, little monster, do you dare?"

EPILOGUE

Bianca

Two.

That's the number of pink lines on the pregnancy test in my hand and the second one sitting on the basin beside me.

Two pregnancy tests, and both of them positive.

I smile at my reflection in the bathroom mirror, giddy with excitement.

I'm pregnant with Massimo's baby.

He doesn't have any idea. Hell, until ten minutes ago, I had no idea. I thought the occasional bout of nausea and my sudden disinterest in coffee meant I was a bit run down.

Turns out it means so much more.

Our baby.

I place my palm against my flat stomach. Just when I thought my crazy life was entering a quieter stage, it's about to flip on its axis again.

We've been married for ten weeks.

Ten cozy weeks that seem to have floated by in a haze of deep kisses and post-orgasmic bliss.

Ten weeks of waking up in Massimo's muscular arms with the heat of his warm body wrapped around me and the safety of knowing I am loved by the most powerful man in the city.

We were married in a park the week after he asked me, on a cool but sunny fall day with clear blue skies and a sharp crispness in the air.

It was low key with just Eve, Natalie, Matteo and Dante in attendance.

I wore a knee-length white dress, strapless and pinched at the waist. My hair was down, with tiny diamond flowers woven through the beachy waves, and I held a small posey of white and soft-pink roses.

Massimo looked like all my dreams rolled into one. A well-fitted button-up shirt. Black pants. Hair dark and inky. His facial hair trimmed to utter perfection.

Standing across from him, I could barely keep my hands off him. I was eager for the ceremony to finish so I could get him naked and spend the rest of the day in bed with him as husband and wife.

We honeymooned in Misty Lake Mountain and watched the first snowflakes fall as we lay in bed wrapped in one another, with a roaring fire and bottles of wine for company. It was peaceful, and blissful, and beautiful, and it was over way too quick.

But I married the boss of New York City, and if our life is one thing, it's crazy busy, and we had to get back to it in the city.

I have school, while Massimo has De Kysa business.

Since marrying, he has moved farther away from Lair and spends more time on the interests of the De Kysa. When I graduate, I will stand beside him at the helm, and together, we will rule the De Kysa empire.

The two of us.

Correction, the *three* of us.

I hear the front door open and close. I hear his familiar footsteps on the Italian tile floors and feel my heart skip with happiness, which it always does when my husband walks through the front door.

I quickly hide the tests, putting one behind my back and knocking the other into the basin, just as Massimo walks into the bathroom.

I swing around to face him. I don't know how I'm going to tell him. Will he be as happy as me?

He's so busy; will this be another thing on his plate?

"Massimo." I breathe his name, excited and full of anticipation at the same time.

My heart feels like it's going to beat out of my chest.

He walks over and kisses me and slides his hands around my waist. His kiss is warm and welcoming. When he breaks it off, he nips my lower lip. "What are you hiding behind your back?"

I try to keep my voice light. "What makes you think I'm hiding something behind my back?"

"You have the guilty look of a shoplifter." He pulls me closer and kisses me again, this time with lots of tongue. He nuzzles my neck. He's trying to distract me. "Do you have something to confess, little monster? You don't have a scarf back there, do you?"

He cocks an eyebrow and I swat him with my spare hand. The one not holding the pregnancy test.

Which tells my observant husband which hand is holding the suspected contraband. He reaches around and grabs hold of my wrist and holds it up between us. He sees the pregnancy test.

"What is this?"

"It's a pregnancy test."

His eyes flare. "What kind of pregnancy test?"

"The positive kind."

The smile on his face fades, and his eyes darken. "Are you sure?"

"Yep, see." I hold the pregnancy test up to his face so he can see the two pink lines.

"But these can be wrong, right?"

"Sure, it's not unheard of for one to give a false positive." I pick up the test I knocked into the sink. "But two? I don't think so. I think you need to face facts, Mr. De Kysa. You knocked me up."

It takes a moment for it to sink in. But when it does, his face breaks into a smile so big it's eclipsing. Eyes. Mouth. Teeth. Cheeks. They're all smiling.

He takes my face in his hands. "You're pregnant."

"Apparently so."

"With my baby."

"Well, I hope so."

He narrows his eyes, but he's smiling. "We're having a baby."

The way he speaks is soft and gentle, and I feel the affection all the way down to my bones.

"Yes, we're having a baby."

He kisses me, and its sweet and tender, and it tells me everything I need to know. He wants this baby as much as I do.

He breaks off the kiss and presses his forehead to mine. "I love you, little monster."

"And I love you, Don De Kysa."

Without warning, he lifts me up in his arms and carries me into the bedroom.

"What are you doing?" I cry.

"I'm taking my pregnant wife to bed, and we're not coming up for air until I've given you at least three orgasms."

"Three?"

"Yes," he says, gently placing me on the bed. "At the very least."

He pins me to the bed with his powerful body, and I lace my fingers around the nape of his neck.

Feeling a surge of happiness, I look up at him. "How is this my life?"

"What do you mean?"

"Less than a year ago, I was broke, had no place to call home, and then you came along."

"Technically, you came to me." He grins mischievously, but then it fades, and fireworks take off in my belly as he places himself between my legs and gives me a look of pure love. His eyes soften. "Because we're meant to be, Bianca, and no amount of war or bloodletting or wickedness will ever be able to keep us apart. We're written in the stars, little monster. And no one can ever take that away from us."

He leans down, and when he kisses me again, I know I am home.

EXTENDED EPILOGUE: MASSIMO

Three months later

I DIVE into the crystal blue water and skim along the sandy seabed before swimming back up toward the sunlight and breaking through the surface again. I close my eyes and float on my back, letting the sun warm my face. It's another perfect day in paradise, and life is pretty fucking perfect. I can see why my brother gave it all up to live on this island.

Since coming to Nico's island hideaway, I feel lazy and relaxed and fucking alive.

It's been a week of late sleep-ins and lazy afternoon naps, followed by daily swims in the ocean, nightly dinners of fresh seafood and good red wine, and lots and lots of sex with my wife.

Swimming back to shore, I walk up the beach to where Bianca is sunbaking on a lounge chair. She's wearing big sunglasses over her eyes and her face is turned toward the sun. When she sees me, a contented smile parts her lovely lips.

Five months pregnant, she's wearing a tiny black bikini, and I've never seen her look so beautiful.

I lean down to kiss her, and she squeals as droplets of cool sea water sprinkle across her warm skin.

"You fiend!" she protests.

"I am, but admit it, you love it."

I kiss her, and she kisses me back with deep longing, and immediately my body responds.

These days it seems I only need to be close to her and my cock gets hard, and today, her tiny bikini isn't helping matters. It shows off her deep tan and barely contains her growing breasts, and it would require no effort to remove those tiny bottoms. Which seems like a fucking fantastic idea.

I climb onto the lounge chair and kneel between her legs to press a kiss onto her pregnant belly. My fingers slide over her warm skin and my cock throbs harder. I can't lie. I'm obsessed with my wife, but when she's pregnant there's something even more sexy about her. It must be some kind of hormonal voodoo that has me wanting to be inside her all the time. A primal instinct that keeps me hard.

Thankfully, Bianca is consumed by the same affliction. Permanently aroused with an insatiable appetite for my cock.

She removes her sunglasses and glances down to where my erection is jutting out of my shorts like a rocket about to ascend into space. She looks around us. We're the only ones on the private beach. It's just us and miles of white sand and sunshine.

She crushes her teeth into her lower lip. "We can't—"

"We most certainly can."

"Someone might see."

I move lower down the sun lounge and bend my head so I'm eye level with her bikini bottoms. "If anyone can get through Nico's sophisticated security systems, then they deserve to watch."

She chuckles. "I'm serious."

"So am I." I push her tiny bikini bottoms to the side and slide a finger inside her.

She groans. "What if Nico or Bella come looking for us?"

She's wet and my finger makes an enticing suckling noise as I move it in and out of her.

"Lucky them. They'll find more of us than they expected."

My thumb brushes over her clit, and her breath quickens.

"Massimo," she protests. Though by the way she's gripping the arm of the lounge chair, something tells me it's an empty objection.

"Relax, little monster." I remove my finger and glide my tongue through her sweet pussy, and she drops her head back with a moan. "Tell me to stop, and I will."

She lifts her head. "If you stop, Massimo De Kysa, I will murder you in your sleep. Now put your tongue back in my pussy and make me come."

"Your wish is my command, my love," I say, burying myself between her legs. While my tongue teases her clit, my fingers release the bows holding her bikini bottoms together, and they fall away, giving me more room to feast.

A trembling moan of appreciation leaves her sweet lips.

God, the way she whimpers. The way she tastes. I want her so bad I can barely think straight.

She starts to rock her hips, shallow little bucks to meet my lips as I suck and lick and penetrate her with shallow dips of my tongue.

Damn, I could do this all day, she tastes so good.

Her fingers push through my damp hair.

"Oh God," she cries out, arching her throat. "I'm going to come—"

Her thighs clamp around my head as her orgasm burns through her, but I don't stop. I keep worshiping her with my lips and my tongue, and when she finally softens and relaxes, I shove down my shorts and thrust my aching cock deep into her warm, wet pussy.

Fuck. I could do this every hour of every day for the rest of my life and never grow tired of it.

I thrust in and out of her body getting harder and harder with every single moan falling from her lips. Images swirl in my head. Pictures of her. Of us. Of our baby. Of our life together. She is my everything.

"Mine," I growl, feeling a rush of possessiveness burst through me as I thrust into her. "You are all mine."

"Yes," she moans. "All yours."

Her head falls back, and her eyes flutter with the surge of a new orgasm rolling through her body. Her pussy clenches around my cock, and I can't take it. I explode into her with a primal cry, my body tensing and jerking to a halt as I'm overwhelmed by the intense rush of ecstasy.

I spill into her, my body shuddering with the release until I'm empty.

Goddamn, I am in heaven.

Soft and lax and heavy with contentment, I sink onto the lounge chair and rest my head against her thighs. It won't be the last time I make love to my wife today.

She tangles her fingers in my hair, and I close my eyes.

My unborn son stirs in his mother's belly, and I am reminded of the adventure that lies ahead. *My son.* I can't wait to hold him in my arms and watch him grow, and the thought sends warmth and happiness spreading through me.

"I love you," she says.

"I love you too."

And I do. With every piece of my heart.

I press a kiss to her sun-kissed thigh and sink deeper into my contentment.

I don't know what lies ahead for us.

But I know that no matter what, with Bianca by my side, anything is possible.

ABOUT THE AUTHOR

Penny Dee writes contemporary romance about rock stars, bikers, hockey players, mafia kings, and everyone in-between. Her stories bring the suspense, the feels, and a whole lot of heat.

She found her happily ever after with an Australian hottie who she met on a blind date.

ALSO BY PENNY DEE

De Kysa Mafia

The Devil's Den (De Kysa Mafia book 1)

The Kings of Mayhem Original Series

Kings of Mayhem

Brothers in Arms

Biker Baby

Hell on Wheels

Off Limits

Bull

The Kings of Mayhem Tennessee Series

Jack

Doc

Ares

Made in the USA
Coppell, TX
04 June 2024